## THE SPRINGERS

'All you'll have against you are the cops, three assorted branches of our alleged Intelligence service, the cops of any countries you move through, and the Russians trying like hell to hijack you en route.'

So went Wainwright's final briefing for one of the most astounding missions ever given to an Intelligence agent. His task: to spring a prisoner from a top-security gaol in England and spirit him out to Hong Kong. There the prisoner, a leading Russian agent, is to be exchanged for a British agent in the hands of the Chinese. And the whole operation must be carried out in the *strictest* secrecy . . .

D1434410

BERKELY MATHER

# The Springers

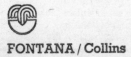

FONTANA / Collins

First published by Wm. Collins 1968
First issued in Fontana Books 1970
Second Impression July 1973

© 1968 by Berkely Mather

Printed in Great Britain
Collins Clear-Type Press London and Glasgow

# Chapter 1

Charlton was talking as we walked up the Strand. It's compulsive with him at the start of a job—like some parachutists can't stop yawning before a jump. Smoking helps, but he'd heard somewhere that no gentleman smokes in the street, and he was strong on gentility. There was a fine soaking rain falling, but he would no more have thought of opening his umbrella than of closing his bottom waistcoat button. Outside the Savoy, thank God, we got a taxi and I gave him a cigarette and said unkindly, 'Shut up, Carlovich,' and he lapsed into a hurt silence for a minute and a half, then, near Somerset House, he said, 'They'll confirm in there that it's Charlton. Deed-poll, sure, but is there any need to be bloody offensive?'

I didn't answer, so he went on miffishly: 'Did I ask for the job? Is it a nice thing to be a party to blackmailing one's godfather?' I told him to shut up again, and added something about his godfather, in fractured Shanghai Russian, which held him in a trembling white-faced rage until we got out in Throgmorton Street. I didn't like doing this to him, but I was even more on edge than he was. I'd never worked in England before, whereas he had not been out of the country for fifteen years and was sure of himself, although *my* name is James Wainwright—not by deed-poll.

I let him pay for the taxi, which I knew would please him. He'd charge the office for the whole distance from Edgware now, and add a two bob tip.

The shop was behind Copthall Court, squeezed between a bank and a fifteen-storey cut-down of the United Nations building, all glass and synthetic black marble. It had one of those round blue plaques over the low doorway—the shop, I mean—that said Josiah Wartnaby had lived here in seventeen-eighty, but one felt that that wasn't going to save its mellow brick and exquisite Regency bow windows for much longer, because there were no windows in the adjacent sides of the bank or the black-and-glass monstrosity, and you knew that some developer was going to bridge the gap in the near future. It was double-fronted, two convexes separated by an Adam doorway, like a jewel between breasts. In one window was a Tsientsin rug draped over an ebony Mandarin chair, a large Sung vase and some jade in a small cabinet. In the other were some good scrolls and one pen-painting I'd have given my eye teeth for. Mongolian horses and Wa-hai ducks in flight or anything else you could have bought in the lobby of the Hong Kong Hilton were out. Yes, this chap knew his *objets chinois*. What we were about to do to him seemed a pity.

Through the glass we could see two men moving slowly towards the door, and Charlton jerked at my sleeve.

'Let's move,' he said. 'The other feller's old Chavers. High Court judge. That's the sort of customer he gets. Top class.'

We looked into a clockmaker's window until an old man in a long overcoat and the sort of broad-brimmed black felt hat that judges, top lawyers and Petticoat Lane crockery salesmen wear, had gone down the lane past us, then we went back. Hand on door, Charlton said, 'In Russian to begin with? It sometimes amuses him.'

'Who wants to be amused?' I asked. 'English.'

We heard a buzzer sound softly as we went inside. Everything was soft—the wall-to-wall carpeting, the light from the (real) dragon lamps and the smell which was a mixture of unburned joss-sticks, old leather and the crushed Tonkin beans I could see mixed with camphorwood chips in a big porcelain censer in the middle of the floor. He came out of the shadows at the back of the shop, a tall man with a slight stoop in dark tweeds, old but expensively cut and as mellowed as the bricks outside. He was clean-shaven and his white hair was well barbered, almost cropped, and you had the feeling that it had always been white because, apart from the stoop, he was ageless, his face unlined and his eyes unfaded blue and alive, and his slightly irregular but very white teeth undoubtedly his own. A well-preserved fifty-five, I'd have said, if I hadn't known that Records had him down as born in Leningrad when it was St Petersburg, in nineteen hundred. He was either a genuinely kindly man or a good actor, because he seemed really pleased to see his godson, who wasn't everybody's cup of tea. *I* certainly wouldn't have kissed the little jerk on both cheeks as this chap did. But that was the only Russian touch. After that we were all as British as lukewarm bitter.

Charlton said: 'James Wainwright, Uncle Paul—we just happened to be passing. Mr Paul Malcolm—he's not really my

6

uncle, but you remember how it was with us kids in Shanghai? Everybody who didn't have slant eyes and a flat nose was uncle ——'

I tried to get a word in as I shook hands with Malcolm, but Charlton was nervous again and wouldn't stop talking. He went on: 'James is still interested in all this bloody Chink stuff. Me, I hate it—sorry, Uncle. How's Auntie, and Sonia and Nicky? I've been trying to get around some Sunday for tea, but you know how it is. Anyhow, we were just passing so I thought——' and in the end I had to do it the rough way. I said: 'Shut up, Charlton, for Christ's sake. It isn't necessary. Just vouch for me and beat it, will you.'

Malcolm was still smiling indulgently, but I sensed the change immediately. It was as if a transparent curtain had dropped between us, and surprise tactics, with all their advantage, were out.

'He's from the office,' Charlton mumbled miserably and looked down at the floor. 'I'm sorry, Uncle. The bastards made me do it. I didn't tell them. They knew.' Then the buzzer sounded, the door slammed, and he was gone. Malcolm was still smiling. He said, 'A peculiar boy. He always was. What can I do for you, Mr Wainwright?'

'A spring,' I told him and he looked politely blank.

'A spring? I'm sorry—I'm afraid I'm not with you.'

'Charlton's broken the ice,' I said. 'Shall we start from there, and save some time?'

But he was over the initial shock now, like a boxer who has taken a count of eight and is back on his feet, rested and wary.

'I still don't understand,' he said. 'Suppose you come to the point, Mr Wainwright. I'm a *reasonably* busy man, fortunately.'

'Then we don't save any time,' I answered. 'Very well. From the top. Paul Melkelm, anglicized on naturalization to Malcolm. Father Ukrainian—medical officer in the Czarist forces. He escaped after the nineteen-seventeen Revolution into Mongolia and from there to Shanghai—together with your mother, you and your younger sister. He practised medicine there until his death in nineteen-thirty-five. Correct?'

He nodded slowly. 'All on record. But we're still no nearer the point.'

'We'll skip it whenever you wish,' I said. 'I mentioned a spring. Does that refresh your memory now?'

7

'Not in the slightest.'

'So we go on. From the age of five to your seventeeth year —the time of your family's escape—you were educated at the Imperial Academy for Pages in St Petersburg. You specialized in English and Mandarin, as you were intended for Diplomacy after your military service. Correct?'

Again he nodded.

'Your father sent you to England from Shanghai. Two years' private tuition and then up to Oxford, where you took an honours degree in English. You then returned to Shanghai and taught at St Michael's College for a couple of years.'

'Three, actually. Nineteen-twenty-three to 'twenty-six.'

'Thank you. Then you came back here and taught for a time in the School of Oriental Languages, Bloomsbury. You became a British subject in nineteen-thirty.'

'And as such I have certain acquired, if not inherent, rights,' he said tartly. 'One of which is to refuse to answer questions put to me by unauthorized persons. Who are you, Mr Wainwright, and what the blazes do you want with me?' He was losing his temper. It cheered me a little.

'I told you—a spring.'

'And I told *you*—I don't know what the hell you're talking about.'

'Up to you. We recruited you in nineteen-thirty-five.'

'Who is "we" and what are you supposed to have recruited me for?'

'With respect, sir, you know perfectly well what I'm talking about—and where I come from. Your nephew has vouched for me.'

'Godson,' he corrected. 'A doubtful honour I inherited from my father. It's a custom in the Orthodox Church to sponsor the children of servants. *His* father was our gardener. I'm sorry if that sounds horribly snobbish, but I neither like nor trust the little rat.'

'Yet you kissed him upon both cheeks as he crossed the threshold,' I said in Russian.

'As Judas kissed Christ,' he answered in the same language, and added in English, 'So you're another of the bastards, are you?'

'That all depends on which bastards you mean. I'm from the office. The same old firm you belonged to for eleven years—and into which you recruited the little rat you neither like nor trust.'

'Grade Three courier, *under* supervision—and only because we were desperately short of screened personnel who could speak both Russian and Chinese. They seem to have promoted the bloody moujhik if they're sending him round to vouch for people.' Yes, the old boy was a snob. All the real Whites were—but the bloody moujhiks seemed to love them for it.

'A spring,' I said gently. 'Ready to discuss it yet?'

'No,' he snapped. 'Nor anything else. I left all that in 'forty-six—cum laude and a gratuity of two thousand pounds, and a bullet in my arse. The two thousand started this business and my arse aches in wet weather. It's aching now. If you're lucky you might beat a stockbroker to a taxi in Throgmorton Street, but not after five-thirty.' He moved to the door and held it open, the buzzer sounding a sustained note. I sat down on a carved camphorwood chest. He closed the door and came back to me.

'Finished, Mr Wainwright,' he said softly. 'Go back and tell them to read my file again. I saw them draw the red line the day I signed the Official Secrets Act. We split a bottle of inferior champagne and old Farrow gave me an even more inferior cigar. He'd have been before your time, I should imagine. The office was still in Ealing in those days.'

'They've read it,' I told him. 'So have I. Up to the red line and past.'

'There's nothing past the line.'

'A two-page addendum,' I said.

'Routine snooping, no doubt.' He nodded as if recalling something. 'Yes, of course, I'd forgotten that. What does the addendum say, Mr Wainwright? What could it say? That I've been in business here for twenty years——? That I've married? —no, that would be above the line. I married before the war. Two children—a boy of twenty-two, a girl two years older —the former a makee-learn lawyer, as we'd have said in Shanghai, in good chambers in the Middle Temple—no briefs yet, but excellent prospects. Sonia, poor lass, looks after her invalid mother. She did six years at the Royal School of Ballet, but she's never even *looked* reproachful. But they wouldn't have all that, would they?'

'Actually yes. Sonia and Nicholas. Not about their characteristics, of course. Just that Sonia is very beautiful and that Nicholas is well-thought of—and that you're very proud of both of them, and that Mrs Malcolm is an arthritic.'

'Christ! Is there any limit to the impertinence of the Civil

Service?' He was really angry now. 'That's all you are, you know. Civil servants, and as such, with a certain vulnerability. Does it mention my friends? Forgive another display of snobbishness, but I number a round dozen on the Bench, in the Cabinet and in the higher echelons of Fleet Street. I've never used any of them. I hope I'll never be tempted to do so, but just drop the hint back there, Mr Wainwright—in case they think of sending you, or any other—er—other——'

'Moujhik,' I supplied.

'*You* said it—around to talk riddles.'

'I'm afraid they will.'

'Right—then I shall complain. I've done all they ever asked me to do, and more. Now I want to be left in peace.'

'Then suppose we come back to this spring? I'm sorry, I can't go until we've discussed it.' And I was sorry. The Gaffer had warned me that he was likeable, with his mixture of donnish primness and longshoreman's profanity. And I'd seen both his kids and had heard what his poor complaining devil of a wife meant to him, and how he loved this business he had built out of nothing. And his record, above the line, was magnificent—and he had guts and humour. At that moment I would have settled for shovelling ordure in a sewer in preference to this.

He sighed. 'Anything to terminate this distasteful interview. All right—the verb "to spring"—to get somebody out of prison. What about it?'

'Your speciality,' I said, and curiously that eased things. We all have our vanities.

He grinned impishly. 'The best in the business,' he said, and it didn't sound vainglorious because we both knew it was a straight statement of fact. 'Forty-seven agents and a hundred and thirty-eight R.A.F. and American navigators brought out safely. They could train pilots, poor dears, much quicker in those days, so they had to make it on their flat feet or stay where they were. All right—once again, what about it?'

'We'd like you to do another. Just one.'

He smiled sweetly and said sorry.

'Ten thousand pounds—tax free,' I said softly.

'Not for a hundred thousand. I'm getting old and stiff, and I don't do any travelling these days.'

'You do,' I contradicted.

'Oh, Hong Kong? That's not travelling. I commute out there and buy some stuff for the shop from time to time, certainly, but you wouldn't want the services of a highly expensive specialist there, for God's sake. Anyhow, important European prisoners are flown home and do their time in Maidstone. But we're talking nonsense. If you had somebody in Stanley Gaol you'd only have to ask for him.'

'Not Hong Kong,' I said. 'Although that comes into it.'

'A Chinese mainlaind nick?' he squeaked. 'Don't be silly, my dear chap. Impossible—even for me.'

'European nick,' I said patiently. 'But we want the client spirited out to Hong Kong—or somewhere near there.'

'Then I suggest Aladdin and his wonderful lamp.' He yawned. 'I'm sorry for my earlier rudeness,' he said. 'Actually I've enjoyed our little talk, but I'm afraid the answer's still no —*non*—*niet*. You are from Shanghai yourself, aren't you? Not Russian, though. I can spot a China-Rusk a mile off. That godson of mine will never be able to clip those long vowels, spurious O.E., tie, rolled umbrella and bowler hat notwithstanding. Awful little shite, isn't he? What *is* your background, since we're both being rude?'

'My old man was a Chief Inspector in the International Concession police,' I told him.

'And you were educated where?'

'St Michael's—after your time of course—then St Paul's on a Mackinnon Scholarship.'

'Army?'

'National Service. Six months in the ranks, six at Mons OCTU, twelve as a Second Lieutenant with the Parachutes. All post-war.'

'Got you absolutely.' He looked pleased with himself. 'How did you get into this murky racket? Or is that *too* rude?'

'A little,' I said.

'It couldn't be the pay. God, they're mean, aren't they? In my heyday I ranked with a half-colonel but got less than an R.A.S.C. major. And the expenses! Do you know what? I once had a taxi bill in Berlin queried—in *nineteen-forty-three*. I was bringing out two clients—Frenchmen. I had to borrow from them to complete the last stage—tube from Victoria to Baker Street.'

'Still the same,' I told him. 'But they're doing *you* all right. Ten thousand quid—*and* expenses.'

'Ten years ago it might have tempted me,' he said.

'I'm afraid you'll still have to be tempted.'

'I don't have to be anything I don't choose to be,' he

flashed. He was getting angry again. 'Good night, Mr Wainwright. I'd like to say drop in again some time for another little talk, but that would be insincere. You wouldn't be a really interesting conversationalist until you had been redlined for the statutory fourteen years, and you'll probably be found dead in highly discreditable circumstances up a dark lane or in a bawdy house long before then. I had enough sense to get out while the going was good—and I'm not coming back.'

'I'm sorry,' I said, and again I meant it. 'You're obliging *me* to be a shite now. You've been back—as a freelance—two years ago. That's in the addendum too.'

That was my first victory, if you could call it such. His face showed nothing because he was now sitting on another carved chest, with his back to one of the dragon lamps. It was just something one felt. He was silent for a long moment, then he said quietly: 'Prove it.'

'Wally Wharton, the bank robber. Out of the top security wing in Lanchester. You were promised twenty thousand for that, but you only collected five. You should have had a better guarantee. But it was your first experience with real professional crooks, wasn't it?'

He said again: 'Prove it.'

I said: 'I don't have to. Wharton's dead. His pals leaned on him too heavily—trying to get him to tell where the bulk of the loot was stashed. But his wife's alive—under Special Branch protection. She's being paid a pension which is about treble what she'd get under National Assistance. If that was ever stopped she'd go to the Sunday weeklies—naming names. The Yard would act then. They're straining at the leash as it is. You've no idea how vicious regular police can get when they're under political pressure. You could count on seven years.'

'And I'd do them—gladly. And *I'd* talk then—in court.'

'In camera,' I reminded him. 'Interests of the State.'

'Then before the trial.'

'You're talking wildly now. You'd be in custody, and incommunicado from the moment your collar was felt.'

'There are still ways.'

'Name them. Anyhow, why are we talking about *you*? There's Sonia.'

'Leave my family out of it.'

'I wish I could. But Sonia was the plumber's mate on that

job, wasn't she? That's going to lose you a lot of sympathy. She wouldn't get more than eighteen months as a first offender, led astray by her father—but Holloway's a hell of a place for a sensitive girl. Then the effect on young Nicholas's career——'

I didn't have time to dodge it. It wasn't a token slap either. He lifted me right off the camphorwood chest on to my backside. I waited until my ears stopped singing, then I got up and tried to shrug.

'Well, that's it, Mr Malcolm,' I said. 'Think it over. I'll be back this time tomorrow.'

The don was entirely subjugated to the longshoreman now. He cursed filthily for a minute and a half.

'All right,' he growled at last. 'Who is it—and where? And how do I get paid?'

'There'll be somebody along,' I told him. 'I only have to take your answer back. I gather that it's yes?'

'You're the bumboy who shovels the filth in the first place, are you?' he said. 'I'll bet you're good at your job. They'll give you a desk at the end of it all—if somebody doesn't break your bloody neck first. Somebody like me.'

'Your answer please?' I insisted.

'What *can* it be?' he asked bitterly. 'You dirty, scabrous, pustulating lot of bastards. Tell 'em yes.'

'Thank you, Mr Malcolm,' I said.

It must have sounded funny, because he chuckled drily and mimicked me as he let me out, and through the glass I could hear him bellowing as I walked away through the rain.


## Chapter 2

I got a taxi by St Paul's and told the driver I wanted the Lazy Rabbit. He didn't know it, which wasn't surprising because I didn't either, so he got out his little book and we hemmed and hawed for a couple of minutes and decided it was the Hazy Hare I wanted, in Knightsbridge. I paid him off as we were passing the Savoy, hopped out quickly, went through the lounge and down the stairs to the ballroom, and out through the Embankment entrance and grabbed a solitary cab going west. Officially I wasn't working and I couldn't think of anybody sufficiently interested in me to be tailing me on spec—other than the office. They sometimes put a legman on to us in the early stages of a job to ensure the Opposition wasn't shadowing us—or so they said. Charlton swore it was Finance who did it, to check on pubs, meals and taxis and so discourage expense-sheet padding. He may have been right. Tonight I was hoping spitefully that I was giving some poor sod sore feet and a run for his, or their, money.

I did the last two hundred yards on foot, down a cul-de-sac off Victoria Street which has the plate-glass windows of a department store on one side and the screamingly ugly façade of a huge Edwardian tenement the other. The tenement contains a hundred and fifty-three dogbox apartments, mostly let to Members of Parliament when the House is in session, and it is the perfect bolthole, because once inside any of its six street entrances you're in a labyrinth of dark staircases, narrow corridors and usually out-of-order elevators, so unless your tail is right on your heels you can shake him flat.

The Gaffer lived on the second floor. To call one's boss Gaffer or Guv'nor is usually to accord him a certain respect, admiration or even a grudging affection. In this case you can forget the middle and last. He opened in answer to the treble-pause-single ring he always insisted on, and let me into the tiny square hall. The sitting-room was on the left, bedroom on the right, and facing was a door into a six-foot-square kitchen. There must have been a bathroom somewhere, but thank God I never had occasion to ask for it. The whole place smelt of dust, damp overcoats and cheese and looked like a stage set of Sherlock Holmes's Baker Street apartment. I never saw out of the windows because they were always covered by dusty brown curtains with bobbles along the edges, and looked, but certainly never opened, on to an air shaft. There was no aspidistra but there was a po-shaped thing with pink roses on it that ought to have held one, standing beside a fireplace the size and shape of the southern approach to Tower Bridge which framed the smallest gas fire I have ever seen. There was a huge overmantel above it heavily carved with vineleaves and scrotum-like bunches of some weird fruit, through which tiny flyspecked mirrors coyly peeped. Steel engravings covering battle scenes from Balaclava to Rorke's Drift plastered the gamboge cauliflowered wallpaper. Whatnots, chiffoniers and the sort of bookcases which come with subscription sets of encyclopædias filled all the rest of the space that wasn't taken up by an enormous dining table, two 'easy' chairs and a sofa. One chair was occupied by a fat and asthmatic cocker bitch with lumps on its belly like the overmantel carvings, the other I knew was master's. In response to his grunted invitation I took the end of the sofa where the springs hadn't gone, after careful inspection, because I'd once got a punctured behind and a bitten ankle through sitting on a chop bone temporarily abandoned by the cocker.

And the Gaffer fitted perfectly into the whole ghastly setting. They say that some people get to resemble their dogs, or maybe it's the other way round. Here was a case in point. He was fat and asthmatic and his hair seemed to have rubbed off in bare patches rather than normally balded, and you guessed that his yellowing teeth were loose and that he was short-sighted. But in the last you'd have guessed wrong. Those little faded blue piggy peepers behind their thick glasses missed nothing. Age? I don't know. Those of us who suffered under him hoped it wasn't far off retirement point, which in our branch was sixty. He was wearing shapeless, shiny, elephant-arsed blue serge trousers, unbuttoned waistcoat and carpet slippers. His collar and tie were over the back of his chair. He looked like a Tooley Street tally-clerk after a hard shift at the docks.

I thought of that beautiful shop and its likeable old owner and compared both with this place and the slag who was my boss, and I wondered afresh why I could never muster the strength of purpose to quit.

The Gaffer said, 'Well?' and relit a cigarette he had economically nipped earlier. He took a lungful right down, and brought it up again fast. It seemed to come out of his ears as well as his nose and mouth. I waited for the spluttering to subside and said, 'He says yes.'

'Of course he says yes,' he wheezed. 'What the hell else did you expect him to say?'

'I almost hoped he'd say it was blackmail, and tell you to stuff it.'

'That'd be the day. Blackmail my foot.'

'Have you got another term for it?'

'Sure. Face-saving.'

'Call it what you like, it still stinks.'

'Don't talk bloody silly,' he said, and spat at the gas fire.

'You call offering a feller ten thousand *blackmail*? My God! I wish someone'd blackmail *me*.'

'A sick wife——'

'A whining old beldame who makes his life a hell,' he said.

'Two kids——'

'One who takes to grafting as naturally as her old man, the other a useless young bleeder who gets corns on his rump in every discothèque along the King's Road.'

I stared at him. 'If that's the truth, why did you give me a totally contradictory briefing before I went there?' I asked.

'Because that's the line I wanted you to follow—that we were acting more in sorrow than in anger—that we hated to do this to him, but we would if he forced our hands. We'd ruin him, bring sorrow to his invalid wife, and Little Nell his chickabiddies out into the cold, cold snow. If you believed that yourself you'd put it over a damned sight more convincingly than if you were huckstering with your tongue in your cheek. You follow?' He looked knowingly at me with his head on one side.

'I don't.'

He sighed. 'I'll draw you a picture. First of all, I know Malcolm—know everything there is to know about him. I can evaluate him to the last hair. I know what he will do and how he will react in any given set of circumstances—like I know it about a hell of a lot of other people—including quite a few gents who roam in this Babylon.'

'In other words you're good.'

He grinned with one side of his mouth and drew smoke with the other. 'Sarcasm bounces off my hide like peas off a tin roof. You bet I'm good. That's why I sit at the top of the pile and send you young punks legging round the globe when I whistle. You know how I started in this business? I'll tell you. I was a chalk-and-water boy for the Sheffield race gangs back in the middle 'twenties, then I went over to Chicago. I was running a beer truck before I was eighteen. Then I did a bit—more than a bit—of strong-arming for the mobs, until I collected a mob of my own. I quit when Prohibition ended and then it was South America, then China—and finally I came back here in the early days of the war to be a gun-knife-and-general-mayhem professor for the Commandos. Finished up as a full colonel—then came to this crowd——'

'Yes, good,' I said again. 'We agreed on that, but what's it all got to do with Malcolm, and my having my leg pulled?'

'Psychology,' he said profoundly. 'I've never done a day's bird in my life—never even had my collar felt—but boy, do I know how the villains think and act.'

'But Malcolm isn't a villain.'

'Not a fully-paid-up practising villain, maybe, but he's a first class schizo. Two people pulling in opposite directions. Jekyll and Hyde, if you like. He got a lot of the Hyde out of his system when he was working for us, so Jekyll has generally managed to stay on top, but only just. He slipped badly over the Wharton business and it scared him, and he's got enough sense to know that he's too old for those capers now and he's got to stay on the straight and narrow.'

'You mean there have been other jobs—criminal jobs, I mean—besides the Wharton one?' I asked.

'Five that I know of for certain—two that I suspect,' he said calmly, and I felt a surge of anger.

'And you let me go to him like a bloody innocent and——' I began.

'I didn't *let* you. I sent you,' he snapped. 'Shut up and let me finish. I'm not telling you all this just to bum my load. I want you to understand. If you had gone along there and put it straight on him to do this job for ten thousand, he'd have turned you down flat. Jekyll would have been right on top. If you'd mentioned a whole string of jobs he'd have said balls—do your worst—knowing damn well that we wouldn't dare give him away to the police. He's got too much on us. As it is you've mentioned just one job—the only one that we could tip off to the Yard without in any way getting involved ourselves. You've blackmailed him, as you call it, twisted his arm and thereby given him the excuse *he needs himself* to do it. He has to yield to force majeure now.'

'But what if he changes his mind?'

'He won't,' he chuckled. 'I told you—I know him. He wants to do it. He loves it—but he must be able to justify it to himself. If he doesn't do it his wife and kids will suffer. The blame is shifted from him now. Don't you see?'

I thought I did. Anyhow there was no point in going all over it again. I'd been made a monkey of, but I'd completed my part of it. I yawned and stood up.

'Where are you going?' he demanded.

'Sorry,' I answered, 'I thought you'd finished.'

'Finished be damned. I haven't started yet. I'm giving you your full briefing now—then you're completely on your own. I don't want you near the office again until it's all over.'

And I had been hoping that I slipped it to somebody else now and went back to my own sector when my home leave was over in another week! I sat down feeling injured.

'Do you know Winterton?' he asked.

'I know *of* him—and I was once introduced to him in the Hong Kong Club.'

'He's not clubbing at the moment, poor bastard. They're clubbing him. He's working on the breakwater in Amoy. They took him off his ship—accused of smuggling refugees out.'

'He'll get four years' rice and the sayings of Chairman Mao if they make it stick,' I said.

'He's got twenty-five,' he answered. 'We've known for a month but we've been trying to do a deal. They found some undeveloped film down in the bilges.'

'How hot?'

'Middling. Harbour installations on the Whangpu—very amateurishly done. Just the sort of stuff an honest China coast skipper would be dealing in, if he wanted to make a few bob from Admiralty Intelligence. We reckoned it would get him ten years, which would be scrubbed if he was willing to talk.'

I began to see light. 'A furbler?' I said.

He smiled sourly. 'Smart feller. Away ahead of me. Yes, a furbler.'

Don't ask me the etymology of the word. A furbler is something an agent sometimes carries as a red herring to disguise his real mission in the event of exposure. If it's to be worth a damn it has to be something genuine—a bishop to save a queen. Once discovered, the agent is at liberty to talk. How much he spills and the degree of resistance he puts up under intensive interrogation is a matter for his histrionic ability and his animal cunning—I don't use the term personal integrity, but all three come into it. To be convincing, he's got to let it go slowly and reluctantly, however hard they may be leaning on him. When he does break he's got to slobber, literally slobber, the lot—almost invariably under lights and in front of a camera. The danger is, of course, that the chap can be pushed to the point sometimes where he is no longer able to distinguish the shadow from the substance, and demarcation lines get blurred, and he babbles on and throws the real thing. The opposition, being fully aware of this, work on it—which is why one can never be really certain of tea and sympathy even after one has sobbed all. They tell you on that part of your training—which takes six months—that a very good furbler in the hands of a resolute man can sometimes save his real mission, but never his skin. It's not meant to. They also tell you that it isn't the damnedest bit of use inventing one of your own. They can be blown too easily—and then you're in real grief. For the reasons I have given, and a lot more I haven't, furblers are strictly for the dons, and on very important business only. Winterton was therefore a don, which surprised me. I knew him, and only slightly at that, as an obscure Hong Kong freighter skipper with a red face, a beer belly and a penchant for wenching in Wanchai.

'What was he really on?' I asked.

'Not bloody likely,' the Gaffer said, 'or we'll have to be giving *you* a furbler—and you don't qualify by a long chalk yet. All you need to know is that front office wants him out.'

'Then Malcolm won't play,' I said. 'You told me, and I told him, that the client was in a European gaol and merely had to be shipped out to Hong Kong. He specifically said that mainland nicks were——'

'If you'll specifically belt up, Wainwright, we might get this finished before morning, and I'll be able to bugger off to bed,' he said wearily. 'Where was I? Oh yes—we want him out. He's sprung his furbler—' he looked maliciously pleased —'which involved five of your blokes being blown.'

'What about me?' I asked bleakly.

'He doesn't know about you.'

'But some of my blokes do!'

'Four leggers and a comprador,' he explained, and I breathed again. We used the old-fashioned five-cell system in my sector. A field man knew only his own cell supervisor, or comprador: a comprador knew his own four and one field man in the cell above. Only in the rarefied heights near the top of the pile did we start knowing each other laterally. Of course one penetrated cell could, through the skill and patience of the opposition—and the bastards had plenty of both—lead to a chain reaction upward, but that took time and

19

we were usually able to regroup before really serious harm was done.

He went on: 'It's at quasi-diplomatic level at the moment. They're willing to do a swap. Winterton for Carter.'

'Carter?' I stared at him. 'But he's been with the Russians for years—right up to the time we caught him.'

'Wheels within wheels.' He smiled twistedly. 'No need to wriggle. They didn't know it at the top—Yanks or us. Carter, like your pal Malcolm, is from Shanghai—and ninety-nine point nine per cent of Shanghai-Rusks are white as the driven snow. Carter's the point one. As English as Malcolm on the surface, but as Russian as droshkis underneath—and as dedicatedly red as the seat of Lenin's underpants right through—yes, all that came out at his trial. What *didn't* come out was that Carter built Mao's intelligence service for him —and was serving him faithfully right up to the split between the Russians and Chinese. He was still serving after the split —but not so single-heartedly. He was leaking to the Russians. The Chinese suspected it, but he got the tip and skipped for Vladivostok before the big chop. He was useless in the Far East then, naturally, but Moscow doesn't believe in passengers. They sent him West. He was out of his element, but he's damn good by any standards. He'd set up three new networks centred in London that not even the Russian Embassy knew of—rubber-heeling on their regular agents—and had suborned a senior civil servant in the Ministry of Power —all inside twelve months. Then the poor bastard walked into a Chink restaurant in Ipswich one night, and the boy who served him happened to be an ex-Shanghai Aliens Bureau dick, two-buttoning for our Special Branch. He recognised him. That bowl of egg-fuyong and noodles cost Carter thirty years.'

'And the Chinese want him back?'

'And how.'

'But what use will he be to them now?'

'Makee-talk in the first place. Oh, sure—the bulk of his Russian stuff will be old hat by now, but some of it will be useful. He could still blow some people in Outer Mongolia —probably a few in China itself. But that's not the point. Come on—you're the expert. What's the most important thing to the Chinese? More important even than respect for ancestors?'

'Face,' I said.

'Exactly,' he nodded. 'Here's a guy who pulled the wool over their eyes for years—then sold them out to people they hate worse than us—worse than the Americans. Plenty of face lost there. Think how much they'd regain that face if they got him back and gave him a bloody big public trial in Peking—Red Guards yowling and all. The long arm of Chairman Mao plucking him right from the heartland of the West and bringing him to justice! Boy! What a triumph that would be.'

'What would they do to him afterwards?' I asked.

He looked at me pityingly. 'Either that question was purely rhetorical, or you're drawing your pay under false pretences. Chop his goddamn head off and stick it on a pole outside the Gate of Heaven. What the hell else?'

'I just wanted to be certain,' I said. 'That, of course, rules out an official exchange for Winterton.'

'That's my boy.' He grinned at me like a jackal savouring a bone. 'He's thinking now. That rules out an official exchange, just like you said. So Malk whisks him over the wall and you take him out there and make a trade—softlee-softlee. Everybody happy.'

'Except Carter.'

'Except Carter—but you can't please everybody, can you? You're not the Fairy Queen.'

'You're bloody right,' I said. 'Or the Wicked Magician either. All right—even presuming Malcolm gets him out of a top security gaol here—an unwilling man. How do I get him across the globe in secret?'

'Your problem, sonny boy.' He grinned even wider. 'A damned interesting one. All you'll have against you are the cops, three assorted branches of our alleged intelligence service, the cops of any countries you move through and, I'm pretty darned certain, the Rusks trying like hell to hijack you en route.'

I said, 'Suppose we drop the comedy for just a few moments. There are some questions I'd like to ask.'

'I'll bet there are—but you'll hear me out first. After that you can say yes or no. If it's no, well it's been nice knowing you. You'll be red-lined, you'll sign the O.S. chit, draw what you have coming to you and go back to polishing your tail in the bank. The bank will offer you a job in London, by the way. Hong Kong will be *terre interdite* to you, naturally.'

'We come back to a word we were discussing earlier,' I said.

'Blackmail? Sure. It's a tool of the trade. You don't need me to explain that to you, surely?'

'How dirty can we get?' I asked of nobody in particular.

'You'd be surprised—really surprised—if we're pushed,' he said. 'It's a very dirty business. Didn't they tell you that when you joined?'

I lit a cigarette, and he went on talking.

'I'm assuming that it's yes,' he said, 'but you can stop me at any time you wish, and walk out—with the provisos I've just mentioned. All right—you go back to Malcolm and tell him that he'll get two thousand five hundred in advance—in fivers through the mail tomorrow morning. You'll get his plan and list of requirements. We'll help to the limit—short of involvement—other than yourself, of course. I don't want to say "if you're nicked you're on your own" because I hate melodramatics, and anyhow you know that already——'

He was still talking at three-thirty and I was listening glumly. Then I left.

## Chapter 3

The drizzle had turned into a steady pelting rain and I was soaked and savage by the time I reached Courtfield Gardens because the only taxi I saw was in Brompton Road and that was engaged. God, how I hated London. In my grade —I'm talking about the bank now—one got two months' home leave every two years. 'Home' was a loose term and provided you didn't exceed the cost of an air tourist return ticket between Hong Kong and London, you could go where you liked. I'd spent my previous leave in Australia and the one before that in America. I suppose I'd better explain about the bank at this point. It was my permanent front but at the same time it was a genuine job and, surprisingly, one I liked. The 'office' had placed me there, of course, long before I even knew of its existence—the 'office' I mean. Everybody knew about the existence of the bank. It was a monument to the acumen of our great-grandfathers and was as much part of Hong Kong as the Peak itself.

My mother died when I was twelve, and the old man when I was half-way through my National Service. His job had gone up the spout when the Communists took over in Shanghai in nineteen-forty-nine, and he was living in London. The British Government paid him a reduced and purely ex gratia pension and gave him sporadic work as an interpreter at the Crown Agents for the Colonies in Horseferry Road. I was serving in Aden at the time of his death and they let me fly back for the funeral. Of necessity I hadn't seen much of the old boy since coming home to school, so I was surprised and touched to find that he had left me seven hundred pounds, a five-year, fully paid-up lease of a three-roomed flat in Courtfield Gardens, and a letter. The letter asked me to see a Mr Kempson at the London Office of the Hong Kong and Southern China Bank. And Kempson, the Assistant General Manager, offered me a job in their foreign exchange department when I came out of the army—and for the want of something better I accepted. It was as casual and as haphazard as that. Or so I thought.

I had been a glorified office boy for a year before anybody approached me, and was seriously thinking of slinging it and trying something else, because, gratitude apart, Gloucester Road to Moorgate and return five days a week was beginning to pall, in spite of a half-promise from Kempson that in due course I might be considered for that plum of plums, a posting to the Head Office in Hong Kong.

Again it was casual; a kindly boss invited a rather lonely junior employee to spend Christmas at his Sussex home. I didn't particularly want to go but I couldn't think of an excuse quick enough when he asked me, so I went down for four days, and his son and daughter tried to interest me in golf at Rye, and on Boxing Night I was inveigled into a yum sing contest—a stupid Chinese drinking game with very simple rules. You just swallow half a tumbler of Scotch every time someone points at you and bellows 'Yum sing'—then you point at somebody else and do the same—and the winner is the last on his feet. I have often wondered if it was intended as some sort of test. If it was I didn't pass it, because I crawled under the billiard table and went to sleep while the rest of the guests, hearty taipan types home on Christmas leave for the most part, were still only getting warmed up.

But I must have had other unsuspected potentialities, certainly by myself, or maybe it was a poor vintage year for recruits, because Kempson invited me to his study the following day, ostensibly to talk about my prospects with the

23

bank, and there were two others of the guests there—and when I came out three hours later, feeling prickly and uncomfortable at some of the questions they had fired at me and even more so at the number of answers they seemed to know already, I knew I had two weeks in which to think things over. I didn't need the two weeks, because I was bored stiff with my job and I was already vacillating between trying to sign on as a deck hand for a long trip somewhere or flogging second-hand cars in Great Portland Street. But they insisted on the pause, and, in fact, Kempson was really very fair. He gave me a rundown on my prospects with the bank if I turned this new proposition down, and they weren't at all bad by any standards. I'd get my move out to Hong Kong before long, and thereafter it would be a steady climb up the seniority ladder with an increment in pay every two years as long as I kept on the ball and off the liquor—an ever present hazard for the Far Eastern businessman—until retiring age in the sixty bracket and a comfortable pension. I ventured a question about the prospects of the other job at this stage, and the three of them smiled kindly and went on with the interview. One thing I did learn, though; my father had been in the business ever since he went out East in the 'twenties, his police job providing the perfect front. Perhaps the answer to my question lay right there. He left, as I have said, seven hundred pounds and a five-year lease on a small flat in Courtfield Gardens. So it can't have been the money that swayed my decision. That, for the record, was the exact equivalent of an army captain's pay, plus allowances but minus tax. Who the hell paid the tax I didn't know then or now, because I never saw anything that remotely resembled a payroll in the 'office'. You got what you had coming to you in cash, through the mail once every fourteen days for some reason or other, in envelopes on which the handwriting and postmarks varied from time to time.

I took some figures in for Kempson to see on the due date, and muttered yes please I'd like to try it—and he nodded non-committally. Three days later I was posted to one of our subsidiaries in Manchester 'for experience', because, although the bulk of our interests lay in China we were also involved in cotton. I actually went to Manchester, too, where I posted wish-you-were-here views of the Ship Canal to two typists in Foreign Exchange and then caught a bus to Chester and another on from there to a picturesque market town on the Wirral. There's a black-and-white timbered country house which overlooks the wild estuary of the Dee, a mile outside the town, and there, except for brief educational excursions, I stayed for a year.

There were eight of us on the course, of whom three dropped out fairly early. We all had one thing in common, and that wasn't sex either, because two of the remaining five were girls. It was just that none of us had a single tie in the world. We were orphans, unmarried and completely rootless. Our ages ranged, I should have said at a guess, from a very fit forty down to myself at the bottom of the scale, just pushing twenty-two when I arrived. The girls were something under thirty, and one of them was attractive—to look at, anyhow. I never got the opportunity to explore the beauties of her mind. It wasn't that the teaching faculty discouraged things. One just didn't have the time, because the scope and pace of the course was murderous. The staff numbered over a hundred although no more than fifteen were ever in residence at any one time. They always arrived by car at night, and departed the same way, and what the hell they did in the interregnums I just wouldn't be knowing. But by God they were thorough. Half-way through the summer they gave us a merciful break. Each of us was booked on a different fortnight's package tourist trip. I drew fourteen days down to the Canaries. I would have settled for two weeks with my feet up in London, but they were adamant on this point, as on all others. The Canaries, they said, and like it. Come back with a tan and all batteries recharged—nothing like a complete break. They were so solicitous that I thought it was a prelude to being fired.

I met a girl on the ship. She was dark and intense, a little older than I but bloody good-looking. She was just getting over the break-up of an unhappy marriage. We discovered depths of understanding in each other, and I found I could talk to her as to no other woman I had met up until then —not that there had been many—and she had a single cabin to herself and we got politely drunk in Funchal. We exchanged addresses when we parted in Liverpool and arranged to meet when I was next in London. I was called in on the mat two days later and told, quite kindly, that my Courtfield Gardens flat was a comfortable and secure little pad but if I wanted to remain there I was not to give the address to casual acquaintances, particularly ones I slept with. I met her again a couple of months later when she came down to instruct on ciphers—sorry—I *saw* her again, but she apparently had forgotten me. Yes, they were thorough.

But at least that must have been my only bad break, because I finished the course and went back to the bank for six months, where I had to slog my guts out on legitimate business during the day and receive a final polish on other things—at Kempson's country house in the weekends and at various addresses round the suburbs in the evenings, including the 'office' in Edgware which fronted as a furniture depository. This is where I first met the Gaffer. He dislocated my shoulder and all but ruptured me during that part of my training. He had already graduated to higher things by this time, but he was a vain old bastard in matters pertaining to his original trade and liked to keep his hand in. His assistants were much better at it and rarely hurt the postulants seriously, although one of them nearly perforated my eardrum during pistol practice.

All this part of the training was treated apologetically—almost tongue in cheek. We should never need it, they told us; if we did it would be because we had made a balls of something and had got into what should have been avoidable trouble. But, as in everything else, they were thorough in it. Mons OCTU was not exactly a bed of roses, and parachute training was even tougher, but neither came anywhere near this. I don't know whether the girls were put through it, because by this time the Wirral house-party had split up and I was entirely on my own. As a matter of fact I've never seen any of them since. I once made the mistake of idly inquiring after them from the Gaffer. He turned a fishlike orb on me and said, 'If you ever met anybody else during training, which I doubt, they were probably makee-learn income tax collectors. Forget 'em.'

And then one day Kempson called me in and congratulated me on my progress—in the bank—and told me they were posting me out to Hong Kong a little ahead of schedule to replace a chap in the Exchange Branch who was being invalided home. Since I had not taken my current year's holidays and would get none for the next two, I was given a month's vacation, to take effect forthwith.

But again there was a catch in it. The Gaffer would call me at all hours of the day and night and tell me to go to such widely diverse places as the Eltham Golf Club, Guildford

Cathedral or a factory in Stepney by any method I chose, buying three packets of cigarettes and a pair of gym shoes, or some other such damned silly things, en route. The object was to throw unseen and unknown shadowers. If he could tell me afterwards the addresses of the shops I'd called into, he'd won. If he couldn't, I had. At the end of the month I was winning twice in five times, which I've learned since is a pretty good average.

I arrived in Hong Kong by air and was met at Kai Tak by a rowdy but good-natured crowd of my fellow juniors. We were called cadets and we lived in Mess, a relic of the East India Company days which many of the older banks and merchant houses still follow. If I expected any of these to make mystic signs and start slipping passwords to me, I was disappointed. Actually I was allowed to stew in my own juice for three months, just getting hep to my job in the bank, before someone approached me. He was an assistant manager in one of the commercial branches who was keen on sea fishing. He invited me out on his launch one Sunday. Six miles out on the South China Sea, and free from bugging, he made himself known and told me as much as I needed to know at that stage. He was purely a Transmitter, he informed me, and as such passed on orders and received reports from me. If I have given the impression of the bank being one big spy network, let me correct it here and now. Actually on the bank payroll I knew of only three, Kempson, this chap, and somebody much higher up in the hierarchy who could post me at the drop of a hat from one branch to another, or send me on a trip to Singapore, the Philippines or India, or indeed any other place where the bank had business. Since they liked the cadets to get around the territory, sadly shrunk since Chiang Kai-shek took off for Formosa in a hurry in nineteen-forty-nine, there was nothing unusual in sending juniors on sometimes quite important bank business at short notice. But none of this came my way until much later. For the nonce I was just to get on with my ordinary job and merge into my social background which, as a cadet, was by no means dull. The Mess paid a blanket subscription for us at the Hong Kong Club, the Yacht Club on Kellet Island and, of course, the Rugby Club at Happy Valley. I was to swim at Big Wave Bay on Sundays, get mildly tight on occasion, dance, play a little golf, lose an unremarkable amount of money at the races and get to know a couple of acceptable girls—this last not easy, because they are thin on the ground in proportion to the stag population, competition is correspondingly keen, and Hong Kong mothers are as Victorian in the management of their daughters' love lives as they are—some of them I mean—broadminded in their own. I enjoyed it all, and I was sorry that I couldn't have landed a job like this without sidelines. But I couldn't—not now. That was made abundantly clear to me at the outset. If I proved a flop in the sideline, the cover job went up the spout and Hong Kong was out as a domicile. Anybody at all can come into England from any part of the Commonwealth, but you try to squat in the Commonwealth if somebody in a Government office doesn't want you there.

And so my first two years went happily by. Wasted time? Maybe, but who was I to argue? I certainly wasn't straining at any leashes to get started. I did improve my Cantonese and Mandarin though, steadily and unostentatiously. The bank ran classes in both these and we were encouraged to attend them. I also kept very fit, not because I was under orders, but because I like being that way. I played a lot of squash and rugby, swam and practised advanced karate. I was a bit doubtful about this last as I thought it might draw attention to myself, but the cult was sweeping the Colony at that time and every young penpusher in Hong Kong was fancying himself as a dan.

Things were different when I came back from leave, though. They started to move me around—sometimes purely on legitimate bank business, more seldom on a real but unimportant 'office job'. Let me clarify here; an 'office job' is a mission. A mission can be anything to delivering somebody's pay to them or, as the Gaffer once put it, somebody's bloody pay-*off*. Can be, I said. My earlier missions lay somewhere in between the two, and for the most part were extremely dull. The only one in the first six months that involved me in any rough stuff was a delivery and pick-up job in Penang when I was jumped by a couple of big Chinese on the waterfront—Northern Province men—and was badly beaten up. But even then I believe it was a straight attempted robbery because they were satisfied with my watch and wallet and I didn't get the expert rolling I'd have got from a real pro looking for papers.

But the tempo was increasing the whole time. The Vietnam escalation kept us busy because the Americans were using Hong Kong like the rest of us were using West Berlin back in Europe—crossing point, clearing house for information, watch-tower and finance centre—and that brought in the opposition in shoals, Chinese and Europeans, and our job was primarily one of tabulating and tagging. So when I got my next leave—this one—I felt I'd earned it. But now they'd jumped the gun on me and were making me work in my own time.

I slept until ten o'clock and woke with a stinking cold. I phoned Malcolm and told him he'd be getting a parcel in the mail and that I'd call round later. He said with icy dislike that he'd rather I didn't, not two days running, and that *he'd* get in touch with *me*, and asked for a telephone number. I felt so lousy that for a moment I thought of giving him my own at the flat and staying in bed, which would have been a gross breach of security, but caution prevailed, as I injected even more dislike into my voice and told him I'd call him again later. The old sweats loved pulling ones like that on the rookies.

I called him again in the afternoon and it was his turn to be awkward this time. He said he'd pick me up in his car outside the Earl's Court tube at about four—a grey Rover 2000, and gave me the number. The old bastard kept me waiting in the rain until half-past and he looked quietly pleased when I squelched in alongside him. I told him I hadn't asked for this job any more than he had, but since we were lumbered with each other how about behaving like adults?

'Splendid with me, Mr Wainwright,' he said as he eased out into the traffic. 'How about a safe number where I can call you, and so dispense with this exaggerated security nonsense until it's really necessary?'

'I'm on leave,' I told him. 'Or was until they sprung this on me yesterday. No time to arrange things.'

'Who's in charge?' he asked. 'You or me?'

'Me,' I said positively.

He shrugged. 'Fine. All you've got to do is to get a prisoner out of prison then. I'll be happy to help in any way I can —in an advisory capacity.'

I blew my inflamed nose and told him to drop me by the next phone box. He said: 'Tell your boss I've got the parcel of money in the car. You can have it back and he can do what the hell he likes about it. I'm not working under the orders of an amateur, Mr Wainwright. Not until the merchandise is this side of the wall, anyhow.'

He pulled up at the box outside the Victoria and Albert. There's a double yellow line there so he said he'd drive round the block. I knew he'd be watching me in the rear vision mirror so I crossed to the box briskly, fumbling for change, although I had no clear intention at that point of making myself a chopping-block for the Gaffer's ponderous wit. But what the hell else was there to do? The position was impossible. Maybe this was it. This was where I quit and went back to ledger-keeping full time—until somebody decided to pull me back again, like they were pulling Malcolm, I thought bitterly. But then *he* was vulnerable to blackmail. I wasn't —yet. I'd done nothing the wrong side of the law for my own profit. Again—yet. I still hadn't got my intentions formulated when I stabbed viciously at the dial.

But the Gaffer was surprisingly mild when I had said my piece. He did mention something about going to Covent Garden when he wanted to listen to prima donnas, certainly, but even so the shot was directed more at Malcolm than me—or so I chose to think.

'You'll have to take *some* direction, of course,' he went on conversationally. 'Stands to reason, don't it? But the can still remains yours, and there's no bloody refundable deposit on it. Tell him that. Tell him he's in charge until the goods are delivered—and you hope, and *I* hope, that you'll pull together like two good troupers, blah, blah, blah.'

'I can see his face as I'm saying it,' I said glumly.

He chuckled fatly. 'So can I. But it'll probably work. He *is* a prima donna. You say he's got the parcel of dough in the car?'

'Yes.'

'I bet he hasn't. It'd be easier to squeeze tooth paste back into the tube than to prise him loose from it once he's felt it.'

'Shall I call his bluff?'

'You can if you like—but you're out on a limb if he calls yours and gives it to you. No, I'd try it my way if I were you. All sweet reason and logic. If that fails——' He stopped.

'If that fails?' I prompted.

'If that fails,' he said slowly, 'tell him you'll be taken off the job—and Richworth will be put on.'

'Richworth?' I repeated.

'Yes. But, I'd rather you didn't. Not unless the velvet glove doesn't work. But if you do mention that name—now or at any time in the future that he gets awkward—you watch *his* face.'

'I'll remember it,' I said.

'Once again, I'd rather you didn't—except as the ultimate sanction. So long.' He hung up.

I got wet again waiting for Malcolm. He tut-tutted solicitously as I got in the car, and we did two circuits of the Park after I had eaten crow and he had accepted our altered status with a graciousness that had me prickly with resentment. He suggested going back to his place then.

'I thought you said you'd rather I didn't, two days running?' I said.

'That only applies during normal business hours,' he told me gently. 'I have several simple basic rules in these matters. I'll explain them as we go along.'

He did, like a kindly schoolmaster. I sat hunched in my misery, thinking longingly of hot whisky and lemon and aspirin for myself, and even more longingly of strychnine for this old devil.

## Chapter 4

A lane ran past the backs of the two bigger buildings which flanked his shop. What had once been a small garden opened on to this, but he'd had it roofed over and a double garage door had been let into the outside wall. He pressed a button on the dashboard and the doors swung back revealing a single car bay with the rest of the space piled with packing cases. I felt him looking sideways at me like a clever schoolboy expecting applause, but lots of taipans are installing remote controlled garage doors in their Peak mansions in Hong Kong, so I wasn't impressed, and even had I been I wouldn't have given him the satisfaction of showing it. Slightly miffed, he closed the doors with the same button when we drove in, and switched on the lights with another. We got out and I followed him through the piled cases to an inside door. There were no gimmicks here, but there was a burglar-proof mortice lock which he opened with a key he kept on a chain, and I noticed in passing that although the door was oak and seemingly as old as the building itself, it was backed by a sheet of steel, and once inside he had to move fast to switch off, then reset, a burglar alarm which was just clearing its throat before blasting off. It was quite a moated keep.

We were in a small square lobby. Another door opened off this, I assumed into the shop, and a flight of carpeted stairs led upwards. Half-way up there was a landing with a window that looked into the shop. The glass had the slightly silvered effect which I knew meant it was one-way. A tired-looking old boy in black jacket and striped trousers was sitting on a mandarin throne almost nodding off. Malcolm put his mouth beside a small mike and said quietly: 'Thank you, Mr Brewster, I'm back now. Would you be so good as to lock up. Good night.' The old boy jumped like a startled rabbit, gazed round wildly and said: 'Thank you, Mr Malcolm. Certainly, Mr Malcolm,' his voice a frightened squeak in the return amplifier.

Malcolm chuckled. 'Poor Brewster,' he said. 'He's been with me for twelve years, but he still hasn't got used to my little tricks.'

He led on up the stairs, past another reinforced door, and then we were in his apartment. Through an open door I could see into a small exquisitely furnished dining-room with an opened serving hatch affording a glimpse of a white-tiled kitchen the other side. He opened yet another door which led into a cloakroom, and helped me off with my overcoat, clucking solicitously over its soggy weight, then he showed me through into another room which I guessed was directly over the shop, and was almost the same in area. There was nothing Chinese here; just good, supremely comfortable period stuff, oak, with the soft dull polished gleam of age on it which robbed it of heaviness, and good leather. Books which, despite their tooled leather bindings, didn't look as if they had been bought by the running foot, covered two walls. There were some pictures on the third, flanking an open wood fire in a cut steel grate and each hung at the correct height to be looked at. I recognised at first glance a Canaletto and a Constable, and they certainly weren't reproductions. Ceiling-to-floor tapestry hangings covered the bow window which formed the fourth wall. There was an alcove to one side of the fireplace in which I could see stairs leading up to the floors above. All in all it was the sort of place to make one who had lived most of his life in schools,

32

barracks and commercial messes ache. He waved me to a deep chair by the fire and took Scotch, glasses and a silver cigarette box from a court dresser and put them beside me. In spite of my efforts to maintain ascendancy I found myself relaxing. He poured two stiff drinks without insulting them with soda, sat opposite me and raised his glass. And he grinned—and for the life of me I couldn't help grinning back.

'That's better,' he said. 'And I'm really sorry about all this nonsense this afternoon—but there *was* a reason for it. I found that out last night.'

'Found what out?' I asked.

'That our property is hot. Very hot indeed.'

'I haven't even named the property.'

He didn't actually tap the side of his nose with his fore-finger, but he gave the sort of smile which goes with it.

'Oh, come now, Mr Wainwright,' he said archly. 'Who else *could* it be?'

'You tell me,' I snapped, feeling angry again.

'Carter.' And he wasn't fishing. He just knew. All I could do was to shrug and feel a fool.

'Bluffing does become a habit, doesn't it? And so it should. It bespeaks thorough training.' He was being kind to me and I was hating him again, and he knew it and was pressing his resultant advantage.

'All right, Carter,' I said. 'An easy enough guess from what I've told you already. Shall we stop sparring?'

'Any time you like.'

'Why is Carter hot?'

'Because the Russians want him out also.'

'We know that,' I said. 'But wanting and getting are not quite the same thing. My guess is——'

'I'm not guessing at anything,' he interrupted. 'I'm just tellng you. I was approached by them ten days ago.'

'What did you say?'

'I told them I'd need a bit of time to think it over—then I passed it on to the Gaffer.'

'The *bastard*!' I spat.

'Why, didn't he tell you?' He chuckled. 'I'm delighted. That means he's puzzled. Passing the tip back to him wasn't meant as an assurance of my loyalty so much as a feeler. I thought perhaps he knew there'd been a Russian offer.'

'I don't give a damn what *you* thought,' I answered. 'He

should have told *me*. Anyhow, if the Russians made the offer, why should you assume that the Gaffer would know about it?'

'The Russians didn't—not directly. It was through a middleman, naturally. A fellow called Wates—a real pro—freelance. The sort of man who might quite easily have leaked it to the Gaffer if he thought it worth while. Anyhow, it tidies things up a bit. I'm reasonably certain now who Wates came from.'

'When did you have to give him your answer?'

'I gave it last night—after you left. I accepted, and I have to see him later on tonight to discuss preliminary details and to haggle about my fee—although I must say that they are much more generous than your people.'

'Why don't you work for them then?' I asked.

He waved his hand round the room. 'This. If I did a job for the Russians I'd exchange it for a twelve-by-eight cell. I'm sorry if I shock you, but I'm damned if I'm going to give you a spiel about loyalty. People who pay less than the rate for the job and threaten one with blackmail, haven't the right to expect it. Still, that needn't worry *you*. Loyalty to the faceless ones and loyalty to the man you're working with are two different things.' He looked at his watch. 'I'm afraid we're wasting a lot of time. I'm meeting Wates at nine o'clock. I hope to be back here by ten. I intend to fix a provisional date with him, which will, in turn, fix *our* date.'

'Better later than sooner,' I said. 'There's a hell of a lot to do beforehand.'

'I'll do what I can, without running the risk of rousing his suspicions.'

'Why should he be suspicious?'

'No reason at all, if I don't depart from my usual form. I'm a better sooner-than-later man myself, and he knows it. We've worked together before.'

'Yes, but what I mean——' I began, but he shut me up with another of his schoolmasterly hand-raisings.

'Let me finish, Mr Wainwright. If the Russians have their escape route planned for a certain date, they'll want me to conform to it, within a reasonable margin. If I start finding fault with any suggested date at this early stage, I *wouldn't* be running true to form. No—my cue at the moment is if he says things are laid on for, say, the fifteenth of next month, to accept it and work out something together on that basis— while you and I fix it for a day or two earlier. You follow?'

Again he was wresting the lead from me. I grunted and tried to think of a brilliant crusher that would re-establish me, but as always in these cases, none came. He rose and pushed the decanter towards me. 'Do make yourself comfortable until I get back.'

I was comfortable but I saw in this a chance to reassert myself. I rose also. 'I think I'll go back to my flat,' I told him.

'Is that wise?' he asked gently. 'I take it you'll want to know what we've arranged—so that will mean either another meeting or a long telephone conversation—both of which I'd rather avoid.' And, of course, he was right. I sat down again.

'What about your family?' I asked.

'My wife is in a nursing home. You'll be quite on your own,' he said. 'You can disregard the telephone. I'll switch it over to the answering service.'

'Sonia? And your son?'

'My son doesn't live here. If Sonia should happen to arrive before I get back, just introduce yourself.'

'As what?'

'As James Wainwright, lately of Hong Kong—seeing me on business, but I was suddenly called out. Tell her I'll be back at ten, and ask her to get us some supper.' He flashed another smile at me and went.

I helped myself to more Scotch, stretched out my feet to the fire and sank back in that wonderfully comfortable chair —and those three things combined must have sent me straight off inside a minute.

I woke in a panic of choking. A girl was standing over me thumping me between the shoulder blades. I struggled to my feet and stared at her through streaming eyes. She was doing her best to look contrite, but the laughter was bursting through.

She said, 'I *am* sorry—I really am——'

'What happened?' I gasped.

'Your head was right back—and your mouth was open— and—well, I'm afraid I chucked a salted almond into it. It was so stupid of me.' And then the laughter took over, but at least she poured me another Scotch so I joined in, albeit a bit hollowly, and we introduced ourselves.

Russian beauty, like olives, is the sort that most men either go for in a big way or leave strictly alone. I mean there is no middle course. Personally I'm a leaver-alone. There were so many of them in Shanghai and they all looked the same, just like the Chinese do in a different way. Dark eyes, chalklike colouring, high cheekbones, wide mouths and identical hair-styles—swept back into a Madonna bun at the nape of the neck. Look at an old picture of Pavlova and a current one of Fonteyn, and try and spot the difference. There isn't any. This girl was just another off the assembly belt. Every movement—the way she poured and handed me my drink, then sank into a chair without looking round at it, feet crossed at the ankles, hands loosely clasped in her lap—looked as if it were the result of long training. Even if I hadn't known her background I would still have been able to pigeonhole her. And the name was just as right—or trite. Sonia. It couldn't have been anything else, except perhaps Natasha. Oh yes—I knew the type so very, very well—like a Holly-wood casting director knows blondes—and was as bored by them. And I was angry at her because the first fall was hers and she was still laughing at me behind her eyes.

I said stiffly: 'Your father was called out suddenly. He asked me to wait. He hopes to be back before ten.' I left out the bit about supper because I had no intention of staying, but she asked me if either of us had eaten. I said Malcolm hadn't, but please not to bother on my account as I wouldn't be staying long after he returned. The smile came out from behind her eyes then. She said, 'You're really angry, aren't you?'

'I'm not,' I said shortly.

'Yes you are. I wonder what makes Shanghai Rusks so thin-skinned.'

I took a deep breath and screwed the safety valve down tight. 'I'm not a Shanghai Rusk,' I told her.

'You sound like one. Like one trying to be terribly English. Am I being rude?'

'Yes.' But it didn't suppress her in the slightest. She lit a cigarette and carried on her detached scrutiny of me through the smoke. I had nothing more to say and I didn't know where to put my hands. She was doing it on purpose, of course. It was disconcerting. She looked so stereotyped, but she was acting right out of pattern and making me feel a fool. I was about to do the sensible thing and break it off and go, but then a bell whirred softly somewhere and she said it was her father arriving back, and went through to meet him at the top of the stairs.

Malcolm came into the room alone and closed the door
36

behind him. He nodded curtly, crossed to the fire and sat opposite me. He said: 'Tricky, I'm afraid,' and rubbed his chin slowly.

'What's tricky?' I asked.

'The whole bloody thing. Listen. As you probably realize, I have a team—three besides myself—completely trustworthy for the simple reason they know that if I am ever nicked through any shortcomings or doublecrossing on their part I can take the lot of them with me upcreek. You follow?'

I nodded.

'But of course that only applies as far as the police are concerned. If the inducement was great enough they could always sell me out to the Opposition—and I might never know who had fingered me. That's if they knew there *was* an Opposition—and who they were. You see what I mean?'

'This is all a bit elementary, isn't it?' I said. 'You take damned good care they don't know.'

'But they do know, unfortunately. Wates has already approached them directly. They thought originally of doing it on their own and cutting me out.'

'What stopped them?' I asked.

'Not loyalty,' he said drily. 'They're all splendid leg and muscle men, but experience and a little—' he tapped himself on the side of the head with his forefinger—'is still very necessary, and fortunately they know their limitations. After some deliberation they told Wates they would rather papa was in at the head of things.'

'But it's still a straight job as far as they're concerned,' I said. 'They don't know *we're* in it.'

'There's more to it than that.' He was still rubbing his chin, and it irritated me. 'The Russians want it done this month —between the twenty-first and twenty-eighth. There will be a Polish ship in the Pool for that week—with a specially built hidey-hole under the bunkers that not even our rummagers could find without taking her apart. First port Gdynia. Just too easy, damn them. Things never work out like that for *me*,' he finished complainingly.

'Where's the problem?' I asked. 'You don't take him to the ship. You take him to wherever I have arranged.'

'Oh, for God's sake, Wainwright,' he said impatiently. 'Don't you realize that before that man comes over the wall every last-minute foreseeable detail has been studied—every step gone over—every yard of the course covered and timed?

If I suddenly depart from the plan with no apparent reason, instant suspicion will be aroused. Don't forget that I will be one against three—four, counting the customer. Oh, I could have two or three good convincing reasons ready, but sooner or later they're going to know that I've pulled a swift one on them—and I've got to live here afterwards.'

I could see his point. *I* was rubbing my chin now.

He broke a long silence: 'Since you've mentioned it yourself, what *have* you arranged, by the way?'

'Nothing yet,' I said lamely. 'I thought that was what we were going to discuss tonight.'

He looked at me in shocked unbelief.

'*Nothing*?' he repeated. 'Listen, my lad, my contract ends when I deliver the man to some prearranged point. The Russians had *their* point arranged before they ever approached me. You and that ape you work for had better start thinking, hadn't you?'

But he'd pushed it just an inch too far, and I had him.

'Your contract is to deliver him to a point near Hong Kong. I made that perfectly clear when I met you,' I said. 'So don't let's waste time and breath, Malcolm.'

'Listen——' he began.

I stood up. 'I've listened all I'm going to tonight,' I said firmly. 'You and your team, as you call it, have made the balls-up—not us. All right, you can get it sorted out, or not, as you like. In the meantime I'm reporting back to the ape. Now let me out of this crazy bloody monkey-puzzle.'

I stalked out to the hall and got my coat from the cupboard. Sonia looked through the kitchen hatch and wailed that she was cooking Russian omelettes and making salad. I didn't mean her to hear my answer—I swear I didn't—but she had good ears, and when I turned back from the cupboard, shrugging myself into my damp overcoat, she was standing behind me. She had the frying pan in her hand. Her eyes should have warned me.

The omelette was the size of a large dinner plate, beautifully souffléd and topped with sour cream and anchovies.

She gave a flick of her wrist and the whole damned thing wrapped itself lovingly round my kisser.

Malcolm gently pried it loose and dabbed my face with olive oil afterwards, clucking his disapproval and tearing strips off her in Russian, but it wasn't doing much good. The bitch was sitting on the top stairs, helpless with laughter.

Then I noticed that the corners of Malcolm's mouth were twitching, try as he might to control them. And then—well what the hell does one do in a case like that? And after all I'd asked for it. I grinned sheepishly, and the rot set in quickly, and the three of us sat round the fire and belly-laughed for a good fifteen minutes before full sanity returned. She went out to make more omelettes.

'I'm sorry, Mr Wainwright,' Malcolm said as the door closed. He looked around quickly, leaned forward and lowered his voice, like one about to impart a guilty secret. 'It's her mother's blood coming out in her. Tashkent. You know what those buggers are like, don't you?'

I didn't actually, but I let it go. He pushed the decanter towards me. 'Well, at least it's served to clear the air a little,' he went on.

But I wasn't letting him off as lightly as that. 'It hasn't solved anything, though,' I reminded him.

'Maybe not—but the ghost of an idea was coming to me even as we were talking. First of all I must know what resources the Gaffer is allowing you.'

'Anything within reason provided there is no lead back to him. I mean, I can have what money I want, but no facilities that we can't arrange ourselves.'

'A job for Kjaer then,' he said.

'Who's he?' I asked.

'You know Finnav, surely?'

'The shipping line?'

He nodded. 'They've got four smallish but fast freighters —Baltic ports to the Far East. Kjaer's the part owner and skipper of one of them. They don't carry passengers, but he would sign on a couple of extra crew members and fiddle the list for a thousand pounds a head.'

'There'd be the three of us—you, me and the customer,' I reminded him, and he looked blank.

'But you wouldn't want *me* to travel with you?' he said.

'Carter won't be a willing passenger,' I said, 'and I couldn't watch him night and day for four or five weeks on my own.'

'You wouldn't have to at sea—and Kjaer would know what to do with him at intervening ports, and going through the Suez. Look, I'm not trying to sidestep anything, but my alibi in this country will be for an air trip out to Hong Kong and back again after a week or so. I couldn't explain a ten or twelve week absence.'

'You wouldn't need all that. You can fly home at the end of it.'

'Still too long,' he said doubtfully. 'And then there's the timing of the thing. I have no idea where Kjaer's ship is at the moment. We might have to keep the client under cover for weeks before he comes through Le Havre.'

'Le Havre?'

'Le Havre and Genoa are the only European ports Kjaer touches at after leaving Helsinki.'

'How the hell do we get across there?' The size and complexity of this thing was appearing in its true proportions for the first time. But this one didn't worry him.

'That's easy,' he told me. 'I've got a safe route from the South Coast. It will cost another five hundred. Not per head —just for the trip.'

'The Gaffer will be delighted,' I said. 'All right then—we assume we get across safely. If we have to wait a long time in Le Havre—what then?'

'Easy again,' he assured me. 'A safe house. Board and lodgings a hundred pounds a week per head, and handy for the docks. Well—so much for that. Now as for——'

But Sonia came in then to tell us supper was ready.


Chapter 5

The telephone was ringing when I let myself into the flat next morning. A girl's voice told me that the two books I'd ordered were now in, but if I was calling for them myself would I please remember that they closed at one o'clock today. 'Books' meant the Gaffer's rabbit warren, and one o'clock minus two meant that he wanted to see me there at eleven. It was already a quarter to, and by the time I'd got the District from Gloucester Road to Victoria and walked the three blocks down I was five minutes late, which gave him the opportunity to needle me about the way I spent my nights. I didn't rise to it and that annoyed the dirty-minded old devil, and in the end he had to ask me where the hell I had been, anyhow. I looked virtuous and told him I'd been at Malcolm's place.

'Did you have to stay all night? I've been trying to raise you since six o'clock yesterday evening,' he grunted.

'I didn't think it advisable to walk through the City looking for a taxi at two o'clock in the morning,' I said smugly. 'Particularly in view of what Malcolm told me about the Russians.'

'What did he tell you?'

'Something you overlooked. That they're trying to spring Carter also.'

'I didn't overlook it,' he said. 'I wanted to see how much Malcolm would volunteer—if anything. If you'd known about it you might have prompted him.'

I was about to ask him just what sort of bloody fool he took me for, but I bit it back. Losing one's temper with the Gaffer was tantamount to swinging a Sunday punch at a judo dan. He just turned it back on one.

'All right,' he went on. 'So Malcolm told you the Russians were in the market too—and that he'd passed the word on to me. Quite correct, he did. But he could have been trying to raise the price. Do *you* believe him?'

This was a new Gaffer. He'd never asked my opinion on anything before. I felt a certain importance.

'I do. He told me the middleman's name and gave me the escape route. There'll be a Polish ship in the Pool between——'

'The *Skagadam*—and between the twenty-first and the twenty-eighth—and Wates—that the feller?' he asked. I stopped feeling important. 'Could be, of course,' he went on ruminatively, as I nodded. 'It fits—but then Malcolm could have *made* it fit—and then again he could be playing us off against Wates, couldn't he?'

I nodded glumly. This was getting just a shade too complicated. Over bacon and eggs this morning I had been trusting Malcolm. Now this old bastard was cutting the ground from under my feet again.

'Well, we've got to start from somewhere,' I said. 'We've got something laid on—in broad outline.'

'Let's have it.'

'He's accepted the Russians' proposition—they're offering double ours, by the way. His fellows make the spring—and then he wants us to hijack Carter very authentically before he reaches the London docks.'

The Gaffer suddenly grinned widely. 'Lovely,' he said. 'If there's anything I like, it's having an intelligent surmise substantiated. That's just what I thought he'd do. You see why, don't you?'

'If we jumped the gun the Russians would be pretty certain to find out,' I said. 'Naturally he wants to avoid that.'

'He doesn't give a monkey's for the Russians,' said the Gaffer flatly. 'If it comes to that he doesn't give a monkey's for us either. He pretends to. To be afraid of somebody disarms them. No—don't you see? He'll jack the Russians up to the hilt for something in advance, so he'll be that much up. I wouldn't put it past him to stick it on them for the lot afterwards, on the grounds that he'd carried out his contract in getting the client out, and if the Rusks couldn't look after him from then on it was *their* fault.'

'They wouldn't be mugs enough to fall for it, surely?' I said.

'I don't know. Twenty thousand quid? Petty cash really. If they paid him in full it would keep his mouth closed—and those of his helpers. If, on the other hand, they felt themselves welshed on through a technicality, they might get vocal about it afterwards. The Rusks would hate that.'

'You mean to say that he'd have the nerve to pull something as raw as that?' I asked.

'I prefer to call it gall,' the Gaffer said. 'And you bet he's got enough of it. Don't ever underestimate Malcolm's gall. Oh well, just let it be clearly understood that he doesn't get a blind sausage out of us until the job has been successfully carried out.'

'What about expenses?'

'He won't have to worry about them. You'll be carrying the bag.'

'He's not going to like it,' I said dubiously. 'He was discussing expenses last night. His team will want two hundred and fifty pounds each beforehand. That's in case——'

'They get nicked on the job and their everlovings and God-forbids are left on National Assistance. Yeah, yeah, yeah, we know all that. How many helpers is he using?'

'Three.'

'Good—so he gives you three addresses. It will go to them through the mail the morning after, *if* there've been no slip-ups.'

'What if he won't wear it?'

'Then he can wear a nice blue battledress with yellow high-escape risk patches sewn on to the arse, knees and elbows of it. Tell him that. Tell him it's the one thing he *can* be certain of on this job.' He leaned forward, emphasizing his points with a stubby forefinger. 'Tell him that his trial will be in camera in the interests of State security, so he can involve anybody he wants to, and it won't do him the bloodiest bit of good. Tell him that even if he has any little ideas beforehand about writing it all down and getting it to the papers after he's been nicked, it still won't do him any good—because we'll slap a "D" Notice across every editor in the country. Tell him that the same goes for his helpers—who are three gents by the names of Maudsley, Ansel and Hessiker. Tell him, in short, that we've got him by the tight and curlies, and if he forces us to twist 'em then, by God, it's going to hurt him more than us. But he shouldn't need telling. He knows it already.'

I nodded and got up. I didn't feel like speaking at that moment. In fact I was feeling just a little bit sick. The man we were talking about had worked well and faithfully for us for half a lifetime. What he had done in the war alone would, in any branch of the service other than this Augean stable, have earned him a chestful of gongs. Granted he had put a foot wrong, but for that he should have been dealt with at the time, not kept on ice until we wanted him again, then blackmailed. Something of what I was thinking must have shown in my face. The Gaffer peered up at me from the depths of his busted chair, like a weasel from a burrow.

'You're not doubting any of this, are you?' he asked. I shook my head.

'Good,' he said. 'Just so as we understand. Because all that *would* happen if he tried to play it crafty—with us, I mean. He can put any bloody thing he likes over on the Rusks—as long as it doesn't jeopardize our interests. Oh yes—make no mistake about that. It'd happen all right—*if there was time for it*, and it seemed expedient—and if he was lucky. If there wasn't time for it, and it didn't seem expedient, then he mightn't be so lucky. The rug might have to be pulled from under him a bit quicker then. It has been known.'

He grunted up out of the chair and moved to the door to let me out. The cocker bitch snarled at me as I passed. Yes, by God, they *were* alike. The Gaffer paused with his hand on the latch, and turned and looked at me again.

'I'm glad we've cleared up any lingering doubts,' he said softly. 'If we haven't, just talk it over with Malcolm. You'll find *he's* a believer. My bloody oath he is. Get him to tell

43

you about what happened to Saunders one of these days. Right —call me here at six each evening—or six in the morning if anything stops you. Be seeing you.' He opened the door, checked that the corridor was clear and let me out. I felt my flesh creeping under my sleeve where the obscene old devil had touched me.

I spent the rest of that day on my own—that is bank—business. There was a hell of a lot to do, and this was something I had to fix up myself as, thank God, the Gaffer had found out that Kjaer's ship didn't call at Le Havre until the tenth of next month. That meant that we would have to stay under cover there for a fortnight to three weeks—and add the voyage of five weeks to it. Seven or eight weeks in all—which would put me a whole month over the top of my leave.

But things worked out much easier than I hoped. My original boss was still there and I went in to see him, and within an hour he had fixed a six-week course for me at the Midland works of a company that was experimenting in a new method of computer accountancy. We both trusted that I wouldn't be called upon to lecture on it when I got back to Hong Kong.

The bank was only a matter of a couple of hundred yards from Malcolm's shop, and it seemed a damned nuisance to have to go back up west in order to reach it, but Malcolm was insisting on full security. He was working for the Rusks now, he said when I phoned him, and they would quite likely put his place under at least sporadic surveillance just as a matter of routine. It would be better if I didn't come to the shop again openly. So he left his mini-van on a meter in Bryanston Square and went off for half an hour, and I got in the back and stayed there until he returned and drove off to his garage. It was a simple ruse but one I'd never heard of before, and he guessed it and gave me a scholarly lecture on the art of tail-shaking all the way back to the City. There was a jack-handle on the floor of the van beside me, and he never knew how close he got to having it wrapped round his skull. But in spite of my techiness he was impressing me. The old devil was a professional of professionals, and if you've got to stick your neck out there's something very comforting in doing it in expert company.

The apartment was again an oasis of warmth and soft light, and this time I didn't have to rough it, because Sonia had been

44

prepared and she'd got the guest bedroom ready for me, even to pyjamas, razor and toothbrush, and she was cooking something in the kitchen that smelled damned good. I sat and drank some more of his Scotch and heard six o'clock strike and thought to hell with the Gaffer; I'd give myself the pleasure of spoiling his early morning sleep tomorrow.

Malcolm said: 'Did you settle the matter of my advance?'

'I tried to,' I told him. 'But he said not a sausage. You can give me three addresses and he'll mail it to the helpers the morning after, providing there have been no slip-ups.'

He grunted something about untrusting bastards spoiling ships for ha'porths of tar, but didn't appear to be too upset about it, for which I was thankful because the acrimony of the whole affair to date was getting me down. Something else was getting me down too, and that was the uncertainty of how much Sonia knew about it. Malcolm never broke off or covered up if she came into the room when we were discussing details, but she never joined in. Yet the Gaffer had told me that she actually drove the getaway car when Wally Wharton came out over the wall. And the Wharton job wasn't the only one, I had been given to understand. Had she helped in the others also? And what was more to the point, was she going to be in on this one? The idea frightened me stiff. I had never worked with women, other than the few specialist instructresses during the course. I put it to Malcolm squarely while she was out of the room, but she wasn't out long enough for me to get his answer. She came in just at that instant to tell us supper was ready, and this time he did cover up. Apropos of nothing at all he asked me if I liked chrysanthemums and then went off into a learned discourse on their symbolism in Japanese art. The whole bloody thing was getting more Alice in Wonderlandish every hour.

But I slept well that night and woke early enough to phone the Gaffer on time on the bedside telephone. I didn't know whether Malcolm was listening in on another extension, but it wouldn't have availed him of anything if he had because all I said was that I'd been needing an extra two pints tomorrow, which meant I had nothing special to report, and the Gaffer said he'd attend to it, which told me that he had nothing for me either. I hung up, then, purely as a matter of routine, I unscrewed the dial of the thing and there, sure enough, was a scriber underneath it. A scriber is a circular piece of paper-thin copper which fits out of sight under the moving part of the dial which has a tiny sharp point set in it. The pressure of the dialler's finger is sufficient to bring the point down on the copper, but it springs back when the finger is removed. The resultant marks on the copper can tell anybody who wants to know just what numbers have been called. The Gaffer's number was, of course, ex-directory. I removed the copper, defaced the marks on it with a nail-file, scratched a rude word on it and put it back.

Malcolm took me up west again in the mini-van after breakfast and left me in the underground car park at Marble Arch, and I took a cab back to Courtfield Gardens. I packed a bag and went off to the computer people since I'd be needing the alibi for the bank later on, and Birmingham was as good as anywhere to kick my heels until I was wanted. I attended a few instructional sessions and even managed to stay awake at some of them. I called Malcolm and gave him the number of my hotel. Then I just waited—and waited.

Have you ever spent ten winter days in Birmingham with nothing to do except call someone you didn't like on the telephone at six each evening? Don't. I'd almost reached the point of going sick and asking to be taken off it by the tenth call, but as it turned out it wasn't necessary. The Gaffer said he didn't like the way things were dragging and told me to come back to town.

I felt a surge of relief. I hung up, then called Malcolm's number. Sonia answered and she told me the old man was away on business and she didn't expect him back that night, but she'd like to see me right away. I said I couldn't make it before the following day. She said what a pity because it was about Timoy scrolls, and I felt a prickly sensation start at the nape of my neck and run down to my Achilles' tendon. 'Timoy' means 'peach' in Cantonese—and 'peach' in any language at all meant 'Stand by—urgent'. But how the hell did she know that? Or did she? Maybe there were such things as Timoy scrolls and she'd just used it by chance. But I couldn't risk it. I told her I'd call her again when I'd found out about trains and I ducked round to the station. There was one in twenty minutes that would get me back just after ten, but when I called her the second time the number was engaged. I couldn't waste any more time so I went back to the hotel, worried and puzzled, and collected my bag.

It was sheer bloody-mindedness that held me from calling the Gaffer again. What would have been the use, anyhow? He obviously knew nothing about recent developments, or he would have told me when I spoke to him at six.

I got the answering service from Malcolm's number when I called on arriving in town. It was raining like the devil and there was a taxi queue a mile long, so I humped my bag along the Euston Road until I found a prowler, and I was wet through and in a filthy mood. It would have been stupid to go to the shop openly after all his previous precautions, so I did the sensible thing and went home. I paid the cab off and was just letting myself in when I heard light steps behind me and a hand came out of the darkness and touched my elbow. I turned. I could just make out that it was a woman, but no more.

I said, 'You're miles west of your beat, sweetheart. This is a respectable neighbourhood, not Jermyn Street.'

'Save the humour,' she snapped. 'Let's get inside.' It was Sonia.

Raging, I whipped her through the front door grabbing at the automatic switch inside that lighted up the hall and stairs when the inner vestibule was opened. I led her up through the darkness and into my flat without speaking. I drew the blinds, then switched on the lights and opened up on her.

'What the hell do you mean by coming here?' I blazed. 'How did you know where I lived? Has that old beat been tailing me?'

'Is that meant to be funny?' She loosened her wet raincoat and shook water like a poodle. 'Light that damned gas fire, for God's sake. I'm frozen.'

'Answer my question,' I said.

'I came here because you told me to.'

'*I* told you to?' I stared at her. 'What on earth are you talking about?'

'You said——' She broke off and it was her turn to stare. 'Well, didn't you?'

There are two ways to get answers from a woman. Gentlemen aren't allowed to use the quick one, so I took her hands and pushed her gently into a chair, put a bob in the meter and lit the fire, because she *was* frozen. Then I poured two drinks and gave her one.

'Right—slowly. From the beginning,' I told her.

'Father went off into the blue two days ago,' she said. 'He

rang me tonight and gave me your Birmingham number and told me to tell you that he had some Timoy scrolls. I was just going to do so when you came through.' So that explained *that* part of it.

'All right,' I said. 'But this address that I'm supposed to have given you——?'

'Well, not you, but the reception clerk——'

I nearly switched to the quick way. '*What* bloody clerk ——?' I began, took a deep breath and a deeper drink, and got hold of myself again.

'The one at the hotel. He said you had just left for London and would I please leave home *immediately* and meet you at this address as soon as you arrived—and to be very careful of the traffic. He rang about twenty minutes after you did. You mean to say you didn't send that message?'

I shook my head and tried to get things into focus. This phone, like the Gaffer's, was ex-directory. The office were the only people who knew the number—or so I fervently hoped. But why would the office uncover my modest hideout to somebody they didn't trust?

Sonia was talking again. 'I took "immediately" to mean just that, and the bit about the traffic as a warning that I might be followed——'

'So what did you do about it?' I shot at her.

'Left immediately, took the Circle round to Euston, bought a ticket to Crewe, went out on the seven-fifteen and slipped off at Willesden and doubled back to Gloucester Road on the Underground—and I've been cooling my heels, literally, in the bloody laurel bushes across the square for nearly an hour and a half watching this place of yours.' She held out her glass. I refilled it for her. She deserved it. I wouldn't have done it as thoroughly if the Gaffer himself had been on my tail. But that still didn't answer my question. Who the hell had leaked my address to her, and why? Then the telephone rang. There was a drill for answering it if you should happen to have somebody else present. You merely let it ring eight times, then you lifted it and said, 'No, I'm sorry, you've got the wrong number.' You then rang the office when things were clear again. But now I was worried, and I answered the first time. It was the Gaffer.

He said, 'Took your time getting back, didn't you? Is that girl with you?' He must have been worried too, because he neither bawled me out for the procedure breach nor made a dirty crack when I told him she had just arrived.

'Were you the reception clerk?' I asked him, and breathed again when he said yes.

'Keep her there, for Christ's sake,' he told me. 'She's not to go back to the shop under any circumstances whatsoever. Do you understand?'

'No,' I said flatly. 'Maybe I would if I knew what the hell was happening.' I waited for the answering blast but it didn't come. I heard him take a deep and gusty breath—the sort of breath a fat saint would take when praying for patience if the bloke operating the thumbscrews was rather stupid.

He said, almost mildly, 'The goods came over the wall an hour ago. No bother apparently, but the maestro rang me just beforehand and said he thought the vodkas were a mite suspicious and would I get the girl shacked up safe with you somewhere just in case anybody called round at the shop. With it so far?'

'Yes,' I said, 'but——'

'*Stay* with it,' he begged softly. 'Maybe we might meet again sometime in the future, though on your present form that seems unlikely. This number and that of the office is dead, as of now, so it's no use calling again. Sorry and all that but you're far too hot.'

'Thanks,' I said bitterly.

'Don't mention it,' he answered. 'Draw what funds you require from your own bank and the best of British luck to you. Further instructions in your own territory out there —if you make it that far.'

I said meekly: 'May I speak?'

'Keep it very short,' he said.

'You're a bastard,' I told him. 'You're hamstringing me before I even start, but I'll get the goods there if it kills me— just for the pleasure of rubbing your bloody nose in it.'

'I'm sorry,' he said. 'But you know the rules. You got out of touch, let him jump the gun on you, failed to keep me informed, disclosed my number to him, and you're breaking security at this very moment. So am I, but I can tear down and build again—you can't. You're on your bloody own. Sleep tight—both of you.'

# Chapter 6

She said as I put the telephone down, 'It would be manners to pretend I hadn't heard anything—but I did, and I'm worried about my father. Can you tell me anything, please?'

I stalled. 'About your father? Not a thing. I was hoping you could tell *me* something. Any idea where he is?'

'If everything went according to plan—' she glanced at her wristwatch—'at least fifty miles away from Lanchester prison, and travelling fast. But I gather from your talk with the Gaffer that everything *hasn't* gone according to plan. Has Father been caught?'

I picked up my empty glass and stepped across to refill it, so that my back was towards her.

'Quick thinking,' she said. 'But not quick enough. Your eyebrows shot up to your hairline before you turned. Yes—I know all about the Gaffer. I know all about you too.'

Naturally I mumbled something about not knowing what the hell she was talking about, and she came back with Oh, God, anything but that, or words to that effect, but I was saved from further floundering by her going to the television and switching it on.

'Shut up,' she said. 'It's coming up to news time.'

The announcer's face swam up out of the grey mush and his lips were moving soundlessly because she hadn't turned the volume control up sufficiently. I pushed her to one side and adjusted it.

'. . . a Home Office spokesman would neither confirm nor deny that the prisoner was, in fact, Robert Carter, the Russian master spy sentenced in 1965 to thirty years' imprisonment . . .' And then his desk telephone rang and he excused himself and listened, nodding ponderously and looking wise. He went on, 'No, I am sorry. There is no further news at the moment, but our reporter, Dominic Sutcliffe, is travelling down to Lanchester with an outside broadcast camera team and we will give you further details and possibly pictures before the end of the news.' Then he went off about the current rail strike.

I turned down the sound a little and looked at her. I'd recovered a bit now, but she had lost ground. She was white and strained. I was thankful.

'How much do you know about this?' I asked.

'The old devil told me that it was only a final run over the course,' she said. 'He wouldn't let me go with him in case you rang.'

'You mean to say that he just went down on spec and sprang this fellow?' I said aghast. 'Without any preliminary plans?'

'Oh, don't ask such damfool questions,' she snapped. 'Of course he didn't. He had it all worked out to the last detail. He's been on it ever since *you* first turned up and started him off again—blast you. He's behaved himself for four years now.'

'He's *behaved* himself?' I said. 'My information is that he hasn't and *you've* been up to the neck in it too.'

'I've done the driving—twice. In each case it was because of a last-minute slip-up with one of his apes—and it was an attempt to keep him out of mischief.'

'But you've known about the other times?'

'What other times? Are you trying to trap me into something?'

'Why should I want to trap you?'

'Don't give me that starry-eyed piffle. Everybody who works for the Gaffer is in some sort of trap. The more any of you can get on another underling the safer you make it for yourselves. Well, I'm *not* one of your underlings—and neither is my father. You forced him into this. Oh, I know he was a pretty willing victim, but that's not the point. It was just like dangling a bottle of whisky in front of an alcoholic—and just as filthy——'

'Oh, come off it,' I said, 'In this particular case he was all set to make a deal with the Russians. At least he's working for his own side now.'

She looked at me scornfully: 'What's the difference? You both stink, and on balance your side is the worse. You're blackmailing one of your own people, and if anything goes wrong you'll stand by and see him sent down for years without lifting a finger to help him.'

I'd had enough by this time. 'Listen, sister,' I said. 'If he goes down I'll probably go down with him, and there won't be any fingers lifted for *me* either. If it comes to that, you aren't such a hell of a good risk yourself. Suppose we stop fighting and do something constructive?'

'Like what? All I'm interested in at the moment is finding

51

out where my father is. When I've done that I'm going to drag him out of it by the ears——'

And then we saw the announcer lift his telephone again, and I brought up the sound, just as the picture changed to one of a dark and rainy village street with a sheepskin-coated young man holding a mike.

'I'm talking to you from the High Street of this sleepy old Dorset town. The grim, top-security prison of Lanchester lies a mile away through the darkness, but the police are stopping all traffic and pedestrians from approaching it until a thorough survey of the ground has been made. No official statement has been released as yet, but I think we might take it that it *is* Robert Carter who has escaped. Apparently he was missed before eight o'clock, but no alarm was raised until a thorough search had been made inside the prison first, which took about an hour. It would appear that Carter, although an extremely important prisoner, was not regarded as an escape risk and was, in fact, a blue-band, or trusty, with full privileges and a wide measure of freedom inside the actual walls. We are going to move up to the police cordon now, and in the meantime we are returning you to the studio. This is Dominic Sutcliffe speaking to you from Lanchester . . .'

I heard her sigh with relief as I turned the sound down again. It was almost a sob. She started to button her raincoat, moving towards the door.

I said, 'Where do you think you're going?' which probably wasn't the most tactful way of phrasing the question in the face of her present mood. She told me to mind my own bloody business. I got my back to the door, twisted the key behind me and dropped it into my pocket. She stood facing me, perfectly composed now, but I could see a tiny vein throbbing at the angle of her jaw.

'Let me out, Wainwright,' she said. 'Or I'll raise such a huroosh that you'll have the fire brigade round.'

'You'd better hear what I've got to say first,' I answered. 'You're here at your father's express wish. He rang the Gaffer and told him that the Russians were suspicious and he was afraid that they might drop in on you.'

'I don't believe you,' she said. 'If he had any such instructions for me he'd have got in touch with me direct.'

'Believe what the hell you like. That's what the Gaffer just told me. It was he who did the reception clerk act.'

I could see doubt dawning in her face. 'But why didn't Father tell me so himself?' she said uncertainly. 'He'd only been speaking to me shortly before—when he told me to ring you in Birmingham.'

'Maybe he tried but couldn't get through. *I* tried to call you twice again after I'd spoken to you the first time. Once the phone was engaged, the next time I got the answering service. He was no doubt pushed for time and did the only thing he could.'

She nodded slowly, convinced against her will, and I could see her relaxing a little.

'I'd like to know where the devil he got the Gaffer's number, though,' I went on. 'Certainly not from me, although I've just had my ears removed for it.'

'He did get it from you.' She looked spitefully pleased. 'You called the Gaffer on our phone.'

'Yes, but——' I began.

'You scratched it out on the scriber and wrote a filthy word on it. But you didn't look underneath. Ours works on both sides. You're not terribly bright, are you?'

And I must have looked it. 'All right,' I said glumly. 'Don't rub it in.'

A newsflash was interrupting the weather report. I turned up the sound. They were confirming that it was Carter, and there was a photo of him. It was an anonymous sort of face, that of a man anything between thirty and fifty, completely expressionless as all professionals are when they are being officially mugged. It was about as much use for identification purposes as a passport photo. And they still weren't giving any details except that he had floated and a close watch was being kept on sea and airports. Then a picture of the Home Secretary, who wasn't available for comment, was flashed on. As a matter of fact they didn't look unalike. Both could have been anybody.

I said, 'The bedroom and bathroom are through there. I'd advise you to get some rest while you're waiting.'

'Waiting for what?' she asked coldly.

'Daylight,' I answered. 'If there *is* anybody laying for you on your doorstep you'd at least see what hit you. Anyhow, since your father asked——'

'Oh, damn my father—and you,' she blazed.

'If childish rudeness is all you can contribute, we'd both better shut up,' I said.

'All right, Confucius. What can *you* contribute?'

'I was going to say,' I said with icy dignity, 'that since your father asked you to come here it wouldn't be unreasonable to expect that this is where he will try to get in touch with us.'

She considered this for a moment, then nodded and sat down and rummaged in her handbag for a cigarette. I lit it for her.

'Maybe you're right,' she agreed grudgingly. 'But when I do want to leave, don't try to stop me.'

I went over to the door and put the key back. 'You can go whenever you like. I only wanted you to hear what I had to say.' I picked up her glass. 'Another drink?'

She shook her head. 'You wouldn't be able to raise a cup of coffee, would you? I missed my dinner.'

And that reminded me that I'd missed mine too. I went through to the kitchen and looked into the refrigerator. There were bacon and eggs there which looked sound enough after ten days, even if the milk was a bit doubtful, and a wrapped sliced loaf was no more repulsive than when it was allegedly fresh, so I put on the percolator and set about getting a scratch supper. It smelt all right, and she was a healthy gal, so she came through and took over from me. We didn't talk much until we had finished it, but she wasn't sulking. She looked deathly tired and I felt sorry for her. I was just about to suggest that she went and got her head down when the telephone rang again. We looked at each other. I took a deep breath and picked it up. A man's voice said, 'A Mr Tim Moy is calling Mr John Brown from a call-box in Christchurch. Will you pay for the call?' I said I would and nodded reassuringly at Sonia, and then Malcolm was on the line.

He said, 'Who's with you?'

'You-know-who,' I told him. 'She's just cooked an omelette, but hasn't chucked it in my face this time. Nobody else, so you can go ahead.'

I heard him chuckle faintly. 'I understand. Put her on, please.'

But I boggled at that. 'I want a few details first,' I said.

'Don't waste time, for God's sake,' he said crisply. 'Put her on.'

I handed her the phone. She listened and said yes at intervals, frowning in concentration, but I could see that she was gathering her forces ready to let him have it when he had finished speaking, and I got ready to grab the phone back from her. But he must have guessed it and he hung up on her before she had a chance. She swore and slammed the phone back. I swore too.

'Well?' I said.

'Have you got a car?' she asked.

'No—I hire one when I want one.'

'That's a hell of a lot of good. We want one now—tonight.'

'Where have we got to go?'

'Dungeness.'

'Where's that exactly?'

'On the South Coast, between Hastings and Folkestone. Near Rye. He's on his way there with the goods now.'

'Sounds just the sort of place they'll be watching,' I said.

'It's as safe as anywhere else,' she answered. 'A couple of coastguards and about four policemen to cover the whole of Romney Marsh.'

'Used it before, have you?' I said, which was stupid of me because it gave her the opportunity to tell me to mind my own business again.

'Train any good?' I asked helpfully.

She shook her head. 'We wouldn't get one before morning, then we'd still need to hire a car in Rye—and that would be asking for trouble.'

'What about your mini-van?'

'He's using that himself. Oh, blast him! We'll have to take mine. He said I wasn't to go back home, but there's nothing else for it.' She was getting into her raincoat. I didn't like the idea of going to the shop either, but, as she said, there seemed nothing else for it.

It was still raining like hell when we went out. I made her stay in the shadow of the portico while I did a quick recce round the square. If anybody was watching the place he had my sympathy, but apparently nobody was because I walked round a corner and waited a full three minutes to draw him without results. I collected her and we padded miserably along to Gloucester Road tube, then separated and travelled in different coaches, and didn't join up until we came out at Moorgate.

I didn't like this part of it at all. You know how deserted the City is even on a fine night. Tonight not a thing moved anywhere, except us. We stuck out like sore thumbs. I

55

suggested that she waited at the station while I went off for her car, but she turned that one down flat. Anyone trying to enter their place without the proper drill could start all sorts of things buzzing and ringing apparently. So I did the best I could think of and made her walk one side of the street while I took the other, a dozen yards to the rear, feeling naked and helpless.

She made it to the shop without my seeing anybody, but that didn't mean a thing. This was different from Court-field Gardens. There were side turnings, alleys and deeply-recessed shop doorways by the hundred here, and we could have been under observation from any of them. She reached the front door, let herself in and switched things off inside, and I walked across quickly and followed her. She relocked and led me through the dark shop and up to the flat above. She checked the answering service but there were no messages on it. We didn't waste any time, but went straight down to the garage. Her car, a little blue M.G. Midget, was standing where the mini-van usually parked. She switched on and checked the fuel gauge. It showed three-quarter full, so she got a two-gallon can and topped up, then started it and warmed on full choke. I went to open the sliding door, but she said it was all right, and then I saw that she was equipped with the same electric eye business as the old man had, so I climbed in alongside her. We backed out into the lane and the door slid down into position again—and then I saw movement at the top of the lane. Two figures were running quickly towards us through the driving rain. I yelled a warning to her. She completed the backward turn, whipped into first and stepped hard on the gas and drove straight at them. She had to, as they were coming from the direction we wanted to go. One of them managed to jump clear, but we hit the other and knocked him flat back against the wall. I heard his yell above the roar of the engine, and there was a bump on the side of the car, then we were clear of the lane, and she was through the gears into top like a flash and we were on our way down Throgmorton Street.

'It looks as if Pop was right,' she said. I glanced sideways at her. I couldn't see her face in the darkness, but her voice was quite steady. In fact it was bright and perky as if, now started, she was enjoying the picnic.

I said, 'We might have killed him,' and all she said to that was 'Too bad.' I felt rattled.

'That's all bloody well,' I said, 'but they might have been plainclothes men—in which case we're going to have a shower of squad cars on our tail in a matter of minutes.'

'I doubt it,' she said coolly. 'Tell me when you last saw a British detective in a belted trenchcoat, except on TV. Those two were Ivans.' And I felt sure she was right, but I didn't love her for it. The wretched woman was taking the show over.

She knew her way and she drove well, with the sense not to go too fast and attract attention. We crossed Blackfriars Bridge and headed for the New Kent Road and the A.20, with me tapping the water off the talc rear window and squinting anxiously behind us from time to time.

'There's no need to get jumpy,' she said. 'They'd have caught up long before this if they were police.'

'Who's getting jumpy?' I snarled.

'You. We're quite safe in the suburbs, but the police sometimes make routine checks on the main roads. If we're stopped we use our own names, because they'll want to see my driving licence. You're my fiancé, and we're going down to the Mermaid Inn, Rye, for the weekend.'

'God forbid,' I said fervently, and felt that the shot had gone home because she maintained a miffish silence thereafter.

But she was right. I *was* jumpy. There was more traffic about here and we had overtaken and been overtaken by several cars, but the lights of one were far too steady for my liking. This fellow was a hundred yards or so behind us and was maintaining the distance, and he switched his headlights off once, and ran on sidelights, then went back after a time to dipped headlights, then on to full again—and always when there were a couple of cars between him and us. This is standard practice when car-tailing at night, to confuse the quarry into thinking you are different cars.

I hated doing it, but in the end I said: 'Jumpy or not, there is someone on our tail.'

'I know it,' she said. 'I've been watching him in the mirror. Light-switching.' The bitch was still a jump ahead of me. 'They're not police or they'd have had us by now. This is somebody who wants to know where we're going.'

'What are you going to do about it?' I asked.

'Throw them if I can.' And she did, as neatly as I've ever seen it done. There were three cars between us and the tailer, and a bus in front of us, just pulling away from a stop. She nipped in between it and the kerb and turned down a side street and went like the clappers with her lights switched off. She turned left at the next turning and left again, crossing the main road we had been travelling on and diving into a dark labyrinth the other side. We threw them all right, but then she was a bit too clever and she found herself in a cul-de-sac and had to back out. Then she got lost, and told me to do the same when I jeered at her.

We stayed off the main road until we found ourselves in Eltham, but then, on the dual carriageway, I became aware of the same guy on our tail again—or someone damned like him. Of course they knew what we looked like and had our number, whereas they were only a pair of lights behind us. I told her about it.

'Have you got a gun?' she asked.

'Don't talk like a fool,' I snapped. 'Of course I haven't. This is Eltham, not Arizona.'

'Well, I have,' she said calmly. 'And I intend getting to where I'm going without these people on our tail. Hang on.'

Her foot went down hard.


## Chapter 7

God! What a drive that was. Those sports toys are fast, but they're not heavy enough for the really high brackets—certainly not in rain like that which was coming down now. There was too much water on the windshield for the wipers to cope with and the headlights were a drowned blur in the slanting downpour, but that didn't slow her down any. It was more like water-skiing than motoring. She didn't have the panel lights on, so I couldn't see the clock, but she must have been needling over a hundred in places. I was scared rigid.

But they were no chickens either, and their car, I judged from the spacing of their headlights, was heavier and faster and generally more suited for this sort of lunacy than ours. They kept right on our tail and finally crept up abreast of us and tried to force us on to the verge, but an oncoming truck saved us and they had to brake hard and slide in behind us again and we gained quite a bit of ground as a result. I just had time to see that it was a big dark car and the fellow beside the driver was leaning out through the open window making urgent signs to us to pull up. I felt Sonia fumbling for something on the floor between us. I said, 'I'll get it, whatever it is. Keep your hands on that damned wheel.'

'The gun's in my handbag,' she said.

I groped and found the bag, opened it and fished out a silly little nickel-plated .22 revolver.

'Good,' I said. 'It's in my pocket now, and it's staying there. Of all the silly, stupid——'

'It must be quite obvious, even to you, that we'll never shake them off,' she interrupted. 'But if you hit one of their tyres——'

'With this scent-spray? You don't know guns. It would bounce off like a pea. Anyhow, who do you think I am? Deadeye Dick?'

'Well, their windshield then.'

'Sheer murder? No thank you. The whole damned works are not important enough for that.'

'We've got to do something. My father's out there in the blue relying on us.' There was a catch in her voice.

'Pathetic,' I said. 'But it's the old goat's own fault. He shouldn't have jumped the gun.'

'You rat!' she raved. '*You* forced him into this. He's done his part of it, and now you want to leave him in the lurch.'

'I don't want to do anything of the sort,' I told her. 'But I'm damned if I'm going to start blasting off with a gun on an English road, especially since we still don't know whether or not they are police.'

'Of course they're not police,' she snapped. 'If they were they'd have whistled up road blocks by radio long ago.' And she was no doubt right, but I still wasn't prepared to risk it.

I saw the traffic lights as we screamed round the next bend, and they were red. I yelled a warning and my hand shot forward to find the ignition key but it was too late; we had already overshot them. They were controlling a long one-way stretch of road, one side of which was under repair, cluttered with graders, rollers and heaps of ballast. And the lights of an oncoming vehicle were blinding us.

Don't ask how we made it. I'm still not prepared to credit her with skill and judgment. Not at that particular instant, anyhow. It was sheer blind luck. She wrenched the wheel over and missed the oncomer by the thickness of a cigarette-paper, skittled a barrier and a row of hurricane lamps, threaded between a miniature mountain of tar macadam and a huge yellow bulldozer, and then was back on the single roadway. But it just wasn't the tailers' night. They didn't make it.

Peering back through the talc I saw the following lights swing to the near side and then soar up and over as the car mounted a steep bank. Then they went out suddenly, and I heard the crash even over the scream of our own tortured engine. The other fellow seemed to have got away with it. It was a huge lumbering truck and it had managed to stop in time.

When I was able to control my voice I said: 'Slow down. You're asking for trouble at this speed, and there's no need for it now. They won't be following anybody any more, except maybe a harp band.'

She didn't answer, but I felt the speed slacken as she lifted her foot, and we proceeded thereafter at a sober fifty.

The reaction set in, as far as I was concerned anyhow, after we had got through Maidstone. A police car with its blue light came towards us, and I waited, prickling. But they swept past us with their sirens wailing. The truck driver must have got to a telephone somewhere. I realized how tired I was then though I did at least make a gesture and offered to drive, but she declined it coldly, so I went to sleep.

I woke as I felt her hand shaking my arm. She said, still coldly: 'We're nearly there.'

I rubbed the moisture off the window and peered through, but could see only dark flatness through the rain which was still bucketing down. There weren't even hedges between us and the fields, and we might well have been in the middle of the steppes. Not even a distant light showed anywhere in a three-sixty degree sweep. I didn't know anywhere as desolate as this existed in England any more—certainly not close to London, and I knew we couldn't be that far away because a glance at my watch told me I'd been asleep less than half an hour.

'Where the devil are we?' I asked.

'Romney Marsh,' she said. 'We should be coming up to a turn-off on the left shortly. Keep your eyes open that side. It's easy to miss it on a night like this.'

And almost immediately I saw it. Two white posts marking the entrance to a cart track. She pulled up, skittering in the wet, and switched off the headlights, then she blipped the side-lights twice. Away to our left a pinpoint of light came up in answer. She turned on to the track and squelched at a snail's pace along muddy ruts until dimly in front of us I saw high mounds silhouetted darkly against the sky, and between them the glimmer of water. She ran the car slowly round the first mound and stopped and climbed out stiffly. I followed suit even more stiffly, feeling damp, cold and miserable. Malcolm loomed up out of the gloom and said testily, 'What on earth kept you?' and I could have hit him. He didn't give us time to reply but just took over like a colonel from a couple of rather dim subalterns.

'Right, this car——' He leaned forward and peered at it. 'Tch, tch! It's yours, Sonia? I told you not to go and collect it. You might quite easily have been followed. You *must* take notice of my instructions. Switch off the lights and leave it. Terry will collect it later. This way, both of you.'

He padded off through the mud and we followed. I could hear Sonia swearing horribly in a choked voice, but for myself I was past it. Just speechless. He led us into a gaunt open-sided shed on the bank of what I could now see was a big pond, and I realized that it was a gravel pit. The rain drummed hollowly on the tin roof of the shed and a cold, salt-laden wind blew through it, bringing with it the distant murmur of the sea on a shingly shore. He used his torch. It fell on the mini-van. He got in behind the wheel.

'You'll both have to cram into the front seat,' he said. 'The back's full. Take Sonia on your knees.'

I'd have preferred to take her by the scruff of her neck, but there was nothing for it. I opened the other door and a rich ripe smell assailed us—of fish. The back of the van was piled high with wooden trays. We squeezed inside, and notwithstanding the discomfort of it, it was good to get out of the cold wind, and close up Sonia was warm and smelled nice. He started up and backed out, then went off down the track. I was bursting with questions but the overladen little van was making heavy weather of it in the mud, roaring its head off in low gear, and anyhow my mouth was pressed hard between Sonia's shoulder-blades. We got back on to the road and he went off at a hell of a clip, but the ride only lasted five minutes or so, for which I was thankful, because although Sonia wasn't a heavyweight, my legs were rapidly going to sleep. We stopped again and extricated ourselves, and I saw we were in another shed—a sort of lean-to arrangement, and the stink of fish was even stronger, and there were more wooden trays stacked tidily along two sides of it.

A door opened and I saw the bulky figure of a woman out-lined against a dim light.

'Look, Malcolm——' I began. His hand shot out and I felt my arm gripped.

'The name's George, you bloody fool,' he hissed. 'Just George. My daughter is Jessie, and if I have to address you at all, it will be as Tom. Please remember that—and talk as little as possible.'

'I want to know what's going on,' I demanded.

'And so you will—at the proper time,' he told me. 'Now will you please shut up and wait here.' He crossed to the woman. Sonia had melted somewhere into the gloom.

Malcolm said, 'Tickety-boo?'

'The boys is down at the boat,' the woman answered complainingly. 'They waited as long as they could—but the *tide* don't bloody wait, you know.'

'Orlright, orlright,' Malcolm said. 'I haven't been picking daisies for the bleeding fun of it. How'm I going to get the stuff down?'

'The 'andcart's there,' the woman told him. 'But be quick about it, for Cri'sake. It'll be light soon and the coastguards will be manning the tower.' She sniffed loudly and closed the door, cutting off what light there was and leaving us in complete darkness.

'Come on,' said Malcolm briskly in his own voice. 'Help me get the van unloaded. Sonia, hold the torch.' He opened the rear doors and started dragging out the fish-trays. They were piled right to the ceiling, but there weren't many of them —just a wall one tray thick in the front and rear.

In the intervening space there were two men, coiled ser-pentinely heads and tails and squashed in tight—very tight —because you know how small a mini-van is. They were very still, and I couldn't see their faces. But Malcolm could see mine and it evidently was a study.

'Don't stand there goggling, man,' he commanded. 'Help me get 'em out—and be careful with this one. He's still alive.' He leaned into the van and pulled one of the heads round. 'No, my mistake. The other's our man.'

I heard Sonia say in tones of deep reproach, 'Oh, Father— no—' as if she were taking him to task for spilling mustard on the clean tablecloth.

'*I* didn't kill him,' Malcolm said. 'It was that creature Wates.

He lost his head and threatened me with a gun. Chaworth jumped at him, and the fool pulled the trigger and got one of his own people. Come on—out with them.'

He got hold of the twisted forms and hauled. I was beyond coherent speech by this. I was almost beyond thought. I was just moving mechanically under his directions. We slid them out. One, a heavily built man in a gaberdine raincoat, had stiffened into the shape of a question mark and was difficult to handle. The other, slighter and dressed in blue battledress trousers and a windcheater, was more supple, and he groaned faintly as we moved him.

'A thiopentone injection, followed by a massive dose of paraldehyde,' Malcolm said conversationally. 'It will hold him for at least another two hours. Excellent stuff. Now where the hell is that handcart?'

We found it outside the shed and we wheeled it in and strained and heaved to get the two of them on to it. There was some tattered tarpaulin in one corner. Malcolm tore off a hunk of it and covered them.

'Right,' he said briskly. 'Outside and straight down the beach path. If we pass anybody, let me do the talking.'

We trundled the cart out. The sky had lightened perceptibly to the east and I could see that the shed was built on to the side of a house formed by a couple of old railway coaches, and that there were other similar houses scattered irregularly over the wide shingle strip that ran down to the shore. Away to our right was a huge concrete building that looked vaguely like the Battersea powerhouse.

'The nuclear power-station,' Malcolm told me. He was still being brisk but his earlier testiness had passed. 'Biggest of its type in the world. It makes one proud to be British.' And it sounded so off-beat under the circumstances that I giggled like a fool, which was a good thing because it helped me throw off the almost cataleptic trance in which I seemed to be moving.

The wheels of the handcart were sinking in the shifting shingle and it was hard work to keep it going. Sonia came up and lent her strength to it and then we were at the top of a steep slope and the tumbling surf was at the bottom, and we could see the bulk of a boat in the shallows. In fact we could see several boats, some already under way puttering out to sea on their noisy diesels, and others, like the one immediately in front of us, still half aground—the nearest a bare fifty yards away. Men with hurricane lanterns were moving about the decks of most of them.

Malcolm said, 'Keep the wretched cart moving or it will bog down,' and ran forward into the loom of the nearest boat, and as we toiled and shoved we heard him talking in a low tone to somebody. We panted to a stop at the water's edge. The boat was a sturdy, bluff-bowed fifty-footer, towering high above us. Somebody let down a rope ladder. Malcolm said, 'Up you go, Jessie,' and without a word she climbed up nimbly and vanished over the bows. A rope came snaking down. 'Give me a hand,' he said, and we got the end secured under the arms of the live one. Malcolm whistled softly and the rope jerked tight, took the strain and bore the chap aloft, then, after a few moments, it came snaking down again.

'They'll probably be a little awkward about this one,' Malcolm said as we made fast. 'It's not in the contract, and they're law-abiding people. You might have to pay anything up to a couple of hundred extra.' He whistled again, and the grotesque bundle swayed aloft, twisting obscenely against the rapidly lightening sky. I felt a little queasy.

'And now,' Malcolm said briskly, 'what money are you carrying?'

'About nine quid,' I told him and he tut-tutted again irritably. 'You can't blame me,' I went on. 'How did I know you were doing it tonight?'

'I had no choice,' he said. 'I'll tell you all about it later. Meantime, what about funds? You've got an awful long way ahead of you, and in this business everybody wants paying on the nail.'

'What the hell can I do about it now?' I demanded angrily.

'It's no good losing your temper,' he said primly. 'How *were* you to be financed?'

'I can draw what I want from a bank in London,' I said. 'I'd better go back, and join you later.'

He shook his head vigorously. 'That would mean leaving Sonia to make the crossing with the goods alone.'

'Aren't you going?' I asked.

'I can't disappear from my business just like that,' he said. 'That would be inviting suspicion. I must be back in town before my usual opening hour. I've got to keep to my ordinary pattern—attend to routine matters—brief my assistant—go down and see my wife—then leave on a normal business trip. All that will take at least three days. I should be able to join you on Wednesday.'

'What the devil do I do in the meantime?'

'Leave it to Sonia. She knows exactly where to go the other side. Can you depute your drawing powers at the bank to me?'

I thought hard for a moment, then nodded: 'I'll get through to somebody by telephoning,' I said. 'They'll get in touch with you. But what about these boat people? Won't *they* want paying on the nail?'

'They've had half. They get the rest on completion, though as I say, they'll probably want a little more on account of our departed friend—but you can leave all that to me.'

A voice from above said hoarsely, 'Hey! What the hell's going on down there? Think we've got all day?'

'Coming,' Malcolm called, then added hurriedly to me, 'You shouldn't have any trouble with Carter when he comes round —*provided he thinks he's going to the Russians*. As far as he's concerned *you* know nothing. You're just an underling. Play it off the cuff, Wainwright—as intelligently as possible.'

'I'll do my damnedest,' I said, and hoped it sounded sufficiently sarcastic. 'You're the one that'll have to do the cuff-playing, though. There *were* two of them watching your place—Russians, we think. They followed us in a car, but Sonia shook them and they crashed near Maidstone.'

Far from worrying him, it seemed to afford him some satisfaction, because I heard him chuckle and murmur something about always being right in these matters. The old devil was certainly playing it cool, I'll say that for him.

He climbed the ladder, and I followed. The oil-skinned figures were waiting for us—one very tall, the other short, stout and choleric. The boat was flush-decked from high bows to blunt transom, broken only by a winch, a square hatchway amidships, a stumpy mast and a cramped wheelhouse aft. Sonia was nowhere in sight.

The short man said furiously, 'What's the bloody caper, George? One of 'em's a stiff.'

'Sorry, mate,' Malcolm said. 'They rung him in on me. What was I to do? Leave him on the road?'

'That's your pigeon. I'm not having him on my boat——'

'Well, I'm not taking him back to the Smoke. What if I was stopped? Blimey!'

T.S.—C 65

'It's not right,' the short man complained, and appealed to me. 'Is it?'

I said, 'Ah' profoundly, and scratched my chin.

'Get 'im orf,' said the short man.

'And leave him on the beach?' Malcolm asked. 'Up to you, of course, but I shouldn't have thought it advisable myself.' And the short man chattered with rage. His mate looked gloomily over the rail, spat, and said, 'The bloody tide'll be 'aving the 'andcart next.' It was only that which settled matters. Malcolm swung down the ladder and rescued it, hauling it up the shingle slope.

'Give us a hand to shove off,' the short man growled. He went aft and opened up the idling diesel in reverse, then we pushed against the shingle with a thing like an overgrown barge-pole, and slid off into deep water. The taller one jerked his thumb at the hatchway.

'Better get below, mate,' he said. 'We only got two of a crew, and you don't look like neither of us.'

I dropped down over the coaming and found myself in a fish-hold which ran from the bows to a bulkhead about two-thirds of the length back. There was a door in the bulkhead and a light the other side. I looked through into a cluttered and smelly cabin which extended the breadth of the boat. It had a couple of rough wooden berths, a table, a form, and an iron stove. A ladder led up into the wheelhouse and a door abaft of it gave access to the engine-room. Sonia sat at the table, hunched into her raincoat, looking sulky and resentful.

A man lay on one of the berths. I recognized the blue trousers and windcheater, and crossed to look at him closer. His eyes were still closed but he seemed to be breathing more naturally, and I had the impression that he was beginning the long climb back to consciousness. I looked round the cabin but could not see the other, and I gathered with relief that they had had the delicacy to put him out of sight somewhere in the fish-hold.

The boat had completed its sternward swing and was now headed offshore and was feeling the long ground-swell. I tried to look out through one of the small portholes which were now greying with the dawn, but they were salt-grimed and opaque. For the want of something to break the silence I offered Sonia a cigarette, but she shook her head and turned away from me. I lit one myself and tried once or twice to make something that resembled normal conversation, but it was no good, so I gave it up and stood on the table and looked out of the open skylight.

The wind had dropped a little and it was no longer raining, though there was promise of more to come in the lowering clouds sweeping up from the south-west. The sun was just appearing over the eastern horizon, gilding the Dover cliffs far away on our port beam. This part of the Channel looked as busy as Piccadilly. The other fishing boats were fanning out and there was a round dozen deep-sea freighters and tankers hove to, picking up and dropping their pilots off the Dungeness Trinity House station, with probably twice as many coasters beating up and down the Channel further off-shore. The boat was beginning to dance now in the short, sharp chop and I had to brace myself against the edge of the skylight. From the wheelhouse just in front of my position I heard the bleeps of the seven o'clock BBC time signal, and strained my ears for the news that would follow, but then somebody below banged my leg to attract my attention.

## Chapter 8

It was the tall man. He was holding up a battered kettle and an untidy newspaper bundle to me as I looked down at him.

'A drop of tea like,' he said hospitably. 'And some nice cold bacon sandwiches.'

Sonia exited rapidly from the swaying cabin, her hand over her mouth, and I was louse enough to feel malicious satisfaction. You just can't be superior and seasick at the same time. I climbed down and joined him and we sat each side of the table and ate and drank in silence. He saw me straining my ears to catch the newscast from the wheelhouse, so he obligingly went up the ladder and turned the volume up.

'. . . the prisoners watching television until eight-thirty. Carter, who had been doing some clerical work in his unlocked cell on the third floor of J Block, was not missed when prisoners returned to their cells and were locked in for the night, because of a note on his table which stated that he had gone to the catering office to complete some entries in the ration ledger, so it was not until the night duty officer noticed his still-unlocked door at ten o'clock that a check was made. It is still not known how, or from what point, he actually made his escape, and Scotland Yard states that the possibility of his still being inside lying low in some hiding place cannot be ruled out. Meanwhile the search is being stepped up by the Metropolitan Police and all county forces, while sea and air ports are under the closest surveillance. It is expected that the Home Secretary will make a statement when the House reassembles on Tuesday next and will have to face some searching questions from Opposition members. A report that Carter was seen leaving a plane in Warsaw and boarding another for Moscow has been discounted . . .' He went on with the rest of the news and mentioned, without apparent connection with the main item, an accident on the A.20 near Maidstone involving a car and a lorry, in which a man had been killed and another seriously injured and was still unconscious. No names were given.

So, I realized with relief, unless the bland tone of the announcer was masking some really deep skulduggery on the part of the police, we were in the clear—so far. We didn't deserve it. The planning and carrying out of this operation would have disgraced an unpaid-acting lance-corporal on a field exercise.

The tall man finished his doorstep sandwich, swilled it down with tea, belched and pointed over his shoulder with a scarred and spatulate thumb.

'Nothing about 'im,' he said.

'Who?'

' '*Im*. The stiff. Looks like George got away with it again.'

'George didn't kill him,' I said, more to dissociate myself from it than to defend Malcolm.

'Don't matter who done it,' the tall man said. ' 'E's 'ere and we'd rather 'e wasn't. You'll 'ave to put 'im over the side as soon as it's dark.'

'Couldn't you do that?' I asked.

'Not bloody likely. We don't want nothing to do with that side of it, mate. For God's sake see he's got nothing on him that can be checked—just in case he comes up again.'

I shivered slightly. 'Where is he now?'

He pointed with his thumb again, to the fish-hold. I went through reluctantly. Sonia was hunched miserably on an upturned fish-tub under the open hatch. Past her, up in the nose of the boat I could see something under a tarpaulin.

I said, 'I've got an unpleasant job to do. If you'd rather go back to the cabin——'

She rose and pushed past me through the door without a word. I went forward and pulled the tarpaulin aside. It was very difficult to search him because he was now completely rigid, but there's a drill for it, and I went over him as thoroughly as I'd have done a fellow student at the school under the critical eye of an instructor. This fellow had been a professional all right. There wasn't a thing on him as far as I could see that could point to his possible identity, unless one counted the gun tucked tightly into his waistband. That was Belgian but good, a snub-barrelled 9 mm, which told me exactly nothing. His pockets yielded seven pounds in a plastic wallet, a fountain pen, a packet of cigarettes, a cheap lighter, four and eightpence in loose change, an unbroken carton of twenty-five rounds for the gun—from which the label had been torn—and a dirty handkerchief. His clothes were the sort you could buy in any one of a thousand chain tailors, but even so the tags had been carefully picked out.

I kept the gun and the ammunition but replaced the rest of the stuff in his pockets. Maybe the money would have been useful later, but somehow I couldn't face sticking to it. Then I covered him up again, quickly, and went back into the cabin. Sonia had taken my place on the table with her head out of the skylight, for which I was thankful because her company was beginning to pall on me as much as mine, no doubt, was on her. Carter was stirring in his berth. I crossed over to him.

His eyes were wide open, the pupils contracted to pin-points, and his mouth was working drily. I got water from a bulkhead beaker, washed out a tea mug and gave him a drink. He was violently sick. Sonia looked down at us from her perch and turned a pale shade of green. Carter went to sleep again.

We stood up and down in mid-Channel all that day. It was too rough for trawling so they codlined with half-mile lengths of rope with hundreds of baited hooks on them. I would willingly have gone up and helped them in order to get out of that ghastly cabin, but the other boats were all round us and the short man wouldn't hear of it, although he relented to the extent of letting Sonia sit on a box in the wheelhouse. Carter awoke again during the afternoon, looked around vaguely and took another drink. He wasn't sick this time but he certainly showed no desire to talk, and eventually went off once more into a deep sleep. The tall man warmed up stew on the stove and made tea from time to time, and I listened to further news bulletins, which had nothing fresh to offer, and somehow we got through that seemingly endless day.

I went up on deck through the fish hatch when darkness had fallen completely, and leaned on the bulwarks enjoying the breeze, which had freshened considerably, although it was doing nothing to dispel a heavy sea mist which was creeping up from the south. The tall man came out and got a rope rove through a block on the stumpy foremast. He nudged me and muttered that I'd find some net weights down below, then left me to it and went and joined the others in the wheelhouse. I took the running end of the rope and dropped down into the hold. It was now knee-deep in still-wriggling fish and as dark as the pit. I slipped and slithered all over the place but finally got the rope fastened around him, then I climbed back on deck and hauled. He jammed hard under the coaming of the hatch once, and I had to drop down again to free him, then once again to grope round among that damned fish until I found some lead things like crude dumb-bells. They weighed about twenty pounds each, I reckoned, and somehow I managed to get four of them fastened to his ankles with some odds and ends of cordage, but then I had the very devil of a job to lift him up on to the top of the bulwarks. I could see the faces of the two men dimly through the wheelhouse window in the reflected light of the compass, but they didn't want to see me. I slipped on the slimy deck twice and came down hard with the poor devil on top of me, but at last it was done and he went over the side and out of sight into the creaming bow wave. Cold as it was now, I couldn't face that cabin again, so I went up into the nose and sat with my back against the winch and wondered dully who he was, what he got paid and why the hell he, I, or any other of the faceless ones did it anyhow. I went to sleep before I had worked out any of the answers.

It was Sonia who wakened me eventually. I was cold, stiff and wet, though somebody had had the decency to cover me with a piece of canvas. She shook my shoulder and I sat up. She handed me a mug of tea without a word. The fog had
70

closed down solid now and I couldn't see the length of the boat. The wind had died and we were hardly moving. Somewhere in the distance a foghorn moaned at intervals, while nearer, a bell clanged monotonously. I gulped the tea gratefully. It was laced with rum and it pulled me together.

I said, 'What's the score?'

'They're putting us ashore here.'

'Where's "here"?'

'They say we're just to the west of Dieppe.'

'And we have to get to——?'

'Le Havre. That's about a hundred kilometres further along the coast.'

'Three foreign scarecrows stinking like the Billingsgate fish markets! No passports and damned little money! How far do you think we'd get before we had every cop in Northern France on our tails?' I climbed to my feet and started to grope my way aft. 'I'm going to have it out with them. They either take us closer to Le Havre or they won't collect the balance of their fee.'

'You can try it,' she said tiredly, and followed me.

But I was just butting my head against a brick wall. They wouldn't even listen to me, and looking back I can't say that I really blamed them, because now they had their hands full. Another bell-buoy was clanging on our starboard beam, and high above us where the fog was thinner we could see the reflected flash of a lighthouse beam. The diesel was throttled down to a throaty whisper and we were inching forward at a snail's pace, the short man crouched over the wheel, the other now up in the bows with a headline.

I gave it up and went down below to thaw out at the stove.

Carter was sitting at the table. There was only a smoky oil lamp, and that was on the bulkhead behind him, so that his face was in shadow.

I said, 'How are you feeling?'

He didn't answer for a moment or so, as if he were sizing me up and searching for words, but when he did speak his voice was clear enough and he had no trace of foreign accent.

'Not too bad,' he said. 'But I'd be happy to know a little of what's going on.'

'We're going ashore,' I told him. 'Then we've got some travelling ahead of us—to a place where you'll be lying low for a bit.'

'And then?'

I shrugged. 'Don't ask *me*, cocker. Somebody else will be taking you over, I expect.'

'Why was I drugged?' he asked.

'Search me,' I said. 'I took you over like that on this boat. I've got to get you to somewhere. That's all I know—that's all I want to know.'

'I'm sorry,' he said, very quietly, 'but that's not good enough. I was told the form in prison, and what to expect, but now something totally different has happened—and I've a right to know why. I remember a fight starting just after we came over the wall. Somebody used a gun—then this needle was shoved into my arm and I passed out——'

'Passed out is right,' I said shortly. 'You passed out of the nick, so what the hell have you got to belly-ache about?'

'I want to know *who* got me out of the nick,' he insisted, 'and where I'm being taken to—and what my ultimate destination is to be. Unless that is made clear, here and now, I'm not prepared to go a step further.'

'Suits me,' I said, and hoped that I sounded like a reasonable man who had done his best under trying circumstances but was now prepared to wash his hands of the whole affair. 'Stay on the boat and go back with them. They'll dump you somewhere on the English coast and then get the hell out of it—and you'll be back inside within a couple of hours.'

'I'd prefer that to——' he began, then broke off.

'To what?' I asked.

'To, shall we say, travelling further with the wrong people —to the wrong place.' And I knew he meant it—and that his suspicions were fully aroused. This fellow was nobody's fool. He knew what to expect if he was, in fact, being shipped back to the Chinese. Nothing we could do to him would be worse than that. He also knew that being shanghaied unconscious aboard a boat was one thing; being made to travel unwillingly in a civilized country was quite another. He had only to sit down now and refuse to budge, to call my bluff. I could have pulled the gun on him and threatened him, but I felt he'd call that bluff too. His worth was alive, on the hoof —and he knew it. I thought of pleading with him, but I knew that would be worse than useless. Then, just as I was about to fall back on the well-worn gambit of sweet reason and a cigarette, Sonia came down the ladder from the wheelhouse. She looked sulky and tired and her face was dirty and her hair was a draggled mess. Anything less like Lola the beautiful spy I've never seen.

She said to me in English, 'Get up on deck. They want your help to get the boat over the side.' Then she went off into rapid Russian to Carter—so rapid that it left me floundering, though I did catch something to the effect that Carter shouldn't discuss things with sub-human criminal pigs like me. I was only a hired courier, and not a very efficient one at that. And she was doing it perfectly. I grunted and climbed into the wheelhouse. All lights were doused now, but I could feel the short man's sweating nervousness even in the pitch dark.

He said, 'Give me mate a hand to get the inflatable dinghy overside. You can trail a line and we'll haul it back when you've landed——'

But we were saved the trouble. There was a startled yell from the tall man in the bows, and an unprintable blast from the other as the boat struck.

It wasn't a hard strike—just a gentle crunch as her bows ploughed into the shingle beach, but it whipped these two into panic.

'Over the side, you bastards—all of you,' yelled the short man, and Sonia came up the ladder fast, cannoning into us in the darkness, and whatever she had been saying seemed to have been convincing, because Carter followed on her heels. We felt our way forward to where the tall man was pushing off frantically with the barge-pole. Behind us I could hear the diesel being revved up hard in reverse. I didn't waste time looking for the ladder. I just jumped, and yelled to the others to do the same. The drop must have been about twelve feet, and I landed awkwardly, lost my footing and finished on my back in about eighteen inches of exceedingly cold water. And as if that was not sufficient, Sonia, then Carter, landed on me as I tried to get up.

We staggered up on to the beach, spitting salt water and obscenity. Behind us, unseen in the fog, the boat was high-tailing it for deep water. I hoped the bloody thing would hit a rock.

I've never experienced anything quite so bewildering as that fog. It had blanketed us on the boat, but at least one could feel one's way along the bulwarks there. Here there was nothing but the crunch of shingle underfoot and the soft lap of the water behind us that was now covering the receding beat of the diesel. It was only that which gave us direction. We walked away from it until we found ourselves among loose rocks, then hard up against a sheer cliff. Sonia turned left—why, I don't suppose even she knew, because it was anybody's guess now. Anyhow, we followed dumbly and blindly, and after a time I stumbled over a concrete ramp jutting out from the cliff bottom, and it was surmounted by an iron rail. We climbed on to it and found that it was the foot of a path leading upwards, so we toiled onwards until suddenly and dramatically we came out of the fog into the clear. We were about half way up the cliff, and above us a lighthouse stabbed the darkness four times, waited, then flashed again twice, waited, then repeated. Professional sailors and keen yachtsmen know the flashes of all the Channel lights, I believe. None of us was either, so we were none the wiser until finally we reached the top and found ourselves on a road. There was a signpost here and in the flashes of the lighthouse we read that Veules-les-Roses was six kilometres to our left and St Valéry-en-Caux two the other way. We chose the latter by common consent, mainly, I think, because it was downhill.

It was getting light and the fog below the cliffs was clearing with the dawn, and I was getting increasingly nervous now that I could see the others. Carter and I each had three days' growth of beard. With his windcheater he might have passed as a hippy—but his hair wasn't long enough to sustain the role. I, on the other hand, must have looked just what I was—a gent who had started out in a decent suit and overcoat but had spent a couple of nights in the hold of a dirty little fishing boat and had been dropped in the sea at the end of it. Sonia, also, was looking terrible. The three of us together would have attracted unwelcome attention anywhere. And to make matters worse Carter was beginning to have trouble with his feet and I noticed for the first time that he was wearing flimsy prison hospital slippers and they weren't standing up to the strain. A signpost on the outskirts of the village which told us that Le Havre was seventy-four kilometres off was the last straw. Carter sat down in the ditch and started to vomit, which gave me the opportunity to take matters up with Sonia.

'We'll have to get under cover somewhere before the local law is about,' I said, and for once she didn't give me a sour answer. She just nodded and said we'd better get down to the seafront.

We walked on through the village. It was set in a chine running down to a tiny harbour between towering cliffs and it would no doubt have been picturesque had we been in the mood to appreciate it. We passed an old woman carrying two milk churns on a yoke who twisted her head round like an ancient tortoise and stared at us, but she was the only one astir in the single street, although below us on the quay we could see fishermen moving about. We skirted round the harbour to avoid them, and reached the wide plage which stretched for miles ahead of us to the west, and walked along the hard clean sand—and then had our first break. We saw a cluster of small wooden beach chalets nestling in the curve of the cliff, deserted and heavily shuttered for the winter. We crossed to them and I went from one to the other cursing the French habit of fitting shutters like the doors of bank vaults. But there's an Achilles' heel to most propositions if you take the trouble to look for it. The window frame of one of them had warped sufficiently for me to get my fingers in and wrench the gap wide enough for the slim hand of Sonia to reach the bolt inside. We climbed in and pulled the shutters closed.

It was a single-roomed place, cluttered with the usual beach gear—deckchairs, mattresses and umbrellas, overlaid with a pall of dust that showed that it had not been disturbed for a long time. It matched my mood. There is something unutterably miserable about summer toys laid up for the winter. Carter staggered across to a corner and lowered himself painfully on to a mattress. He looked dreadfully ill and he was shivering like a wet dog. I helped Sonia drag out another mattress to cover him, and I stood looking down at him helplessly. She caught my eye and moved away to the window and climbed back outside. I started to follow her but then realized that she probably wanted a few minutes' decent privacy, so I dumped myself down on another mattress.

I would have to have things out with her when she returned, I decided. This was ridiculous. The whole thing was falling apart. Here we were stuck out in the blue, miles from anywhere, with a sick man who was going to get a damned sight sicker unless we did something for him pretty soon. But what could we do? Three scarecrows who would invite questions from the first rustic gendarme we ran into—no

French money, passports—no anything. If I could have seen any way whatsoever out of the mess at that moment, even the base one of quitting cold and leaving them to it, I'd have taken it. We shouldn't have left the boat, I reflected savagely. We should have gone back with them and forced them to hide us up until things could have been arranged properly.

But even in misery there are priorities. Obviously our first was French money. With that I could at least go out after dark and make a call to London. But who to in London? I'd been virtually fired by the Gaffer, so he was out. There was always the bank, of course, though I shuddered at the time lapse that would mean—but money was the first thing. I'd have to change my few pounds to francs. It would be asking for trouble to attempt to do so here in the village. Le Havre—that was it. Spruce up a bit as best I could and thumb a lift in——

But that was as far as I got. I remember thinking that Sonia had been gone a long time, and that was all. Except for uneasy catnaps on the wet deck I had not slept for forty-eight hours. I must have gone out like a light.

I woke stiff and chilled. It was getting dark. I sat up and looked round. Carter was thrashing around on his mattress, muttering deliriously—but there was no sign of Sonia. I peered round the cabin, then climbed out of the window. No sign of her out there either. So the bitch had quit. The thought that I had been ready to do just that myself was no comfort.

Well—that was it. I'd have to extricate myself as best I could. But what about Carter? I couldn't leave the poor devil here to die. An anonymous call to the police once I had put a reasonable bit of distance between myself and this ghastly place——?

I was turning this over when I saw the two figures approaching along the darkening beach.

## Chapter 9

One of them was Sonia, and my first thought was that she'd got herself pinched and had brought the law back with her, but the other turned out to be a silent gent in a plastic mac and a beret, carrying a basket.

76

She said: 'How is he?'

'Not too bright,' I told her. 'Where the hell have you been?' But she didn't think that worth answering. She climbed through the window, and we followed. There was just enough light to see Carter. He was still muttering. She knelt beside him and felt his forehead and his pulse, then she gestured for the basket. She took a bottle of brandy and a metal cup from it and raised his head and got a little of it between his lips. It was probably the wrong thing since he was in a burning fever, but it did seem to pull him round a little. She passed me the bottle then, and I took a double swallow too quickly and nearly choked. It certainly pulled *me* together. She rose to her feet and said, 'We've got to get him along the beach. We've got a car waiting by the harbour wall.'

'Fine,' I said. 'But who's "we"?' I jerked my head at the silent one.

'Suppose we leave that for the moment,' she said impatiently. 'Help me to get him up.'

We raised Carter to his feet, but his legs buckled under him, and the other man and I had to lift him bodily through the window. Outside she made me put my overcoat round him, then we got one arm over each of our shoulders and half carried him. I was bursting with questions but she didn't volunteer anything and I assumed she didn't want to talk in front of the other man, so we walked the mile down the beach in silence—a weird-looking quartet, although by some feminine miracle Sonia had managed to tidy herself up considerably. It was raining hard again when we got to the harbour, which was all to the good because not a soul seemed to be out. We came up to a battered black Citroën in the shadows, and eased Carter into the back seat. Sonia got in beside him and I rode in the front with the other fellow. We drove soberly up through the village on to the clifftop road, then he put his foot down hard and he had us in the outskirts of Le Havre in something under the hour.

I tried, mainly as an exercise to get my fuddled wits to work again, to keep track of the turns we made after entering the town, but it was hopeless. We finished up down in the dock area, bumping over railway lines and waiting for swing bridges to be lowered for what seemed nearly another hour, until finally he dropped us off in a narrow street running up from the Quai Colbert. Sonia and I took Carter's arms again but I noticed that she made no move until the

77

tail-light of the car had disappeared in the rain, then she led us along the street a hundred yards and took an even narrower turning between two warehouses. There was a group of high-fronted stone houses squeezed into a cramped square at the end, through which I could see the arched gateway of a military barracks. The corner house was a café, the next was a laundry, the others might euphemistically have been called hotels. Two military policemen came out of the café, frog-marching a drunken soldier. They had their hands full, but one of them still managed to pinch Sonia's bottom as they passed. She said something unprintable in French and they laughed and offered to swop drunks as theirs seemed the lighter. Down in this belt we were right in character.

We turned up the steps of the fourth house. There was a light in the basement kitchen but the windows above were dark. I stood holding Carter upright while Sonia fumbled for a bell-push. We waited, the rain trickling down my neck, Carter swaying and threatening to buckle at the knees again and Sonia jabbing angrily at the bell. Then it was opened by somebody I couldn't see in the dark but who smelt of onions and musty clothes. Sonia muttered something I couldn't catch, then we were inside and the door was closed behind us and somebody switched on a light. We were in a narrow and indescribably filthy hallway from which bare wooden stairs with broken banisters ran up beyond the feeble glow of the single bare electric bulb hanging from the ceiling. An old woman in black with a face like a sick and vicious marmoset pointed up the stairs and held up three fingers. We went up, having more difficulty with Carter and stumbling in the darkness until we reached the third and top floor. A door opened letting light out on to the landing and another woman, as old perhaps but not so simian as the first, motioned us to come in.

Surprisingly, there was nothing squalid about this room. It was a plainly but comfortably furnished sitting-room, and a glass-fronted anthracite stove gave out a welcome heat. The woman took us through another door into a bedroom and told us to get Carter undressed. I knew enough French to realize that it wasn't her native tongue either. She stood watching us as we stripped the sodden clothes from him and laid him on the bed, then she came forward with a large bath towel and massaged him with it from head to foot, competently and quickly. She even produced pyjamas and helped

78

us get him into them. Then she got some aspirin between his chattering teeth and we left him to it. Looking back at him as we came out of the room I found myself almost envying him. All he had to do was to lie there and let somebody else do the worrying.

The woman showed us into another room opening off the landing. It was a bedroom furnished like the first one, with a huge double bed, and there were more pyjamas here and a couple of dressing-gowns, draped frankly on a his'n'hers basis on the turned-down sheets. Sonia asked curtly for yet another room, but the woman shrugged and said this was the limit of her available accommodation—unless m'sieur cared to sleep with the sick man, or perhaps share a room downstairs with an Algerian gentleman. But at least there was a bathroom of sorts with plenty of hot water. Sonia told me to take it first and shook her head impatiently and went out with the woman when I tried to be polite. So I stopped being polite and soaked for a glorious half hour. And there was even a razor and a new toothbrush there.

I came back to the bedroom with a towel round my waist. My wet and stinking clothes had gone, but my possessions had been placed on the dressing-table, even to the gun and ammunition I had taken from the dead man, although her .22 which I had been carrying had disappeared. I put on the dressing-gown and went back to the sitting-room. There was brandy and a packet of English cigarettes on the table. I helped myself to a stiff snort and went through to look at Carter. He was sleeping peacefully. Somebody had taken his clothes away also. Behind me I heard a chink of crockery. The woman was setting a meal on the table. There was a cassoulet in an earthenware pot that was giving off a rich spicy steam that started the drools running down my chin, cheese, crusty bread and a bottle of wine. Sonia came in behind her. She was pink and flushed from a hot bath and had changed into the other dressing-gown, but she still looked deathly tired. The woman left without a word, closing the door behind her. I poured a brandy and passed it to Sonia, but she shook her head and helped herself sparingly to wine. We were both ravenous and neither of us spoke during the meal, but when we had finished, the silence became uncomfortable.

I said: 'How did this miracle happen?'

'Quite simply,' she answered tonelessly. She lit a cigarette.

'I went out and made a reverse charge call to these people. They sent the car.'

'Who are they?'

She lay back in her chair and closed her eyes. 'Does it matter? People my father has had dealings with before. We are safe here until he gets in touch with us.'

'Why didn't you tell me what you were going to do?'

'Because I was tired of arguing. I'm still tired. You had better take the other bedroom.'

'You take it,' I told her. 'I can shake down on the couch in here.' And for once we *didn't* argue. She went through to the bedroom and came back with a blanket and an eiderdown and dumped them on the couch.

She said: 'I think our friend will sleep through until the morning, but if you should hear him stir, you might look in on him. Good night.'

I got to my feet. 'Good night,' I answered. 'I'm sorry you've been dragged into all this. Sorry—but at the same time very, *very* grateful. I wasn't doing so well on my own.'

She paused with her hand on the door, then turned and looked me straight in the eyes. 'God,' she said quietly. 'If you only knew how I hated you. You and the rest of these jungle animals—on both sides.'

'It's a job that's got to be done,' I mumbled.

'Nonsense,' she said scornfully. 'You choose it. You're all free agents—at the beginning, anyway. You enjoy it. Each miserable little success makes you feel good inside. You get a kick out of being frightened, like children playing dares. But that's not the worst of it. The really sickening part of it is your damned hypocrisy—the way you see yourselves as brave men and patriots. I can understand an honest criminal. He's in it for himself alone, but you people use the same methods—lying, cheating, blackmailing—then try and justify it to yourselves.'

And she wasn't so far off the beam either, which was why I blew my top. 'Who made you judge and jury?' I shouted. 'What the hell do you know about it, anyhow?'

'You forget. I've been practically brought up in the business,' she said. 'I know. Oh yes—*I* know.'

'And been in on things once or twice,' I spat at her. 'So why put the finger on *me*?'

'I was trapped into it.'

I laughed at her. 'Who's doing the self-justification now?' I asked.

'That's probably what it sounds like,' she said wearily. 'But at least it's true. I saw my father as a Scarlet Pimpernel helping the victims of people like yourself.'

'Sure,' I said. 'Only the Scarlet Pimpernel never got paid for it.'

'And never got blackmailed by his own people either.'

'Don't you believe it,' I said. 'That was only an act. Your father came back into it for exactly the same reasons as you've been ascribing to me—plus the cheque, of course. Anyhow, we're talking in circles. If that's the way you really feel about things why don't you bow out now? As I've already said, I'm grateful for what you've done, but you don't have to stay.'

'I'm staying until my father arrives,' she answered. 'Then I'm taking him home—and I hope I'll never see you again, Mr Wainwright.'

She went through and closed the door firmly, and I sat on for a time chewing on the cud of my anger and drinking brandy, then I switched off the light and went to sleep.

The grey of a winter's morning was showing round the edge of the blind when I woke. I climbed out of the warmth of the couch with reluctance and went over to the window. A thin, cold sleet was slanting down. Over the roofs of the houses opposite I could see the upper works of ships in the *bassin* on the other side. Down below, on one hand, I could see into the barrack yard where troops in scruffy fatigues were greeting the day like soldiers the world over before breakfast —smoking, gawping, spitting and looking browned off. It made me feel nostalgic for those safe uncomplicated days. The other way pea-jacketed, blue-jeaned dockers were filing in through the dock gates.

I looked at my watch. It was just coming up to seven. I wished I had a transistor to get the news. Sonia's door was still closed, and I hoped it would stay that way for a long time. I'd had enough of that uncomfortable female. I went through to look at Carter. He was still sleeping. I felt his forehead. The fever of the previous night had abated. He looked rather pathetic—thin-faced, pinched round the nostrils and with five days' wispy growth of beard framing a rather weak jaw. I went back to the couch and tried to go to sleep again, but the warmth had gone out of it now, as it had out of the room, because the stove was cold, and anyhow I wanted to pee. I tried the door to the landing but found it was locked.

I felt a surge of blind, insensate fury and started to rattle and kick at it with my bare feet. Sonia's door opened. I turned and glared at her. She pointed to the table and closed the door again. The key was there. She had obviously done what I had neglected to do and locked it during the night. I felt a bloody fool. I crept along the landing to the bathroom.

The woman came up with coffee and croissants and some soup in a teapot for Carter. She laced it with what was left of the brandy and went through to him. Watching her from the door I saw her raise his head gently and feed him through the spout. He hardly woke. She grunted her satisfaction and came away. I asked her about my clothes and she said later, they needed much work, and held her nose, then went.

I saw that there were two cups on the tray and that it must obviously be meant for us both. I didn't know quite what to do, but in the end common courtesy prevailed and I took Sonia's share to the door and knocked. She opened up, looked at the tray, then at me—and then actually smiled her thanks and took it from me. Once again I felt a fool—but also, strangely, a darned sight less gloomy. I almost hoped she'd come out and join me, but she withdrew to her room again.

Our clothes came up at mid-morning, washed, cleaned and pressed. I shaved and bathed, then went into Carter's room and dressed quickly—but Sonia had been quicker, and when I came out again her door was open and she was gone. It didn't matter. I knew what I wanted to do. I was going to find a bureau-de-change, get some French money and make a guarded call to the bank in London. But then I found that my English notes, which I had left on her dressing-table the night before, had gone also. I cursed. Probably she had had the same idea about changing the money and would be back soon, but this was wasting time. Then the woman came up again—and this time she had Charlton with her. I stared at him, pop-eyed.

He waited until the woman had gone down again, then said: 'Man, you're not popular with the Gaffer.'

'All right, Carlovich,' I said. 'I never was. Just give me the message.'

He put a briefcase on the table. 'There's five thousand pounds here. Half in francs, half dollars. You'd better check it.'

'I trust you,' I said sweetly. 'The message.'

'He's to be got aboard the ship——' he began, but then I noticed the open door to Carter's room. He still looked asleep, but I crossed and closed it softly and drew Charlton into Sonia's room.

'Go on,' I said.

'——with less ballsing-up than hitherto—Sorry, his words, not mine—and there'll be orders for you on arrival in Kowloon.' He was enjoying this.

'How does he know I've got him?' I asked.

'My uncle, naturally. He's filled him in on all details.'

'Including the balls-up *he* made in springing the client ahead of the gun?' I asked.

'That couldn't be helped,' Charlton said. 'It was the Rusks who jumped the gun. Wates had everything laid on for that night and they were going to do it on their own. The Gaffer says they've been on to Uncle for weeks, probably—sorry, again his words—through your buggering about. Anyhow, Uncle got wind of it in time and went down and hi-jacked Carter. You know the rest, I believe. Pretty good, I think, considering his age.' He beamed with family pride.

'Pretty good?' I raged. 'Shooting me off cross-Channel without warning—without money—briefing—and loaded with a stiff.'

'But he did send Sonia——'

I said something inexcusable about Sonia and he looked genuinely shocked.

'That's about all, I think,' he said stiffly. 'You know the ship——'

'I don't. That's one of the many things nobody has thought of telling me.'

'The *Nurma*. The captain's a man called Kjaer. She's due in here next Saturday and should be leaving again on Tuesday. You'll have to be careful how you approach him——'

'But surely to God he's already *been* approached?' I said.

Charlton shook his head. 'Unfortunately not. My uncle would have been attending to that here, but now with these new developments——'

'*What* new developments?'

'You haven't given me much opportunity to explain, have you?' he said reprovingly. 'I suggest you listen for a moment. Malcolm is being watched by the Russians very closely. That's only to be expected, of course, and we could take care of it ordinarily, but Special Branch are watching the Russians even more closely, and that could be dangerous——'

And how right he was. We wouldn't give a damn about what the Russians suspected, for the simple reason there was nothing they could do about it officially, but the police were a different proposition. If they smelled a connection between the Russians and Malcolm they'd start digging—and we couldn't stop them.

—'and so you see the Gaffer's point in pulling my uncle right off everything,' Charlton went on. 'He mustn't leave London. He mustn't do a single thing outside his normal round of business. The Russians, of course, know that Sonia is tied up in it somewhere—the Gaffer is *most* upset about your going to the shop to collect her car—' he loved getting that one in —'and *you* must be regarded as compromised as a result, but at least the trail has broken short of this point. The Gaffer thinks that if you stick rigidly to instructions from now on you've still got a chance of bringing things to a successful conclusion——'

I said something inexcusable about the Gaffer also. Since family wasn't concerned he didn't looked shocked this time.

'All right,' I said wearily. 'I've got to see this fellow Kjaer when his ship gets in, make a deal with him, get Carter aboard, take him to Hong Kong——'

'Where you'll receive further instructions,' Charlton interrupted. 'I rather gather that those instructions will be to hand over to somebody else, so you have nothing really to worry about.'

'Except explaining my own arrival there out of the blue,' I said. 'Only a minor point, of course, but I'll be expected back by air in the normal way. Friends usually meet one at Kai Tak —there are such things as arrival lists and a social column in the local rag.'

'As you remark,' he said sweetly. 'A minor point. Naturally that will be left to you.' He delved into the briefcase. 'But at least here's your passport.'

'Where the hell did you get it?' I asked, startled.

'From your flat. Where else?' He was pulling flat packs of French and American notes out of the case. 'The Gaffer had it turned over as a matter of routine in case you'd been uncovered and somebody else did it. I don't want a receipt for this money, naturally, but you'll have to account for it some-time. My uncle says a thousand pounds a head for the passages is the correct thing, and don't let Kjaer stick you —and a hundred a week here. The fishing people have been attended to, but I've been asked to clear two points. Did you, in fact, use six lead weights for certain—er—ballasting pur-poses? They've charged five pounds each, which Accounts think excessive—and meals and drinks on board are down at another thirty.'

'Four weights,' I said spitefully. 'Worth, I should say, five bob each—and meals consisted of three bacon sandwiches, a plate of foul stew and innumerable mugs of tea that tasted of seaboot socks. Call it two pounds, and you're overpaying them.'

'Good,' he said, and rose. 'Now, if I could see Sonia for a moment. I've got her passport and a message from her father.'

'She's out,' I told him, and his eyebrows shot up in pained surprise.

'Do you think that's wise?' he asked.

'Ask her yourself,' I said. 'She certainly didn't ask *me*.'

'She is a little headstrong,' he conceded. 'You'll have to take a strong line with her.'

'Me? Why me? She's all yours, brother, from this point on.' That, in fact, was the only thought that held any sunshine at the moment.

'I'm afraid not,' he said, pursing his lips. 'She goes with you.'

'Not bloody likely,' I said firmly. 'Thanks for the offer, but I can manage on my own.'

'It's not an offer. It's an order.'

'Whose order?'

'The Gaffer's, naturally.'

'I'm not prepared to accept it,' I said, and he looked as if I had blasphemed.

'You are aware of the consequences of that, while you are still serving?'

'Actually I'm not,' I said. 'I'm doubtful whether any con-sequences could be enforced—particularly since it would appear that I'm being fired after this anyhow. She's not coming with me, that's all.'

He dropped his prissiness. 'Very well, Wainwright,' he said quietly. 'If you really mean that, I take over—and you can find your way back to London. If you've got any doubts about that I'll give you a number you can call for confirmation.'

Call it outraged pride, wounded vanity, pricked conceit —anything you like—but it was that which shot me down. I just couldn't take that. I hadn't shown up too brilliantly so far, admittedly, but that would have been the ultimate humiliation. It must have shown in my face, but I still tried feebly to bluff.

'It's unnecessary—and she'll be another disposal problem in Hong Kong,' I said.

'Just another minor matter,' he said. 'The reason the Gaffer wants her to go with you is because he is afraid the Russians might try a snatch if she shows up in London, or anywhere else in Europe. You know we haven't the facilities for a round-the-clock watch and ward—not without police assistance. On the ship she's out of harm's way until after the swop's made.'

I suppose it made sense. I loathed the idea but, as usual, the bastards weren't giving me any option.

Then Sonia knocked at the door.

## Chapter 10

'All right,' I said to Charlton. 'Only you break it to her, and for Christ's sake make it perfectly clear that it isn't *my* idea.' Then I went through to the sitting-room to unlock the door.

'There's a relation of yours in the bedroom,' I said sourly. She pushed past me, looking relieved, expecting no doubt to see her father. I went into Carter's room and closed the door, leaving them to it. He was awake but muzzy. I gave him a drink and he asked peevishly when the hell we would be moving—and where? I soft-talked him and said any minute, but first he had to get his strength back—and in that, at least, I wasn't kidding. He was making progress now, but he was still a very sick man. I don't pretend to any medical knowledge, but I rather guessed that in his weakened condition under that massive anaesthetic and subsequent exposure, he had gone down with pneumonia. It made things simpler for us at the moment, though I wondered how long this would last, as I could sense his unease growing as his wits returned. He said he'd got back all the strength he needed and he wanted a bath. I told him I'd go and get one fixed and made it an excuse to leave.

He said: 'What are the honourable names of your esteemed self and that of your village?'—in perfect Cantonese, but he had timed it badly and I was at the door with my back to him so he missed any reaction that might have shown in my face.

I said: 'Sorry, cocker, I don't speak Russian.'

'The girl does,' he said. 'Where is she?'

'She's around,' I told him casually. 'I'll send her in.' I could feel his eyes fixed on the back of my neck as I went through and closed the door. I hoped it wasn't betraying anything. This fellow, sick as he was, was nobody's goat.

They weren't fighting when I joined them, though Sonia was scowling and Charlton looked as if he'd come through a lively five minutes.

'You've heard this stupid idea, I suppose?' she said.

'Don't blame me,' I answered. 'Given the choice I'd sooner travel with a lady porcupine. Nothing personal.'

'I'll need to go out and buy some clothes,' she said icily.

'Sonia, you must keep off the streets,' Charlton said earnestly.

'That shouldn't be necessary while that lasts,' I said, nodding at the money on the table.

'Funny man,' she spat. 'My God! Fancy having to put up with that for six weeks.' She went into her bedroom and slammed the door hard.

'That sort of thing doesn't help, if I may say so, Wainwright,' said Charlton severely.

'—— off, Carlovich,' I told him. 'You've said your piece. And tell the Gaffer he can go and ——' and I went into details. Childish, no doubt, but it seemed to help at the moment, particularly since I knew Charlton would report it word for word.

'Neither does gutter filth,' he said with dignity. He gathered up his hat and briefcase and moved to the door. 'One last thing. The Gaffer suggests that it might be a good idea to give our friend the impression that he is being taken the long way round to Vladivostok, as all European routes are dangerous.'

I locked the door behind him and grinned ruefully. He *would* suggest it, and thereby rob me of even that small satisfaction—because I'd already decided to do just that.

What I did then was purely a matter of conditioned reflex. I moved to the window and looked down into the square to watch Charlton leave. One always did that—just in case. And this time, by God, it paid off—or seemed to. He went down the front steps and turned right towards the narrow alley leading to the dock road. I remember reflecting sourly that he was a bright herb to be warning Sonia about going out, because although not conspicuously dressed, he was still too smart for this neighbourhood, and was therefore noticeable. He passed the café at the end of the terrace, walked briskly down the alley and disappeared round the corner. And as he did so a man came out of the café and went off after him. Just a very ordinary man in a very ordinary suit and a beret. Of course he may have been nothing more than that, and this was pure happenstance—but it was something that couldn't be disregarded. It certainly looked as if Charlton was being tailed.

I tapped at Sonia's door. She opened, still angry. I told her, and she stopped looking angry.

'You've been out too,' I reminded her, 'and you came in on Charlton's heels.'

'I wasn't seen,' she said positively. 'Coming or going.'

'How can you be certain of that?' I asked.

'I used the back way. The yard gate opens right by a tram stop. You wait for a tram to halt, open the gate and step on. If nobody gets on with you you're reasonably certain you're not being followed. Coming back you do the same thing in reverse. If anybody gets off with you, or is already hanging about—you go for a walk and lose them. Daddy's been using it for years.' I stared at her. That was one nobody had heard of at the school.

'Why didn't we use it last night, when we arrived?' I asked.

'Cars aren't allowed to. Trams only. In any case it wasn't necessary. The taxi wasn't being followed. I'd made certain of that.'

'So if we've been blown it's that bloody nit who's done it,' I mused. 'I wonder how long *he's* been blown. All right then, let's assume he's been tailed all the way from London— damn, I wish I knew which way he'd travelled.'

'London Airport to Rouen, then he hired a car,' she

answered promptly, and added innocently. 'I remembered to ask him. Daddy says one should make that a drill when dealing with low security couriers.'

I didn't hit her. I just swallowed hard—because Daddy was bloody well right, and I'd forgotten to do it.

'Question is, then, was this a single tail or a double?' I asked myself aloud. 'If it's the former the guy will note each place of call and have to whistle up reinforcements to take over. That might take a little time. If it's a double——'

'There's another one holed up somewhere,' she supplied. 'We'll test it if you like.'

'How?'

'I'll go out the front way and you can watch to see if I'm followed.' And she meant it!

I said, 'No, thanks. As it is, they don't know for certain we're here. Your way we'd be giving it to them.'

'Not if I led them a dance and lost them,' she said.

But I turned it down firmly. 'This is a brothel, isn't it?' I asked.

'More or less. The girls are free-lancers who rent rooms here. The clients mostly come from the ships and the barracks.'

'So that means practically anybody can walk in and out?'

'Only if a woman brought him.'

'How would they stop a couple of determined blokes—armed?' I asked.

'There are two Algerian bouncers. If they couldn't cope Madame would have the police round in a matter of minutes. They all pay protection money to the local inspector.'

I looked at her with a new respect. Much as she might inveigh against this business, her father had had an apt pupil in her. She never failed to come up with the answer.

'Could Madame be got at?' I rubbed my forefinger and thumb together.

'Can't everybody, if the price is high enough?' She shrugged. 'But Daddy has always paid well—and he used the place right through the war, with the Gestapo quartered in the barracks practically next door.'

'Well, in that case we'd better just play it cool and sit tight,' I said. 'We've got another four days to wait before the ship arrives. It's Carter who worries me. He's getting better, and increasingly more suspicious.'

'Father gave me some stuff in case it should be necessary,'

she said. 'But I'd rather not use it if it can be avoided. In his present weakened state it could be very bad for him.' I stared at her, but she was quite serious. It gave me a nasty taste in the back of my throat. It was like a doctor and a hangman discussing the health of a condemned prisoner.

She had brought the English papers in with her. Carter's escape had yielded pride of place to a particularly nasty child murder in the Midlands, but the leader-writers were still screaming, and a retired general was heading a court of inquiry into prison security, while an 'ex-M.I.5 Agent' who naturally preferred to remain anonymous, detailed with meticulous accuracy, and maps, the entire escape route. It was by means, we understood, of a black Jaguar Mark 10 from Lanchester to a disused R.A.F. airfield in Suffolk, thence in a mystery plane flown by an Irishman known as the Mad Squadron Leader, to Warsaw—and Carter was now installed in a dacha outside Moscow waiting to take up translation duties in the Soviet Ministry of Propaganda. The second Russian in the car smash near Maidstone had since died. They, the author was in a position to state, had been a red herring to draw attention away from the real route.

Poor M.I.5. Any bloody liar could claim ex-membership without fear of being disowned, and the more lurid his imagination the greater its feasibility. The writer of this crap, I reflected sourly, would collect more for a couple of hours at a typewriter than I was paid in half a year. Still, more power to his elbow if it threw dust in anybody's eyes. But this I doubted. It certainly wouldn't deceived anybody who mattered.

Sonia and I took turns at the window in the forlorn hope of spotting a watcher, but we gave it up after a time by mutual consent. Watchers with turned-down hat brims only read newspapers under the windows of the watched in the movies. This fellow, if there *was* a fellow, would probably be in the café—and if they were doing it properly he'd be relieved from time to time.

Carter started to call querulously at mid-afternoon, so I helped him through to the bathroom and gave him his promised bath and then shaved him. When I got him back to his room Sonia had remade the bed and got him fresh pyjamas, and he cheered up somewhat. He obviously trusted her more than me. They started to talk in Russian, so I looked bored and went back to the sitting-room, closing the door behind me. He had a light meal later, and then went to sleep again. She came out and joined me.

'Well?' I asked.

'I've told him the truth—with certain variations.'

'Such as?'

'That Wates was working for the Chinese. We got wind of the attempt and snatched him. Wates did the drugging.'

'How did that go down?'

'He appeared to believe it, but one can't tell with a man like that. His real preoccupation is our next move.'

'What did you tell him?'

'That we were awaiting orders.'

'Who does he think we are?'

'He knows perfectly well what *I* am. He picked me as a fellow Mig immediately.'

I jumped at that: 'Shanghai——?' Mig is their own name for expatriate Russians, and Shanghai, after Paris, is where most of them are concentrated. Mig is a contraction of émigré.

'I'm not quite as dumb as that,' she said. 'I've never been to Shanghai, and he could have shot me down within minutes. No, London. Parents dead—brought up by a White grandmother—recruited by Red agents while studying ballet in Paris, now employed on courier and conducting duties—medium security.'

'You mean you volunteered all that?' I jeered. 'He must be laughing his head off. You wouldn't make *low* on that.'

'Nor that dumb either,' she said coldly. 'He wormed it out of me over the course of a couple of hours. I was in and out to him several times during the night while you were sleeping—with the outer door left unlocked.' The bitch had the upper hand again—and she kept it.

'He had no difficulty in placing *you*,' she went on. 'Criminal working purely for the pay cheque. Limited intelligence but good in a rough-house.'

'Yeah. I heard you priming him on the boat,' I said. 'I speak a little Russian myself.'

'So Daddy told me,' she came back. 'Very badly, I understand.' You just couldn't get the last word with her.

The rest of that first day and evening dragged by in much the same way. She'd be quite reasonable, even amiable, for a time then either she or I would say something that the other took umbrage at, and we'd be back at it like a pair of

Kilkenny cats. Of course it was nerves, and I think that both of us realized it, but that didn't help. And, oh God, there was another four days of it ahead before the ship arrived.

I sat up that night, more to rob her of the satisfaction of sneaking back and forth while I was asleep than for reasons of security, because I managed to persuade myself that the man I'd seen leave the café was just one of those things. Madame was mean with the coal, and the stove went out about midnight, so I draped a blanket round my shoulders. Sonia crept through in the darkness once and I said: 'He's all right. I've just looked,' and was childishly pleased when she jumped. I must have dropped off after that.

I awoke as somebody tried to open the door. It was only the softest click but it was unmistakable, and it was followed by a creak from the warped floorboards as whoever it was moved away along the landing. A second door from Carter's room opened on to it, and I'd had the sense to lock that.

I tiptoed through from the sitting-room. Carter was breathing quietly and evenly. I moved to the other door and touched the knob lightly. It turned softly under my hand. The door creaked as someone evidently tried it with his shoulder then moved away—I went back and collected the gun from the table beside my easy chair, crossed to the landing door, eased the key round and opened it a bare half inch. There was a dim light thrown up the stair-well from the lower landing, and I could see the bulk of a man moving along to the next door—the outer one leading to Sonia's room. He was on his own and his back was towards me. He was small and rattish and was dressed in a pair of dungaree pants and a dirty singlet, and his feet were bare. I motioned him into the sitting-room ahead of me. He started to stammer in bad French that he was looking for the pissoir, but didn't move, so I did, past him and behind him, and I clipped him smartly on the back of the neck with my free hand. He went then, protesting and almost whimpering.

A half-naked tart came up the stairs, saw the gun and started to scream. Sonia came out of her room quickly. She grabbed the tart by the arm and heaved her inside, hissing impolite French. The screams rose in pitch and volume, so Sonia hit her—considerably harder than I'd hit her boy-friend. She stopped screaming and started to snivel. The man was asking in an injured whine whether it was a

92

crime to pee in France? Then Madame came up in a dirty dressing-gown and curl papers. Sonia drew her to one side and they conversed in an undertone and Madame took over, efficiently if somewhat cavalierly. She spat several questions at the girl in French that was too fast for me to follow—shook the answers from her, then backhanded her out on to the landing. She went down the stairs wailing dolorously. Madame told us to wait, and followed her down. The man lapsed into silence—his eyes shifting from me to Sonia and back again, then he delicately brought up the question of the pissoir again. I was about to say something to Sonia, but she signalled me to shut up. I think she was afraid I would speak in English. I prodded the man along to the bathroom. He thanked me with the deepest feeling. He certainly wasn't putting on an act there. His need was of the greatest urgency, and it reassured me a little.

Madame came back with the man's coat and a fistful of papers. They were in Greek and Spanish. She ran a practised eye over them, shrugged and showed them to us. They looked all right to me—but then *my* eye wasn't practised. They were seaman's discharge papers, and pertained to one Yoni Youssakoupolis, engine room greaser, and the photo on them was at least recognizable. His last ship appeared to be the *Stanta Sebastiana*, and he'd been paid off in Brest three days previously. Madame spat more questions at him. Brest was a pig of a port, he said plaintively. He'd come up to Le Havre because jobs were easier here. He had quite a good pay-off—a man needed a little relaxation after a long voyage —the lady had picked him up in a bar near the docks—he'd paid fifty francs for the night, plus another ten for the room rent. Where was the crime in that?

Madame drew us into Sonia's room. I stood where I could still see him through the door. She said, 'I *think* he's all right —but it's up to you, mes enfants. His papers are genuine enough—and I know papers. Of course, he *may* be doing a little snooping job for somebody.'

'What about the girl?' I asked.

'Georgette? Been here three years. Hard worker. Her pattern never varies. Four short times and an all-nighter, six days a week,' Madame said with a touch of pride.

'Never on Sundays,' I said like a damned fool, and Sonia looked at me as if I was something that had just crawled from under a flat stone.

'Well, what about it?' Madame said briskly. 'What would you like me to do?'

'What can you do?' I asked.

'I can get him held for riotous behaviour for three days before he appears in court,' she answered. 'Cost you two hundred francs.'

'Can you make that five days?' I asked.

'Cost you another two hundred,' she said promptly.

'He won't be able to get word out to anybody?'

'Completely incommunicado. That's part of the service. Of course another hundred would make it absolutely certain.' The Gaffer would have loved this. He was always moaning about the stolid incorruptibility of our own police.

'Done,' I said.

Madame went off and did some telephoning, and then came back and took the glum Yoni downstairs, and ten minutes later we looked down into the dark square and saw him being hustled off between two gendarmes. I felt sorry for him. He was probably just what he claimed to be, but this was no time to take risks. The door to Carter's room opened. He stood blinking at the light.

'What goes on?' he asked complainingly.

'Nothing to worry about, cocker,' I reassured him. 'Some burk wandering around outside. He's been taken care of. You get back to sleep.'

We got him into bed but he was as restless and petulant as a sick child and kept demanding to know where he was and why he was being held against his will, so in the end Sonia went down and rustled some hot milk from somewhere, but he wouldn't drink it, and when we tried a little mild persuasion it made him vomit. However, he went to sleep then and we tiptoed out and left him. I was feeling a little pleased with myself. I advised Sonia to get back to bed also, and sat down on guard again, feeling and no doubt looking a bit like Horatius on the bridge. It was I who had been on the ball this time, while she slept. She went through to her room looking sour, and slammed the door behind her.

The fag end of that horrible night dragged on and I got colder, stiffer and more miserable every minute. I'd have given my soul for a cup of coffee and I tried to take my mind off it by chain smoking, until my throat and mouth felt like a lime kiln. Then I remembered the hot milk Carter had refused, so I went and got it, and warmed it up a little by burning newspapers in the cold stove. I've eschewed milk since the age of three, but at least this was more palatable than French tap water. It certainly made me sleep. In fact it took a jug of that same tap water plus a series of stinging slaps each side of the kisser to wake me.

Sonia was saying, seemingly from a long way off, 'Couldn't you have just given him your gun and money and let him walk out? Did you *have* to mickey finn yourself as well?'

## Chapter 11

She swam muzzily into focus. She was standing with her hands on her hips looking down at me, and I've never seen such contempt on a woman's face in my life. Past her I could see Madame moving into range with another jug of water. I got out of my chair hastily and nearly feel flat. It was broad daylight.

'What the hell happened?' I croaked.

'I put something in his milk to quieten him down, and *you* drank it, you bloody fool,' she answered, and Madame murmured something about les Anglais being nice people, but no wonder the General wouldn't let them into the Common Market.

'So he just walked out,' Sonia went on. 'Taking your gun in passing.'

'Clothes——?' I began, but she pointed to the side table where they had been neatly folded after returning from the cleaners, and of course they weren't there.

Please God I'll never go through another five minutes like that again. They spared me nothing—Sonia dealing with me like a vivisectionist working on a live dogfish, and Madame coming in from time to time like a Greek chorus—and when I could take no more and went through to Carter's bedroom to get away from them, there he was in bed, fast asleep. I turned on them, choking and boiling—but they still had me cold.

'That's just what happened,' Sonia said, 'so spare us the righteous indignation. Fortunately he couldn't get the front door unlocked, and the bouncers found him thrashing about in the dark. But he had your gun and he got off two rounds ——'

'One of which went through Hassan's foot,' Madame put in. 'That will cost you another two hundred and fifty—plus, of course, yet another two hundred for the police.'

'The shot brought a gendarme,' Sonia explained. 'Our friend demanded to be taken to the Soviet Consulate. We managed to get things straightened out, and he's now under sedation again—but it was touch and go for a time.'

Well, that's the way it was from then on. I sat there like Joe Soap on guard; feeling guilty if I dozed off, although, fair play to her, she let up after a while and urged me to take a proper relief period off from time to time, but I couldn't. I was on edge the whole time. She went out twice, supremely confident, and I found myself almost wishing that she'd run into trouble, or lead a tail back to us, if only to restore my self-respect. But she got away with it each time. She bought some light but serviceable clothes for herself and a list of things I made out for Carter and myself, and on the second day I saw in the shipping columns that the *Nurma* would be berthing at the Didier Dock the next morning.

She inspected me critically before I set out after dark the following evening. The dungarees, jersey and pea-jacket I was wearing were all new, so I'd damped them and rumpled them up a bit, but she thought my face and hands were too pale for a sailor, so she went down and got some permanganate of potash from one of the girls and I washed in a medium solution of it which darkened me down nicely.

'Take the tram at the back gate—the one going downhill,' she told me. 'Get off when you reach the Boulevard François, then walk down towards the outer harbour. The Didier Dock is at the bottom on your right. Coming back, take a No. 8 tram from the Place Vauban, at the top of Boulevard François. This is the eleventh stop. Here's some small change. The fare is fifty centimes.' I felt like a yobbo being briefed by his mother before going out for an interview for his first job.

'Why don't you give me a cheese sandwich, and wipe my bloody nose for me?' I snarled.

'It's all very necessary,' she said sweetly. 'If I didn't tell you, you'd have to ask directions—and your French, like your Russian, is not terribly good, is it?' Maybe she was right, and I suppose I had asked for it, but my God, it was galling.

I found my way downstairs and through a filthy kitchen. A

dark gentleman sat spitting gloomily on the stove, his foot resting on another chair, bound up like a gouty colonel's. He scowled at me. I assumed him to be Hassan. A fellow who looked like his twin brother loomed up out of the shadows and unlocked the back door, then led me through a cluttered yard to a gate in a high wall. He unbolted it and looked through. Outside was an Arrêt sign, and tramlines ran down a narrow cobbled street. It was again raining and there wasn't a soul in sight. He pointed to a concealed bellpush high under the lintel, then closed the gate again. He waited until we heard the clatter of an approaching tram. He opened the gate and pushed me through. The tram squealed to a halt and I climbed on. It was pretty full, but most of the passengers seemed to be dressed more or less as I was and I felt my nervousness leaving me. It was good to be out again after a week cooped indoors with that hellion.

I got off where she told me and walked downhill to the docks, and found my way to the Didier without difficulty. I saw the *Nurma* in the nearest berth. She was small, clean and streamlined like most post-war Scandinavian freighters, and they were working cargo under decklights. I crossed to her and climbed the gangway. A big blond seaman leaned on the rail at the top. He said 'Yo?' interrogatively and barred my way. I told him that I wanted to see the Capitaine but he shook his head ponderously and told me in French even worse than mine to come back in the morning. I argued that I had an important message for him, and the seaman said fine—give it to him and he'd take it. It wasn't that sort of message, I insisted. I had to deliver it myself—but it got me nowhere. Capitaines didn't see bums out of working hours, apparently. It made me furious. To have got this far and to be balked by a stupid ox like this. I cursed myself for not bringing a letter addressed to the Captain. To have to go back to that damned woman and confess that I couldn't get on board because a sailor wouldn't let me was more than I could face. He had a round, inviting belly and I thought for one desperate moment of bringing my knee up into it and clipping him one as he went down, but there were too many people about. So finally I did what I should have done in the first place, and suborned him with a ten franc note. He pointed over his shoulder to the midship quarters and strolled away aft.

I walked along the deck. A door opened and an officer came out. Past him I saw into a cosy well-furnished saloon where a white-coated Chinese steward was serving food to other officers. I wondered if the captain was one of them, then, as the first man passed me and walked to the rail, I saw he was wearing four gold rings on his cuff. I went up beside him and said, 'Captain Kjaer?' but muffed the pronunciation into 'Kayer' instead of making it rhyme with 'Fire' as it should have done. It seemed to tell him something, because he turned and looked at me sharply, and said, 'Briddish, huh? Naw—we don't have no jobs.' He was a thickset man, built like a Dutch eel barge, with a moon of a face, piggy little blue eyes and almost pure white hair and eyebrows.

I said: 'I don't want a job. I want a passage. I'm willing to pay.'

'You got a passage, mister,' he answered. 'Down the bloddy gangway—for free. We don't have a licence for passengers.'

I turned away from the rail so my back was to the light, and produced a flat wad of American hundred-dollar bills, and riffled the edges with my thumb, like a pack of cards. It must have been the noise that did it, because he certainly didn't turn his head to look. He said: 'Bloddy cold out here. Come and have a drink.'

He led me up a ladder to the bridge deck and into an alleyway that was panelled in polished light wood and smelt cleanly of beeswax. He opened a cabin door and motioned me in with his head. It was panelled like the alleyway, with bright chintz curtains at the ports, and matching covers and cushions on the chairs and settees. A very snug number indeed. He got a bottle of aquavit and glasses from a locker and poured two enormous drinks, then sat down and said, 'Skal. What that crap you're talking outside? I told you —we don't carry passengers.'

'Then why bring me in here to tell me again?' I asked. 'Skal.' The stuff tasted like varnish remover but was very warming when it got down.

'Where you want to go—and how much are you thinking of?' he said. 'Not that I'm open for business.'

'Hong Kong—and a thousand a head,' I answered.

'A thousand what?'

'Pounds—what else? The going rate, in other words.'

'Who said it was the going rate?'

'A friend—who you've dealt with before.'

'What friend?'

I had to take a risk here. 'Malcolm,' I said.

He laughed. 'The Meisterspringer? That old bastard still in business?' He pursed his lips and thought for a moment. 'Hm—I don't mind doing the old man a favour but I'd have to have some guarantee that you do come from him.'

'I'm certainly not carrying a letter of introduction,' I said. 'You'll just have to take my word for it.'

'I don't have to take anything, mister, that I don't want to take. How do I know you're not an Amsterdam pirate?' Which showed he'd been around a bit. 'Amsterdam pirate' is the business term for *agent provocateur.*

'Who would I be working for?' I asked. 'An Englishman coming aboard in a French port? What could I be trying to tangle you up in? You'd only have to holler for the cops and I'd be having my arse tickled by the Sûreté inside the hour.'

'All right then—who *are* you working for?'

'I told you. The Meisterspringer. Who *he's* working for I wouldn't be knowing. I don't ask rude questions.'

He grinned slowly and poured more drinks. 'Touché. You tickle *my* arse now, eh? Okay—but you got the going rate wrong. That was in the old days—before the Gyps took to rummaging the hell out of ships going through the Suez—and asking my *crew* rude questions. I got a lot of itchy palms to grease now, mister. A thousand don't leave much for myself.'

'I said a thousand a head. There are three of us.'

'That makes the risk bigger—and the palms itchier. Call it four thousand. I got to cover my overheads.'

I sighed. The tightwads had only allowed me five for the whole operation, and I'd run up a sizeable bill with Madame already. 'All right,' I said wearily. 'Four thousand.'

He beamed and said *skal* again and added as an after-thought, 'Half now—half when you come aboard.'

'Half when we come aboard—half in Kowloon,' I said firmly.

'I can't argue in Kowloon if anything happened on the way—like the rats chewing your wallet or something.'

'No—but you could hand us over as stowaways or some-thing like that, couldn't you?'

'You're a hard case, mister,' he said. 'All right—so we say a thousand now—a thousand when you come aboard and the rest on arrival. That way we can all trust each other.'

So we settled for that. I fought off another drink and he gave me boarding instructions—very, very precisely.

'I run her tight, mister,' he explained. 'She's a small ship so I got a small crew—me, three mates, three engineers, three Swedes on deck—quartermasters. All the rest is Chinks —six topsides, six below, a steward and a cook and a Marconi guy who does supercargo as well. Him I'm a little doubtful about because it's his first trip with me. The others I slip a little something to on top of their pay when I carry anything I don't want talked about, and then I don't worry. You see what I mean?'

I didn't quite, but I realized that in spite of his heartiness he was nervous. 'What's worrying you?' I asked. 'You just slip the Marconi man something too.'

'Sure, sure, sure,' he agreed. 'And maybe it'll be all right —but I'd still rather he—or the others for that matter—don't know you're aboard until we're at sea. So you'll come aboard the day after tomorrow—dressed like you are now—no luggage—when the stevedores come on for the last bits of cargo. I'll contact you on deck and slip you away somewhere out of sight.'

I nodded slowly. I could see his point, and it made sense, but it also raised a difficulty that I had not foreseen. Carter and I could pass unnoticed among the stevedores—but what about Sonia? I was about to mention this, but then I decided to keep my mouth shut. Kjaer, while more than willing to pick up an easy four thousand pounds, was *not* willing to run too many risks. If he knew in advance that one of the party was to be a woman he might turn the whole thing down, or, at very least, jack the price up beyond the limit. No—let's get her aboard first, and argue afterwards, I thought.

'Anything you say,' I agreed, and started to count American bills on to the table. 'Dollars, two-eighty to the pound. Twenty-eight hundred.'

'Call it three thousand to make it round figures,' he wheedled, but I wouldn't budge. He sighed and gathered it up with stumpy fingers.

'We'll be sailing as soon as they open the dock gates at high water,' he said. 'That'll be at eight in the morning. The stevedores will be changing shift at four. That's when you'll come aboard. All right?'

He opened the cabin door and looked out into the alley-way, then led me through to the open deck and down into the well, and left me without a further word. My friend the Swede was back at his post when I went down the gangway, but he chose to ignore me.

I found my way back through the rainswept docks and up to the Place Vauban feeling pleased with myself. This had been the trickiest bit and so far I thought I'd handled it rather well. Getting Sonia aboard would be only a minor hazard. Men's clothes would take care of that. Four o'clock in the morning, nice and dark, with everybody too sleepy to notice much. Carter? There should be no difficulty with him provided we kept him too muzzy to take interest in things, but still able to walk.

I felt my spirits rising. It was good to be out and about again, with things on the move. I looked at my watch. It was only just after nine. I felt like prolonging things a bit—perhaps dropping into a café for a drink—but then I saw a No. 8 tram coming up through the rain and I decided not to push my luck too much.

Three of us got on the tram; a woman with a laundry basket who had already been waiting at the stop when I arrived, and a man who came up at the last minute—a nondescript-looking guy dressed more or less like myself. It was the woman who held my attention, because she got into a furious argument with the conductor about where she should put the basket. He said it shouldn't go in the aisle where it would obstruct other passengers, and she said for God's sake there were only five other passengers and where should she put it? and he told her, impolitely, and she became even more impolite in turn and appealed to the rest of us for support against this instance of bureaucracy. It was all good Rabelaisian stuff and I found it amusing—so much so that although I was still counting the tram stops subconsciously, I nearly missed getting off at the eleventh and had to jump for it at the last minute. And apparently another passenger was absent-minded also, because I saw him jump off just as the tram disappeared round the next bend. There was an over-head arc-light right at that spot and I saw that it was the man who had got on with me. I went into the ditching drill immediately and ignored the back door to the house.

I continued on up the hill without looking round until I came to a turning off the narrow street. There were no lights here so I was able to peer back down the hill. I saw somebody moving swiftly through the shadows on the dark side, coming up towards me. I went further down the turning and found a deep recessed doorway. The man came into sight again. He stopped and looked round uncertainly. For a moment it seemed as if he was going on, and there would have been no problem, but then the door behind me opened and I found myself bathed in light. A man and an obvious tart looked at me in surprise. The man grunted, pushed past me and went off, but the tart, manifestly, like Georgette, a good worker, fastened on to me as the next client and addressed me loudly and affectionately as *petit chou* and tried to drag me inside. I pulled away and went on down the lane, but the damage had been done. The guy at the corner had seen me.

The lane led into a square which was fairly well lighted, and there were several people about, though the crowd was not thick enough to make tail-shaking easy. I looked round as I crossed a patch of shadow. He was just emerging from the lane. I felt a surge of rage—at myself—because this was sheer bloody inexcusable ineptitude. That back gate had been used by Malcolm for years. The damned girl had used it herself three times in the last couple of days—but I had to go and blow it the very first time I came out. Or had I? Nobody had seen me come out, for the simple reason nobody had got on the tram with me. No—this goon had picked me up outside somewhere—and unless it was somebody who knew me, that could only have been at the docks. That meant the ship was being watched. Somebody had seen me go aboard—probably saw the bit of business with the sailor on the gangway—then my short conversation with the captain on deck—my going off with him to his cabin—then my coming ashore again.

But, with luck, I still hadn't blown the back gate.

Well, there was only one thing for it. He had to be shaken —and there is only one way to do that with any degree of certainty when you're being tailed by somebody who thinks that you know he's tailing you. First of all you've got to rid him of that certainty, and make him think that you *don't* know, because only that way can you hope to get him close enough to deal with him. The interlude in the doorway

102

might have given the game away, but not of necessity. I could have been a man who had mistaken the house—or having seen the wares it had to offer, had thought better of it.

There was a Tabac facing me. I walked in and bought some cigarettes, and then came out and retraced my steps. He wasn't terribly good at it because I caught him unawares and nearly bumped into him. I grunted an apology and went on without a glance at him. I went into a café then and shouldered through the crowd to the loo, hoping I might have a break there, but it was an inside one with no window and a ventilator that wasn't up to its job of admitting air, let alone allowing egress. So I came back and had a drink at the *zinc* and bought a bottle of pastis. There were several brands there and I was choosey, because although I couldn't see him I knew he'd be around somewhere and I didn't want to give anything away by buying the first cheap bottle that came to hand. No, this was something for a man who knew what he wanted and had no other thought than of enjoying it later.

I left the café, stuffing the bottle into the side pocket of my peajacket, and went back up the lane, making up a phrase in my inadequate French that would, I hoped, get quick results. I had to trust to luck now that he was on my heels because I didn't dare look back. I went to the brothel door and knocked. The same tart opened and looked out.

I said quietly: 'You dirty whore. You poxed me last voyage. I'm going to slit your throat,' and stepped forward. She slammed the door in my face. I turned and waited in the darkness. From down the alley he would only have seen the reflected light as the door opened, and would, I hoped, have assumed that I had gone inside.

I heard soft hurrying footsteps and then he was up to the recess, staring in—just a bulk in the dark. I swung the bottle. It didn't break. It would have been better for the poor devil if it had, because that would have proved his skull was the harder of the two, but as it was it sounded like a melon being hit with a sledge hammer.

I dragged him into the recess and left him and then went on to the top of the lane and turned back down the tramlines. I passed the gate and waited in the dark a little further down, just in case there was another of them around, but nothing stirred except a lean cat that rubbed itself against my leg and nearly made me jump out of my skin, so I returned to the gate and pressed the bellpush. It opened after a moment and the Algerian who had let me out admitted me and led me back across the yard and through the kitchen. I gave him the bottle of pastis and he thanked me gravely and the one with the punctured foot said I was *très gentil*.

Sonia let me in. The room was warm and cosy, and, surprisingly, I was glad to be back. I think maybe she was too, because she didn't start an argument and even helped me out of my wet peajacket—which was unfortunate, because all the wetness wasn't rain. She looked at her reddened hand, then at me. I saw her eyes widen with distress and her lip trembled, then the next thing I was conscious of was being sprawled back in a chair and her arms were tight about my head, with my face cushioned in that gorgeous tophamper. She was cursing in three language whoever had done this to me, and crooning sympathetically in turn. I tried to explain—or I think I did—but it wasn't any use, so I let things take their course. This highly improbable and totally unforeseen reaction was worth a lot of the grief we had been through together. It had a curious dreamlike quality about it; a dream that you know is a dream, but which you strive to prolong. My lips traced a track from hers, along the line of her firm little jaw to her ear, and back again.

Of course it was bad tactics to reach out for the light switch—certainly at that moment. I should have let things ride for a bit. As it was, it broke the spell. She pulled away from me and stared at me questioningly. Like a fool I grinned. Brother! I can feel that slap across the kisser to this day.

'You bloody *rat*!' she hissed at me. 'Where did that blood come from?'

'From a bloke I clobbered outside a brothel,' I told her, the grin rather lopsided now, and her lip curled in disgust.

'At least you're frank about it,' she said, 'but I would have thought that this was hardly the time for that sort of thing —or does time make any difference to you?'

'Hey! Wait a minute,' I yelped indignantly. 'I wasn't catting around, if that's what you mean. This fellow followed me from the ship, so I led him a dance and then crowned him with a bottle of pastis.'

'You're certain you weren't picked up leaving here?' she asked anxiously.

'There was nobody in sight—and certainly nobody got on the tram with me.'

'And when you got off?'

'As it happened, nobody got off with me either.'

'Then it's a fair assumption that the ship *is* watched,' she said, troubled. 'But why?—why?—why?—before you even approached Kjaer?'

'I don't know,' I said gloomliy. 'The whole crazy exercise is bugged.'

I actually was going to say 'buggered', but I clipped it for politeness' sake—then something occurred to me.

'Bugged,' I repeated. 'I *wonder*?'

Then supper arrived.

## Chapter 12

But she pulled that possibility to pieces as we ate, although I still gave the place a thorough going over afterwards. If it was bugged, whoever had done it was a genius, because *I* certainly couldn't find a trace of wiring that couldn't be accounted for.

'It would mean that Madame would have to be in on it,' Sonia said. 'And I'm certain she isn't.'

'You yourself said everybody has their price,' I came back at her.

'Maybe, but my God it would have to be a high one in her case. She's got too much to lose—and she knows it.'

'Then it comes back to the ship,' I said glumly. 'We've just got to accept the fact that it's being watched and that I was picked up and followed back from there.'

'But you *did* break the trail?' She put it in the form of a question and I felt my anger rising again, but I fought it down. This needed clear-headed discussion.

'I broke the trail all right.'

'Did you——?'

'Kill him? Quite likely. I didn't mean to, but—well, there you are. Look, let's run over the whole thing. Probabilities first. They know we're here. How? They had a tail on Charlton. Why? He's a known associate of your father's. That sailor the other night. It's pretty clear now that he was one of them—sent in to make a recce. We've stymied them there and they realize that they can't try further strong-arm methods to winkle us out without trouble from the police, but they're watching, waiting for us to make a move—how many of them we don't know, but there's bound to be more than one.'

'We know all that,' she said impatiently. 'But the ship? Why would they be watching that?'

'Pretty obvious, isn't it? China bound—and your father has dealt with Kjaer before.'

She nodded reluctantly, hating to concede too much, but unable to put anything up against it. 'Still, once we're aboard our worries are over until we reach Hong Kong—and then, if your people are on the ball there——'

'I wouldn't be too certain about that,' I said. 'I mean about our worries being over. We've got to go through the Canal, don't forget—and the Russians and Egyptians are friendly at the moment. If they knew for certain we were on board they could hold the ship indefinitely and search us down to the rivets.'

'*If* they knew we were on board. We've got to take damned good care that they don't know.'

'Easier said than done. If they're watching that ship properly they'll know all right.'

'Couldn't we ask Kjaer to——' But I didn't let her finish.

'Kjaer's already told me how we're to come aboard,' I said. 'If I try to vary his very definite instructions he'll know it's because I think we've been blown—and he'll drop the whole thing like a hot potato. No—we've got to get aboard as arranged, but we've got to throw these goons first. Really throw them.'

'Which brings us right back to the beginning. How?'

'Give me a chance,' I begged. 'I need a little time.'

'It's running out. From what you told me, we've got something less than twenty-four hours left.'

'Look—suppose you go to bed,' I suggested, 'and leave me to think.'

'I'd be glad to,' she said waspishly, 'if I thought something might come of it. But on your showing to date you'll have to excuse a certain pessimism on my part.'

And then we were into it again and we wrangled unprofitably until we heard Carter calling sleepily from the other room. She mixed something in a glass and went through to him. He went to sleep again. He must have been as full of dope now as a Flower Child at a love-in. I almost envied him. At least he didn't have to listen to this bitch.

She came out and went through to her room, and I sat on —and on—and on—until finally I had some sort of a plan. A pretty wobbly one, but at least it was something. I tapped at her door. She must have been awake because she opened immediately.

I said: 'You say as far as you know, Madame can be trusted?'

'As far as I know,' she confirmed.

'What about the help?'

'You mean the girls?'

'Actually I was thinking of the Algerians—but I'll need a girl as well.'

'I'd prefer to put it to Madame herself. What is your idea?'

'A car,' I said. 'We'd go out the front way—me, one of the Algerians and a girl, wearing your clothes. If we picked our time, say at half light, and moved quickly, we ought to be able to get away with it.'

'And what then?'

'Lead them a dance,' I said. 'Not an aimless one. We'd make for another town—either Rouen or Brest—and we'd throw them on the way. Then I'd come back and collect you just before boarding time.'

'I don't think much of that,' she said.

'Neither do I, but it's the best I can do. If you can come up with something better I'd be glad to hear it.'

'What if you don't manage to throw them?'

'I don't come back. If I haven't returned or telephoned by a certain time, you'll have to call your father and tell him what has happened. It will be up to him then.'

'I don't like it.'

'I've told you, neither do I, but——'

'If I came instead of one of the girls——'

'Nothing doing,' I said firmly. 'Both eggs in the same basket if anything goes wrong.'

'All right then—if *I* went, with two Algerians, and you stayed here—' she raised her hand quickly as she saw me take a deep breath and get ready to explode. 'No—please—I'm not being offensive. Carter might require manhandling —even carrying at some stage. I couldn't cope with him on my own.'

It was a shrewd one, but I still wouldn't wear it, so in the end she gave in and went down to knock Madame up. She came up snarling and grumbling, and I knew that this was going to cost somebody plenty. I outlined the idea to her briefly, omitting any reference to the ship. She chewed over it for a long moment and then said flatly, 'Too dangerous.'

'It needn't be,' I said.

'If you don't manage to lose them, you lead them back here,' she said.

'I don't,' I answered, playing it off the cuff. 'Mademoiselle takes the client away after I have drawn the pursuit off.'

'And suppose you drive fast and crash, or are stopped? Suppose you fight and someone is hurt—killed?' She spread her hands and rolled her eyes.

'Madame's solicitude touches me, but provided anything like that should happen away from here she need not concern herself unduly.'

'With my *porteur*—one without papers—and a lady from this establishment in the car? M'sieur is naïve. The police would be round in shoals. With our local inspector things —small things—might be arranged, but not with the headquarters flics.' Of course she was only jacking the price up, but it took a long time, although I must admit that once she had squeezed the last franc out of me she got things moving fast. She routed out Georgette and the Algerian with both sound feet and brought them up, yawning and blinking. The girl ventured a timid question or two but got nowhere with Madame, but the Algerian accepted things with Oriental fatalism, and we got them dressed—in the clothes Sonia and I had been wearing when we arrived. I studied them both doubtfully. In the light neither looked very convincing, but a headscarf over the girl's dark hair and my felt hat pulled down over the Algerian's face helped considerably.

'The car——?' I asked.

'The one that brought you here,' Madame answered. 'Driven by my son—so m'sieur can understand my anxiety. A mother's heart——'

We waited a long time for it to arrive. They garaged it half a mile away, apparently, and Jean sometimes had difficulty in starting it in damp weather, although, Madame assured me earnestly, once going it marched in a manner *très formidable*—and had cost a lot of money.

I waited, fuming and sweating, peering down from behind the curtains into the square. Sonia wasn't helping either. She was putting into words that which had been bothering me.

'We don't really know if we *are* being watched here, do we?' she said.

'We damned soon will,' I growled.

'Even supposing your hunch is right and they do follow

you, does that of necessity mean that they'll withdraw the watch from the ship?'

'We've got to assume *something*. If they're convinced we've gone scooting off in another direction they're hardly likely to waste men watching an abandoned bolt-hole, are they?'

'Who's going to tell them, if the people here go scooting off after *you*?'

'Oh for God's sake stop, will you,' I howled—and then I saw the black Citroën arrive outside. I hustled Georgette and the Algerian downstairs ahead of me, hissing last-minute instructions. Sonia came down too, relenting a little and wishing me luck. I said: 'Give me until midnight. If I haven't shown up by then put a call through to your old man, but don't risk going near the ship.'

I opened the front door and slipped through. It was just getting light and early workers were already moving down towards the docks.

I tried to play it as naturally as possible without overdoing it. I took a fairly searching look around the square and then, as if satisfied, hurried back up the steps and collected the other two. Fair play to them, they did it very well —heads down and coat collars turned up, and wasting no time. I hustled them into the back seat and told them to keep down low, then climbed in beside the driver and told him to get going for Rouen and to step on it, but not to be too rash. This was going to be the tricky part. Too fast, and I might throw them in reality. Too slow and it would be obvious that we were laying a trail. As it was it worked out nicely, because the 'costly' Citroën ran true to form. Not yet properly warmed up, it balked and stalled on starting and in the end Jean had to run downhill slipping his clutch in second gear before the engine took up. That, I reflected with some slight satisfaction, would give them time to get properly organized. I set the rear vision mirror so that I, rather than the driver, could see behind and sat back.

We drove down the alley and out on to the dock road. Parking was permitted on one side of it. If they had a car waiting, this is where it would be. There was plenty of truck traffic moving both ways so we couldn't have speeded even had we wanted to, and twice we were held up by swing bridges before we got clear of the docks. But not a thing had moved out of the parking area, and there was no sign of a car on our tail. I felt, once again, a complete fool. My theorizing had been knocked flat, and all this elaborate nonsense had gone for nothing, not to mention a further five hundred francs of my slender resources being down the drain—because there'd be no refunds from Madame. Now I would have to go back and face that damned girl again and give her best—well, half-best anyhow, because she had been no more nor less certain than I about the place being watched —but she'd had the sneaky feminine foresight to voice her doubts, while I'd been cocksure about it. I was about to tell Jean to take a couple of turns round town to make sure, and then turn back, when I noticed the motor-cyclist.

I don't know where he came from, but I was certain we hadn't overtaken him. He was just there—two trucks behind us—and he made no effort to close the distance when first one, then the other, turned off into the docks. He just kept on at the same speed and allowed other traffic to pass him and fill the gap. I thought for a moment of putting it to the test and telling Jean to make a sudden turn down a side street, but I let it go. That would let him know that we knew he was following us, and that was the last thing I wanted at this juncture.

We came out of the Le Havre suburbs into Harfleur, and here the road forks—left to Fécamp and Dieppe, right to Rouen—and I saw him stop. This was textbook stuff. Unless I was very much mistaken he was acting as contact man for yet another trailer further back, and was waiting to point out the turning we had taken. And I *wasn't* mistaken, because I told Jean to stop for petrol at the next service station and I bought a Michelin Grandes Routes map, and while we were halted a green Peugeot went roaring past—and sure enough some distance along after we had got going again, *it* had stopped for petrol also, and looking out of the corner of my eyes as we passed, I saw four men in it.

Thereafter it followed the familiar drill—dropping right back out of sight when we were on a long stretch of road without junctions, but obviously navigating on a map as I was, and closing up when we were coming to a turn-off. Oh, yes—this was the Opposition all right. The question was, what to do with them now?

I started the old routine that sounds so easy at the school, of putting myself in their place. What did they want? Without question, they had fallen for it and they wanted to get hold of Carter. Four of them, undoubtedly armed, should be able to do this without difficulty, given the place and opportunity, and a busy highway in broad daylight was neither. So what would they do? Quite obviously just what they were doing now. They'd keep on our tail until the place and opportunity for a quick snatch *did* present it. Next question—did they know Carter and/or Sonia by sight? Did they, in fact, know *me*? To be on the safe side one would have to assume that they did. That being the case, if they got a close look at the other two they would know they had been fooled, and would immediately turn round and hightail it to Le Havre and resume their watch, and we'd be right back where we started. So I had to shake this tail without their getting that close look. That in itself shouldn't be too difficult, but we were still within eighty kilometres of Le Havre and if we ditched them too soon it would be a reasonable assumption on their part that the whole thing had been a plant, and we intended going back, and the heat would be on again.

No—they had to be convinced that we were to hell and gone out of the area. We could do that, no doubt, by continuing on to Paris and really losing them there, then I could get a train back—but that was too dicey. Theirs was immeasurably the better car of the two, and there was always the chance of their picking a lonely bit of road, overtaking us, forcing us off and blowing the whole thing. There was always the chance, if it came to that, of getting oneself killed. We'd knocked off quite a few of their side so far, and even dedicated Ivans could be expected to show a little exacerbation under the circumstances. Anyhow, I didn't know how the trains ran, and I might be cutting the time factor too fine—and I certainly couldn't risk coming back by a car that was now known to them. And thinking about trains, gave me the ghost of an idea.

As we came through the next town. Yvetot, I called a halt outside the station and sent Jean in, as if *pissoir* bound, to buy a railway timetable. In the mirror I saw the others stop the far side of the Place de la Gare and park unobtrusively among some other cars. Two of them got out and strolled casually in our direction, and for a moment I was almost panicked into sliding into the driving seat and pushing off before they got too close, but I fought it down and muttered to the two in the back to slouch forward, faces buried in collars, as if asleep. Panic now would tell the followers clearly that we knew they were tailing us, and might force their hands. However, Jean came back while they were still a good twenty yards off and we started up and drove away. They turned and hurried back to their car.

I studied the unfamiliar timetable as we drove fast over the last forty kilometres to Rouen. There was a good train in an hour from now—good insofar that it was fast and only stopped twice before Paris, at Les Andelys and Magny-en-Vexin. With a bit of luck that might do it.

We drove down the hill into Rouen half an hour later, and I dropped off in a traffic jam near the station, telling Jean to keep circling the block until he picked me up again, and I ducked into a café. Looking through the window, I saw them drive past on the tail of the Citroën. They seemed to be arguing and for a moment I thought at least one of them might hop out and follow me, but the flow quickened and they had to move with it after the main quarry. I hurried across to the station and bought three tickets for Paris, ascertaining the platform the train left from, and rejoined the car on its second circuit. I told Jean to drive towards the centre of the town and to time things so that he could be passing the station again in exactly ten minutes, which would give us three minutes to make the train. I was beginning to develop quite an affection for Jean. His conversation was limited to a grunted *oui* or *non* as the situation dictated, but he didn't need a blueprint of a reasonably simple instruction. The other two were, however, becoming a little restless. The Algerian wanted a drink and the lady wanted to pee, and both were complaining that they had missed their breakfast. But I managed to smooth things down with glib promises, and give them precise instructions at the same time.

He timed it exactly, and positioned the car well. We were the inner line of a long flow of taxis and private cars, while the Opposition were well to a flank and our rear with a bus and several cars between us and them. I jumped out, ran round and hauled the Algerian and the girl out, keeping myself between them and the Peugeot and hissing at them to keep their faces down. I hustled them through on to the assembly platform, then raced for the Paris train. They were just closing the barrier and we were the last passengers through —the last legitimate ones, that is. As I pushed the others up into the first coach I glanced round and saw three of the men arguing and scuffling with the ticket-collector who was yelling the place down—and a gendarme was bearing down on them. But one of them made it. He streaked for the train and jumped for the steps and looking back I saw him climb aboard.

I pushed the others ahead of me down the corridor until I found an empty first-class compartment. I bundled them into it and slid the door almost closed and jerked the blinds down.

I peeped through the chink obliquely up the corridor. He came into sight through the door from the next coach, looking into each compartment. He reached ours and I slid the door back and jerked my gun hard into his belly. He grunted and looked surprised.

It was our visitor of a few nights previously—Yoni something-or-other. Either Madame or the police were gypping me, because I'd paid for five days in the nick for him.

I pulled him inside and closed the door again and told the Algerian to watch it. I frisked him of an automatic, some money—quite a thick roll of it—and a small but very vicious leather-covered cosh which he carried inside the waistband of his trousers. Georgette seemed pleased to see him, much more than he was to see her. In fact I don't think he even noticed her. He was too busy watching me. I realized it would be a sheer waste of time to question him. These people don't talk when they are caught *in flagrante delicto*—not unless you've got the time and facilities to lean on them really heavily—and I had neither, and he knew it. The Algerian mentioned helpfully that there were tunnels on this line, and glanced at the outer door. Georgette squealed softly, and Yoni's eyes flickered nervously. It would have been a quick solution, no doubt, and one which I might have to take if nothing else offered—but I wanted to avoid it if possible. Beaning a bloke in hot pursuit is one thing—but killing him in cold blood is quite another.

We sat on in a strained silence for a time. Whatever I did would have to be done quickly. This first-class section was empty at the moment, but if a ticket-inspector came along, or other passengers got on at the next stop, I couldn't continue to hold a gun on him, let alone use it, if he chose to make a break.

Georgette started to wriggle, then with a murmured apology got up and made for the corridor. For a moment I thought her womanly heart had been touched at the prospect of an ex-client being done in, and that she had gone to summon help, but she was only going to the loo down the corridor. In the kerfuffle of the last half hour I had forgotten the poor soul's personal needs. But it gave me an idea. I could cosh him and leave him in the lavatory, and we'd get off at the next stop.

But I discarded that one quickly. Coshing, short of the absolute mayhem I had committed with the bottle, is a chancy business at the best of times. He would recover sooner or later, and if it was sooner he might have time to raise an alarm by telephone from Paris. He'd seen the others and he knew they were not Carter and Sonia. No, he had to be kept quiet—really quiet—until after sailing time at least. I found myself looking at the outer door. His eyes followed mine, and again I caught the nervous flicker. He was frightened—which was all to the good—but I still didn't know what the hell to do with him—short of *that*.

The train was slowing down for the first stop, Les Andelys, according to the timetable. We rumbled over a bridge and underneath I could see a muddy canal snaking off to the right where it debouched into a wide river. The Seine, I assumed it to be. It was raining again and the place looked miserable and beautifully deserted. If only I had him down there.

We ground to a halt short of the station. I lowered the window and looked out. Right alongside us on the next line was a stationary goods train. I looked up and down the track. It curved here, so I couldn't see far in either direction and there was nobody in sight. I made up my mind quickly.

I said to Georgette, 'Go on to the next station—Magny-en-Vexin—and stay there until this time tomorrow, then find your own way back.' I gave her her ticket and added a two-hundred-franc *pourboire*. Then I wrenched the door open, hauled Yoni to his feet and spun him round, gestured to the Algerian to follow, and kicked the other in the small of the back. He landed in a heap, six feet below on the tracks, and we were down each side of him before he could yell. I jammed the gun in his ribs and we hustled him underneath the nearest goods truck. Behind us I heard our train jerk forward and run slowly into the station. Peering out between the wheels I saw a line of closed, rain-spattered windows and as far as I could determine, nobody was looking out through any of them. We waited until the last coach had passed and then crawled out the other side. We were just clear of the bridge, and a bank sloped steeply down in front of us to the canal.

I said to Yoni: 'Keep your mouth closed and do as you're told, and you've got a chance.' I think he wanted to believe me. He moistened his lips and nodded.

We slid down the bank. On the towpath under the bridge was, inevitably, a Frenchman sitting on a box fishing with an enormously long bamboo pole. It gave me quite a start, but fishing is more than an avocation in France. It's an all-absorbing way of life, and he didn't spare us a glance.

We walked up the towpath, the Algerian, who knew his job without being told, with Yoni's right arm tucked affectionately and tightly under his left, and me a couple of paces to the rear. I was looking for a lonely shed or, failing that, a good thick clump of bushes, but it just wasn't that sort of country. Here we had the town on the other bank and flat sodden water meadows on this one, with not a hint of cover. But then we passed a string of moored barges—a couple of Dutch ones, a Belgian and three French. I looked at them longingly, but all had the usual living quarters astern and, although nobody was stirring, we couldn't risk sneaking aboard.

But even the longest canal has a turning. We came round the next one and there were more barges—the sort that are towed, without living quarters on them. I went up the gangway of the first one. The hatches were on loosely and I could see grain in bags half-filling the hold. I signalled to the Algerian to bring our friend aboard, and there we struck our first difficulty. He suddenly smelled danger and started to struggle and yell. I went back quickly and beaned him, hard, with his own cosh. He went down like a log and we hefted him aboard and dropped him down on the bags. I took a frightened look round, but there was still nobody in sight, so we jumped down beside him and I tied his wrists behind him with the belt of his raincoat. The Algerian, now thoroughly in the spirit of the thing, and enjoying it, started to gag him with fiendish ingenuity and a mouthful of loose grain kept in place with his own grubby handkerchief, but I stopped that. Grain swells with moisture, and the poor bastard was going to be in a pretty dicey situation as it was if nobody unloaded the barge for a few days.

We walled him in loosely behind some bags, came ashore and walked back towards town. I thought of telling the Algerian to telephone the police the following evening and giving them an anonymous tip about this, but I abandoned that because I knew damned well he wouldn't bother.

We parted after that. I told him, like Georgette, to amuse himself locally until next day and gave him an extra two hundred francs also. With Yoni's unexpected contribution to the kitty, which I found to be just short of two thousand, I felt I could afford it. I went on into town. I didn't risk the train again, but found I could get a bus to Rouen an hour later.

It was dark when I got back to Le Havre. I was crying-weary but I played things safe and went into a long and complicated tail-shaking routine to be on the safe side, finally buying a plastic mac and a peaked cap in place of the knitted one I had been wearing, then I caught a No. 8 tram and came 'home', as I was now thinking of the damned place, and went in the back way.

But Sonia wouldn't leave me alone. She put me through a long catechism about the whole thing while I was having a couple of stiff drinks and a belated supper—then she tried to pick holes in it—but I snarled at her and finally went to sleep in a chair in front of the fire.

She woke me in what I muzzily thought was a bare five minutes later, but when I looked at my watch I saw it was half-past three. I started to rave because that only gave us half an hour before we had to be aboard, and I hadn't even started to think about how we were going to do that, but she told me icily that that had already been arranged, and I noticed her appearance for the first time. She had certainly done it well. She was dressed in slacks, jersey and peajacket and she bulked realistically because she was carrying a lot of spare gear underneath. And she had darkened her face and hands, and her hair was hidden properly under her woollen cap. She looked a typical young longshore yobbo.

Then I saw Madame holding Carter upright. He was able to stand and even take a few steps if he was supported, and his eyes, though glazed, were open. But that was about all. I still didn't see how we were going to take him on a tram, and I said so.

'The trams have stopped running,' Sonia said.

'So we've got to use a car again? From the front?' I shook

my head. I was as certain as one could be that I'd drawn them off, but it still seemed an unnecessary risk.

'From the back,' she told me. 'Ordinary traffic often uses that road when the trams are not running and there are no police around.'

And that is how we did it. It was Jean again, but they'd had the savvy to get a different car. But I was still jumpy and I made him drive round a bit until, *this* time, I was certain there was nobody on our tail.

We stopped fifty yards short of the dock gate. It was just four o'clock and the shift was changing. There were no lights except those on the ship itself, so we had no difficulty in mixing with the gang going aboard. Carter revived a little in the cold air and walked without being too conspicuous, but he had started to mumble. I left them both near the winches of number three hold, which wasn't being worked, and went in search of Kjaer. He saw me as I climbed from the well deck and came and met me. He was in high good humour. I was glad somebody was. He led me into the shadow of a lifeboat.

'We fix our little bit of business, eh?' he said, and rubbed his forefinger and thumb under my nose. I gave him his thousand.

'Count it later,' he chuckled. 'I trust you. Where the others?'

I told him.

'Fine,' he said. 'You'll see an alleyway on the starboard side, leading aft from the well deck. Go down that. I meet you the other end. Pretty small and stinky the place I put you —but that only till we drop the pilot. Maybe two, three hours. Fix you up good then—nice cabin for three.'

'You couldn't make it two cabins?' I asked anxiously.

'Not a chance,' he said, and chuckled again. 'If only one of you had a Marconi ticket you could have Sparks's cabin. The bastard jumped the ship, and I don't see him for two days. Suits me fine—only I got to take the third mate off watches to do his job now. Still, you don't worry about that. This three-berth cabin I give you, bloddy nice.'

That was one problem off our shoulders. He had said his crew was reliable, with only this one in doubt. And it had been worrying me vaguely. Malcolm had used this ship before. If the Opposition knew that—and had planted this fellow—well—even that doubt was removed now.

I went down and collected the others and met Kjaer at

the end of the alleyway. He opened a steel door in the bulk-head and ushered us through as if he were showing us into the bridal suite at the Ritz. It was pitch dark and I, leading the way, went arse over head on a paint drum. He clanged the door to and I heard the key turn outside.

We lowered Carter to the deck and found seats for our-selves on other drums and just sat there in silent misery. Time dragged on. We heard clumping and clattering over-head, then the throb of engines—and more clattering—and once I went to sleep and fell off the drum. Carter came round a little and started to shriek, and we had a hell of a job to quieten him down. Then, after what seemed days, but actually was only three hours, we felt the gentle lift of the deck under us that meant we had reached open water. But it was another hour before Kjaer unlocked. We staggered out, and Carter was violently sick, which at least stopped him asking questions. Kjaer hurried back to the bridge.

Overside I could see a small boat making away from us towards the pilot cutter. The coast was astern of us, with the lights paling in the dawn. A fresh breeze was blowing, which was heaven after that hellish paint-locker. I felt my spirits rising. The tough part was over now. There was just a sea voyage ahead of us—a voyage which could, conceivably, be even enjoyable, now that our tautened nerves could relax a little.

Yes—we'd done it—and my little ploy of yesterday had paid off—and had pulled the whole thing off the rocks. Wherever else they thought us, they would be certain we weren't on this ship.

My spirits rose further, and continued to rise. I even turned and grinned amiably at Sonia. Then I stopped grinning.

A man was looking down at us from the deck above. I thought for a moment that he was an Indian wearing a white turban. But *only* for a moment.

His head was heavily bandaged—but there was no mistaking his face.

He was the fellow I had crowned with the bottle in the brothel doorway.

## Chapter 13

He gave no sign of recognition. From where he was we were no doubt just a group of sailors huddled in the half light under the break of the well deck below him, and anyhow he looked a pretty sick man, his face as pale as the bandages. He continued to lean on the rail for a while, then he withdrew out of sight. Sonia happened to turn at that moment, and I must have been looking as sick as the other guy. She said: 'What's wrong now?'

'Every bloody thing,' I groaned. 'That fellow up there is the one who followed me from the ship.' I felt like a man who has just scaled Everest and come face to face with a Coca-Cola advertisement on the summit. I braced myself for the lash of her scorn, but for once she was at a loss for words. She took a deep breath, like a martyred saint who has been asked to take just that little bit too much, and then Carter, who was being sick in the scuppers, lost his footing as the ship butted into a sharp, steep swell, and rolled on the deck. We helped him up and sat him on the corner of the hatch. We had a job to hold him there, because the breeze was reviving him quickly and I could see panic setting it. I told him to take it easy, but he struggled and tried to break away from us, yelling incoherently. A group of Chinese deckhands came along with brooms and a hose, and when he saw them, the balloon really went up. I think that if he could have made it, he'd have jumped over the rail. Then suddenly the fight went out of him, and he sat hunched with his face in his hands, and he gave a deep, shuddering sob. It was a terrible moment. Up to this point he had been a piece of merchandise on the hoof, but now for the first time I saw him as a human being—a terrified man who was being taken to his death, and who knew it. I may be kidding myself, but I think in looking back that if the pilot cutter had still been within hailing distance I'd have jacked the whole thing in. But she wasn't within hailing distance, so I sought refuge in our carefully planned lie.

I said: 'What he hell's eating you? You're out of gaol and you're on your way back to your own people. All you've got to do now is relax and enjoy the ride.'

'My own people?' he said hopelessly. 'I have no people. Only a wife and two children in Moscow.'

'That would be enough for most blokes,' I said. 'Okay, so you'll be joining them. It will take a bit of time, but at least you're on your way. Why the squawks?' It was apparently too much for Sonia. She moved away to the rail and stood looking out across the sea. From the corner of my eye I saw her drag her woollen cap off and shake her hair free, then turn her face up into the wind and take deep breaths, like someone trying to rid themselves of something that smelt nasty. Carter looked up at me quickly—searching my face—then he shrugged.

'You ask me to believe that?' He gestured towards the Chinese seamen who were now swabbing down the foredeck. 'I know what those people mean. You're taking me back to China.'

'As far as I'm concerned, my orders are to escort you to Vladivostok,' I told him, and again he glanced up at me sharply. I saw a momentary glimmer of hope in his face, but it faded immediately.

'Vladivostok?' he repeated. 'I'm not a child. Why would you transport me right round the globe? I know what my route was to be—Gdynia, Warsaw, Moscow. I was told that weeks ago in prison.'

'I wouldn't be knowing,' I said. 'I get my orders and I carry them out to the best of my ability—and get paid on results at the end of it. I don't ask questions. But things can change,' I went on. 'One door closes, so they open another. The heat was on us the whole time, you know. Pretty fierce. We hadn't a prayer by the European route.'

'Why was I drugged?' he shot at me. 'I was co-operating. I was doing everything I was told to do—while I thought you were working for the Russians.'

'I don't know,' I said. 'You were handed over to us like that. I had nothing to do with your coming over the wall.'

He nodded slowly. 'That I can believe. That is probably the only truth you've spoken so far. I know who brought me out of prison. I knew who to expect. They identified themselves. But then I was hijacked, wasn't I?'

'Not to my knowledge.'

'You're a liar, my friend—and not a very skilled one. You've been renewing the drug at intervals the whole time. You and that girl.' He nodded towards Sonia. 'Why—un-

120

less you knew that I might start to ask awkward questions—might, perhaps, make trouble at the wrong time?'

'I told you,' I said. 'I get my orders—and I don't ask questions.'

'Orders from whom? Who are *you*—you personally—working for?'

'Oh, for Christ's sake,' I said wearily. 'You know better than that. Even if I knew, you surely wouldn't expect me to tell you.'

'What harm can it do now?' he asked. 'I can't escape from this ship before you hand me over to somebody else.' He paused, looking at me directly. 'On the other hand we *might* be able to come to some arrangement.'

'Such as?'

'That depends. You mentioned that you were paid at the end of the job—on results?' I was becoming conscious of a change of manner. His initial weakness had been purely the natural reaction of a man surfacing after days of heavy sedation and finding himself in peril. The fear was no doubt still there, but he had had time to collect himself now, and his guard was up again. I felt a certain relief. Nothing is so demoralizing as dealing from a position of strength with a thoroughly defenceless opponent.

He was watching me closely, waiting for my answer. I rubbed my chin slowly, and flicked my eyes towards Sonia warningly. He lowered his voice.

'If we could discuss that fee—and I offered to double it, with a cast iron guarantee—*on results*——' He let the rest trail off. I looked at him shiftily. I didn't have to act it either. I was feeling shifty.

Then Kjaer arrived. He came to the top of the ladder and beckoned peremptorily. He was looking like thunder. I called to Sonia, who still had her back to us, and they both followed me up to the deck above. Kjaer grunted and led us off to the bridge superstructure. He opened a door leading to a smallish cabin on the port side. I could see it had two berths, one above the other, with a third made up on a settee. We started to go in, but he grabbed my elbow and said, 'Not you. I got to talk to you.' He closed the door on the others and half led, half pushed me to his day cabin. He was quivering with rage.

'So you bloddy put it over me, eh?' he roared. 'You think you going to get away with this?'

'What the hell are you beefing about?' I demanded. 'We made a bargain. I'm keeping to my half of it——'

'That goddam woman!' he stormed. 'You don't say nothing about a woman!'

'I said three *people*. You didn't ask our bloody sexes. What difference does it make, anyhow?'

'Difference?' he howled. 'It makes this difference. If I know you had a broad with you I don't carry you—that's all.'

'Well, you know now,' I snapped. 'What are you going to do about it?'

There was nothing he *could* do about it, except curse—and he certainly did plenty of that. He did say, however, that he wanted another couple of thousand, but I said balls to that. He switched then to almost tearful complaint.

'Three men is all right,' he said. 'The crew get used to seeing you around and pretty soon they don't think about it any more. By the time the voyage is over they've forgotten about it. But a woman is different. Those randy buggers in the fo'c'sle they'll talk about nothing else the whole trip— making up stories they'd like to believe. If she hangs up a pair of drawers to dry they'll blow their stacks, like stopped-up billy-goats. When they go ashore they'll still be talking —then word gets out—then inquiries start—and I'm in the crap up to my goddam neck.'

'You're making difficulties,' I said. 'When we get to Hong Kong we'll be over the side and away—and even if your crew does talk afterwards nobody could prove anything. Anyhow, you said you could trust them.'

'I said I *know* them,' he grumbled. 'I pay them a few bucks extra to stop their mouths—but to stop them talking about a woman on board I'll have to pay 'em a bloddy sight more ——'

'We'll deal with that when we come to it,' I said. 'At the moment I've got something really serious to talk about. You've got a man on board with a bandaged head.'

'Sparks—the Marconi man?' He looked startled. 'What about him?'

*I* looked startled then. 'But you told me he'd deserted?' I said.

'That's what I thought, but the police put him back on board just as we were coming through the dock gates.'

'Oh my God,' I groaned. 'What happened?'

'He got a smack over the dome in some dive, and he was

122

unconscious for a couple of days. When they found out which ship he was off they put him on again, toute suite. They don't like having to look after foreign bums in a French port. But what do *you* know about it, mister?'

'The night I saw you on board here,' I told him. 'He followed me afterwards. I didn't know he was actually off this ship then, but I took no chances. I led him up an alley and crowned him with a bottle.'

He looked as sick as if I'd crowned *him*. 'I knew it,' he groaned. 'What did I tell you? I got a nose for not-right bastards. I had a feeling——'

'Where did he join you?'

'Helsinki,' he answered. 'Just before sailing. I got a doctor's note to say my regular guy was sick. This fellow came aboard on a pierhead jump. His papers looked all right, bastards. I had a feeling——'

'What date was that?'

'The eighteenth. Two days after Carter came out,' he said, and caught my eye. 'Oh, come on, mister—you don't think I didn't know, do you? The Meisterspringer had already sounded me out on it—in Antwerp, on the way up to Helsinki. Only the deal the old sod offered me was for two guys and nothing about a woman.'

'He didn't know then,' I said gloomily. 'Neither did I—or maybe I'd have turned it down myself. Well, that's it, then. They've planted him on us.'

'Looks like it,' he agreed. 'He's not a Rusk, though. German. Hamburg papers—but he could just as easy be East as West.' Then he said, 'Shit!' explosively, and jumped up, fumbling for a bunch of keys on the end of a chain. He opened a small locker on the bulkhead. Inside I could see a large electric switch. He seemed relieved. He relocked it and sat down again. 'Master switch,' he explained. 'When that's out the Sparks can listen all he damn well wants, but can't send. I like to know what goes out from this ship.'

That was certainly a relief, but then a thought struck me. 'In port,' I said. 'Genoa or the Canal? He could get a message ashore——'

'He'll be lucky,' Kjaer said savagely. 'He'll be in a dark hole down below—with you others—when we're in port.' He suddenly beamed like the sun coming from behind clouds. 'Damn lucky that. When he hadn't turned up before sailing I scratched him off articles and had the shipping master stamp it. I
123

haven't had time to put him on again. Officially he ain't aboard, so there'll be no questions if the port doctor called a crew muster.' He rose. 'Well—maybe it could be worse. Bloddy good job you clobbered him. It's put a dhobi mark on him all right—so we know him. But a pity it just wasn't that *liddle* bit harder. You'll all be wanting your breakfast.'

'You can see now why I wanted an extra cabin,' I ventured.

'For the broad? You can shift her in here if you think you're going to be crowded.' He winked lasciviously. 'Briddish? They take a bit of warming up, but it's a wonder what you can do with them in a narrow bunk and the leeboards shipped.'

Unaccountably I was furious. 'Listen, Kjaer, you fat bastard——' I began.

'*Captain* Kjaer on my own ship,' he said with dignity. 'And I ain't fat.' Then he went off into roars of laughter.

We walked along the deck to collect the others. Carter was sitting on a lifebelt rack outside the cabin. He rose as we approached and I introduced him as Mr Jones. Kjaer shook hands and said he was happy to have him aboard, and hoped he would have an enjoyable voyage, and Carter bowed solemnly, and said he was sure he would. He was now in complete control of himself, and it was hard to realize that a short half hour previously he had been sobbing brokenly.

Then Sonia came out of the cabin. She was still dressed in slacks and jersey, but she'd shed the jacket, and with it the bulk she had been carrying beneath it and by some feminine magic she had stepped back into her own personality. She had got rid of the stain on her face and neck, and the cold, brisk breeze whipped the colour into her really beautiful skin even as she came out on to the deck. She used little make-up—just a slash of lipstick and something very faint round her eyes—that was just exactly *right*. Her hair was tidy when she came out, but the wind played havoc with it —but somehow that was just exactly right also. And her figure certainly did things to the slacks and jersey that would have surprised the young fisher boy they had originally been intended for.

Kjaer's objections to female passengers seemed to disappear like the morning mist before the sun. He engulfed her hand in his huge paw and made porcine sounds of approval and

124

welcome. He really was a most objectionable man. He took us into the comfortably furnished saloon. Two of the mates —the second and third—were having a late breakfast. They must of course have known by this time that there was a woman aboard, so they showed no surprise, but just rose and bowed gravely and murmured greetings in good English— two blond and rather lumpish young men in neat blue uniform. The breakfast the Chinese steward served us was English too—a good one of bacon, eggs, toast, marmalade and wonderful coffee. Kjaer left with his officers then, to go about their business, and shortly afterwards Carter, who had lapsed into a stony, expressionless silence, pushed his untouched plate aside and made a hurried exit, looking once again a bit green about the gills.

I could see that Sonia was bursting with questions, but the steward was within earshot in his small pantry, so I signed to her to come out on deck. We walked to the stern and leaned with our backs to the rail and looked forward along the entire length of the ship. The weather was clearing, but the wind was increasing from the south-west, and from time to time a flurry of spray smacked over her bows. The officers and crew berthed amidships and for'ard respectively, and this part was completely deserted. Behind us the seagulls were wheeling and diving over the wake, and the Normandy coast was receding on our port beam. I realized that this was the first time since that second evening in their London home that we had been alone—really alone. Always we had been conscious of the presence of Carter and the necessity of keeping our voices down—of the possibility of ears at keyholes and watching eyes outside. Now, for a time at least, we were free of all that, and ahead of us was the long run south. True, there were the minor hazards of Genoa and the Canal to be got over, then the immeasurably greater one of the handover in Hong Kong, but for the moment we knew only this blessed relaxation of tension.

I brought her up to date with things, telling her what Kjaer had told me.

She said: 'It's going to be difficult keeping Carter and this other man from getting their heads together. We can't watch them both day and night.'

'We'll just have to do our best, that's all,' I said. 'But even if they do manage it, there's nothing they can do about it.'

'He—the Marconi man I mean—can expose Kjaer afterwards.'

'That's Kjaer's lookout. He knows the risk he's running —and he's being paid for it. Anyhow, as you say, that will be afterwards. The Russians are realists. They don't waste time, effort and money purely on vengeance—not unless there's some propaganda value attached to it. And there won't be to this—not if they've been done in the eye.'

'I don't know,' she said slowly. 'The ship does go on to Vladivostok, doesn't it? He'll undoubtedly be searched there.'

'They'll find nobody.'

'The Marconi man?'

'If I know Kjaer he'll put him ashore before that. They stop at three or four Chinese ports after Hong Kong.' I was refusing to cross bridges before coming to them.

We strolled back amidships. Kjaer was being the perfect host. He had turfed the third mate out of his cabin and put him in the radio shack. 'Help keep an eye on the bastard,' he said, 'and now the lady gets a cabin to herself.'

We met the rest of the officers at lunch—the mate, an elderly Finn, the three engineers, two Swedes and a Dutchman, and finally the Marconi man, who came in for some heavy ribbing from the others. There is apparently something exquisitely funny among sailors in being beaned in a brothel. He took it well, with just the right mixture of bravado and sheepishness. He was a well-built, quite good-looking type in the middle thirties, and his name was Wetten. He knew his job too. There wasn't a flicker of recognition in his face as he shook hands—first with me, then with Carter. I was watching Carter. There was no recognition in his face either.

The mate, who was old enough to know better, asked Wetten whether he had had his money's worth before being clobbered, and he answered dirtily in English. English, I found, was the *lingua franca* on this polyglot ship. They all spoke it ungrammatically but fluently, plentifully bessprinkled with the four-letter words—with o doing duty as u. The chief engineer went into a long and very boring story of a similar experience that had befallen him in Valparaiso many years previously, but which due to his wit, perspicacity and super-human strength had turned out differently. Then Sonia arrived and the Captain rapped for order.

I had a hell of a shock that night. I took a stroll up and down on deck with Sonia after supper, then I turned in

126

early. Carter was already in the lower berth, his face turned to the wall. I took my money and passport from inside my shirt and put both under my pillow, then started to clear my pockets. And only then did I realize that the gun and packet of ammunition I had been carrying had gone. Both had been there when we came aboard—in the right and left pockets of my peajacket respectively—and I'd left the peajacket hanging behind the door when I'd gone to have a bath in the afternoon. And Carter had been in the cabin. I make no excuses. That's the sort of silly thing a man lulled into a sense of security can sometimes do after a period when the pressure has been on.

I dived for the lower berth and hauled Carter half out and got his neck in the crook of my left arm while I slid my other hand under his pillow.

'Where is it?' I demanded.

'Where's what?' he asked expressionlessly.

'You know damned well what I mean.' I applied a little leverage and he winced. 'My gun.'

'Your gun?' His face twisted into a wry grin. 'The lady took it from your pocket when she was clearing her things out to the other cabin. Didn't she tell you?'

I believed him, but it still might have been a trick to get rid of me while he recovered it, and I was taking no more chances. I hauled him right out and shoved him hard into a corner while I searched thoroughly—under both mattresses, lockers, drawers and the small wardrobe. He stood looking at me contemptuously. I gave it up at last and opened the door.

'Don't try anything, Carter,' I told him as I stepped outside. 'It will get you nothing except a broken neck.'

He said: 'You're leaving your money on your bunk.'

Furiously I stepped back inside and collected it.

'You're not terribly good at all this, are you?' he went on. 'I'd quit if I were you—while you're still alive. With a tidy little competence there are lots of comfortable places in the sun where a man can live without looking over his shoulder all the time. Let's talk about it, shall we?'

I went out and walked along to Sonia's cabin. There was a light behind the curtained port. She opened the door a chink in answer to my knock.

'My gun,' I said.

She passed it out to me without a word.

'Why the bloody hell didn't you tell me you'd taken it?' I snarled.

'Why the bloody hell did you leave it there?' she asked coldly and closed the door in my face. And once again, after this temporary truce, I was hating her guts.


## Chapter 14

We butted our way down through the Bay of Biscay in bad weather, for which I was thankful because it kept Carter in his bunk. He only got over his seasickness on the fifth day, when we were well into the Mediterranean, with another couple of days to go before we reached Genoa—then he took it up with me again on deck.

'How much do you want?' he said without preamble.

'What for?' I asked.

'To deliver me to the Soviet consulate in Genoa.'

'How would I collect?'

'From them—on my vouching for you. Dollars, sterling, Swiss francs—any currency you wish.'

'And how far do you think I'd get with it?'

He shrugged. 'Surely that's your affair. You could just disappear.'

'You can say that again,' I said drily. 'I'd disappear all right if I started to make deals on my own. My orders are to deliver you to Vladivostok—and that girl's here to see that I do just that. Forget it, Carter.'

'We haven't discussed a price yet.'

'And we're not going to. I said forget it.'

'Ten thousand pounds.'

'I'm getting more than that as it is,' I said.

'I don't believe you, but we'll say fifteen, eh?'

'No—nor fifty.' I broke things off and walked away, but I knew he'd keep at me.

And then Wetten started to give trouble. He complained bitterly to Kjaer about not being able to transmit.

'All you got to do is listen, mister,' Kjaer told him. 'When I want to transmit anything, I tell you.'

'But I got to acknowledge, for God's sake, when anything comes up for us.'

'Don't worry. Just keep on listening.'

128

'I've had two calls from your own damn agents in Genoa, wanting to know our E.T.A. there. What are they going to think when I don't answer?'

Kjaer smiled sweetly. 'They going to think I got a damnfool Sparks who gets clobbered in a joyhouse and can't do his job properly. They'll be damn right too. Just carry on like I say, mister.'

A couple of hours before we got in, Kjaer took him down below in his dual capacity of supercargo, and came up ten minutes later, alone. He winked at me broadly and told me to collect Sonia and Carter, then he led us down through the engine-room and along the propeller tunnel to where a section of the curved bulkhead had been removed. We went up through this and found ourselves in a compartment some eight feet square, and sat and listened while they bolted the bulkhead back into position. We were well below the waterline but it wasn't as bad as perhaps it sounds, because there was a light there, and air came in through a duct. It had obviously been used for the same purpose before. There were mattresses, a tank of water and some canned provisions. There was even an Elsan there, and Kjaer, the perfect host, had had the delicacy to have a canvas screen erected in front of it. It could have been worse—but it was still hell.

They let us out fifteen hours later. It was a cold, clear night and the lights of Genoa were dropping astern. Sonia went off to her cabin without a word, and I leaned on the rail drawing great breaths of clean air down into my lungs. Carter came up beside me and started again.

'There's still Suez,' he said. 'Easier there.'

'You've seen the form,' I told him wearily. 'Even suppose I wanted to do a deal with you, how could I? We'll be down in that damned place and we could yell our heads off without anybody hearing. Drop it, Carter.'

'You've got some money,' he said. 'A lot of money. Lend me a thousand pounds.'

'What good would that do you?'

'Just lend it to me,' he insisted. 'I'll guarantee you twenty in return.'

'Not a chance,' I snapped, but I was intrigued. What the hell had he thought up? I shuffled my feet and mumbled, 'I'd want to know exactly what you were going to do with it— and I'd still reserve the right to turn it down.'

'Piecee-money,' he said. I knew what that meant, but I played it dumb.

'What's that?'

'I'd tear the notes in half and give them to somebody—with a letter.'

'And then?'

'God—you're not really as stupid as all that, are you? The person concerned only has to slip the letter to a port police official, and he collects the other halves of the notes afterwards—and nobody is any the wiser where the tip came from.'

'Sure,' I said. 'So we do that—and some sailor is a thousand pounds up. But what about me? They make a complete search and we are dragged out. *You* may get clear away with it, but I get booked for kidnapping and criminal conspiracy.'

'The letter would completely exonerate you in advance—and would contain a guarantee that you were to get your twenty thousand afterwards. You could read it, of course.'

'I don't read Russian.'

'It would be in English.'

'Sorry,' I said. 'But you've overlooked one thing. The most important thing. As far as I know I'm working for the Russians already. Are they going to pay me twenty thousand over the top for disobeying orders that I've already received? Be your age, Carter.'

'You're not working for the Russians. You're working for the Chinese,' he said flatly.

'You're nuts.'

'Would you like some cards on the table, Mr Wainwright?' he asked quietly. 'My cards, I mean.'

I tried to repress the start, but he was conscious of it even in the darkness. I had never told him my name. I was Smith on this ship—as he was Jones. Then I thought he might have heard Sonia let it slip in an unguarded moment, but he disabused me of that in the next second.

'Oh yes,' he went on. 'I know your name. I know quite a lot about you. You're working for Malcolm—the Masterspringer—at the moment, but your real controller is Henry George Gaffney—or the Gaffer as you call him.'

So much for the school—the years of training—the bloody mumbo-jumbo of schoolboy secrecy they put one through, I thought bitterly. Christ, we were only boy scouts at this game.

'You were recruited in London and trained in England initially,' the flat voice went on. 'Then you were infiltrated into Hong Kong—Hong Kong and Southern China Bank. Not so, Mr Wainwright? or are you going to waste your time and breath in denying it?'

'I don't know what the hell you're talking about,' I said, but it sounded feeble even to me.

'More cards, Mr Wainwright? Very well—here they come —face up—the lot. Your late lamented father—ex-Shanghai policeman. He defected to the Russians in nineteen-twenty-seven——'

I threw the lot then—right into his lap. 'You're a bloody liar,' I said. 'Get back to the cabin before I throw you over the rail, you bastard.'

'Why the indignation, Mr Wainwright? That's what you've done yourself, isn't it?' he said, and that, curiously enough, enabled me to get a grip on myself again. He was clever all right, and what he knew about me had come in the form of a shock that had had me gasping and floundering for some minutes, but this restored the balance. So I had been blown? If he knew my background and cover, then obviously others did too, so I was out of the game—once I had handed him over. But that was *all* he knew. For the rest he was just guessing and probing. He had overplayed his hand in suggesting I had gone over—and the shrewd one he had whipped in about the poor old man was of the same cloth. I felt my anger subsiding. I yawned elaborately.

'I've listened to enough cock for tonight,' I told him. 'I'm going to turn in. It's no good trying to rat me for a thousand pounds while I'm asleep, Carter. My money's in a safe place. Anyhow, you'd never find a man on the ship who'd dare pull a fast one on the skipper—except Wetten, and he'll be down in a hole somewhere going through the Canal—just as he was this time.'

'You're still not convinced, are you?' he said. 'A few more cards——?'

'Shove 'em. Good night.' I turned away.

'A pity,' he said softly. 'This way we both die. I've got rather longer than you, because there's quite a lot they want out of me first. But you're booked out too, you know. Your own people will do it. They've got to now.'

'Things are getting a bit mixed,' I said. 'Who are my own people? First you say I'm working for the Chinese—then you say my father and I defected to the Russians.'

'You're mistaken. I didn't say *you* defected to the Russians. Your father—yes—but when the big split came in nineteen-fifty-five he plumped for the Chinese. You never had that agonizing choice—and it was agonizing for the real, orthodox Marxian—you went Chinese right from the beginning.'

'Well, at least that tidies things up a little,' I said. 'So now the ungrateful sods are going to rub me out, are they? Why?'

'They've hardly any option, have they? You've been blown for the last eighteen months, Mr Wainwright. You're just about the biggest security risk they're carrying at the moment —less perhaps the Gaffer. I had you on the list long before I went inside.'

'You're losing me again,' I said. 'Who was I blown to? The Russians?'

'Curiously enough, no,' he said. 'They'll know by now, of course, since this London interlude, but you got away with it in Hong Kong. Their set-up is not very good there, as you no doubt know yourself. The Chinese breathe too closely down their necks. No—I was referring to the British.'

'Ah!' I said profoundly. 'Now we're getting somewhere. So the British know all about me, do they?'

'Not all. You were on the doubtful list for quite a long time, but when Winterton blew his furbler in Amoy he named you as a *British* agent—under stringent interrogation. Word got back, as Winterton meant it to—and that was it. Through you Kempson in your London office, and Walters and Blackman in Hong Kong, were then uncovered.'

Then cold breezes *did* start to blow around my tail. My God! He'd named the three key people in the whole set-up as far as I was concerned. And he had already brought the Gaffer into it. He had us all in the wrong context, of course, but he *knew* us—and he was being handed over to the Chinese —and he'd probably either try to make a deal—or break under interrogation. They probably knew all this already, but if they didn't this fellow was going to be a pearl of price to them.

But I'd had enough by this time. My head was reeling. I turned and walked away abruptly, but he caught me up by the ladder to the upper deck.

'Look, Wainwright,' he said urgently. 'I'm not scared for my own hide. What these bastards will do to me will be unpleasant, but that, as we both know, is one of the contingent liabilities of the job. But what *is* burning me up is the thought that this can be avoided. Just let me fix that letter—and we're out of it.'

'How could you guarantee that?' I demanded. Any pitiable scrap of information I could pick up out of this lousy affair might be useful to somebody afterwards.

'The letter will be addressed to a certain consular official in Port Said. Within a matter of minutes it will be relayed to Cairo. We'll be off this damned ship before we get through the Canal——'

'And splurged across every front page in the world,' I said. 'What chance would *I* have?'

'What chance have you got now, you bloody fool?' he came back at me. 'You think you're going to hand me over in Amoy or Shanghai or some other Chinese port, and then just drift back into circulation again? For God's sake, haven't I told you enough? The British *know* you. Your rope's run out. You'll be picked up as soon as you show your face in Hong Kong if you've got any ideas of trying to make a break for it there—and if you get away with less than thirty years you'll be lucky. But personally I don't think you'll reach Hong Kong. The Chinese will bump you off.'

'If the British have known about me all this time, why haven't they picked me up before?' I asked.

He laughed shortly. 'I don't want to be insulting,' he said, 'but you've been quite a useful bloke to them, haven't you? You've blundered around so much that you've uncovered everybody you've had contact with. They've been using you as a stalking-horse, for Christ's sake—but now your usefulness is finished. You'll just be swept up into the dustpan. My way you'll come off this ship with me—and Wetten—and there won't be a word on *any* front page. You have a passport. You can take your own chances—or you can be on a plane with me to Moscow the same day.' He laughed again. 'You wouldn't be lonely. There's quite a colony of us there nowadays.'

'What about the girl?' I asked. 'What happens to her?'

'Does that make any difference?'

'It does to me.'

'In which case I can see no objection to her coming with us. *She* hasn't such a hell of a rosy future anywhere else either.'

I said: 'I'll have to think about it.'

'You haven't got much time,' he said. 'None of us has.'

I went to the saloon. Everybody not on watch was there, including Wetten. He looked up and nodded as I entered, showing no resentment for his sojourn in the bowels of the ship. The others were watching Italian television, entranced. It was something they only saw in port and for a couple of hours thereafter.

Kjaer yelled: 'Old Sparks here bloddy good. He get this damn thing to work after the bloddy third pour beer in it. That little piece there with the nice ass—wouldn't mind having *her* aboard. Have a drink.'

I needed one. I felt as though I'd been put through a wringer.

I thought of going along and knocking Sonia up, but I dropped the idea. She would be tired and edgy after our spell in the tank and wouldn't be much help in this. But I couldn't face another session of cross-talk and double-think in the cabin, and I knew Carter wouldn't let up on me now, so I found a sheltered corner right down at the stern and sat on the deck and smoked. The son of a bitch had certainly shaken me.

They knew so much. True, they had misinterpreted a lot of it—but they still *knew*. They knew the Gaffer. Henry George Gaffney. God damn it, not even I had known his real name until tonight. Did *he* know he was blown? If I got out of this in one piece it would afford me the acutest satisfaction in telling him. But then, I reflected sourly, he would without a doubt blame *me* for it. Kempson, my boss in the bank in London—the man who had recruited me in the first place. He was only on liaison work admittedly, but he was still a pretty big wheel. But it was the thought of Walters, the deep-sea fishing *aficionado*, and Blackman, my immediate controller, being uncovered that really frightened me. They, I had no doubt, would be the ones who would be arranging our reception in Hong Kong. If they were in a fool's paradise we were walking straight into a trap.

What a bloody mess!

I tried to sort things out in my own mind. Three parties, mutually antagonistic—the Russians, the Chinese, ourselves.

Carter was a Russian. We held him. We were going to give him to the Chinese in return for Winterton. The Russians were trying to rescue him before the exchange took place. That was the problem reduced to its simplest terms. What were the factors affecting it? First and foremost, for reasons of policy we, the British, had to work secretly—without the knowledge and co-operation of our own orthodox agencies. Factors to our advantage at the moment: A. We were holding Carter. B. Secrecy, insofar as the said orthodox agencies were concerned, had been preserved up to this point. And that was *all* I could find to our advantage. Factors against us: A. The Russians knew we were holding Carter. B. Although we might have broken the trail in Le Havre, it would still be a reasonable assumption that the exchange would be made in or near the only place where the British and Chinese frontiers touched—Hong Kong. Therefore the watches would be on there. C. The Russians knew our people in Hong Kong. D. I had every reason to believe that our people didn't know that the Russians were aware of them. They would therefore, except for normal precautions, be off their guard to that extent. E. Whatever the outcome of this, our Hong Kong set-up was now irretrievably blown. But at least to get another set-up going was somebody else's headache.

Numerically the advantages were overwhelmingly with the Russians.

There was one other factor that remained a wild joker without apparent advantage or disadvantage to either side. The Russians thought that we—that is, the Gaffer, Kempson, Walters, Blackman, myself and others known or unknown —were working for the Chinese. I wondered what the hell gave them that idea? They had been so right—so frighteningly on the beam—about everything else. Was that a deliberate thing on our part? A carefully and diabolically clever smoke-screen laid by our higher-ups?

Then, in spite of the cold breeze, I suddenly found myself breaking into a prickly sweat. *Were* the Russians wrong? What did *I* know about the higher echelons? Just four men. Couldn't I have been a complete catspaw all along? Couldn't those four be working for the Chinese?

I scrabbled round for something concrete to batter at this terrifying new hypothesis. The school? They surely couldn't run as elaborate a thing as that right in the heart of England?

135

Or could they? After all, security had been as tight there as anything I had ever known. The Gaffer? He, of course, could be anybody's meat and I disliked him so much that I would be prepared to believe anything about him. But the three senior bank officials—comfortable, secure, affluent—the epitomization of English upper middle class—? No, that was too fantastic. But what about a couple of senior diplomats and a round half-dozen scientists who were forming the nucleus of the Moscow colony that Carter had mentioned? What about a man who had been at the top of our orthodox Secret Service itself—now living comfortably in a dacha? A consulate official who had been whisked over the wall just as Carter had been——?

The Meisterspringer? Sonia? Where did they fit into it? Just hirelings who would work for anybody who paid them? That was the impression Malcolm seemed deliberately and cynically to give me. But Sonia? Was she here only for her own safety—or was she rubber-heeling on me to make certain there were no slip-ups? Well, whatever the answer to that last one was, I couldn't trust her again.

Then I thought I saw a chink of light at the end of the dark tunnel through which I was crawling. For God's sake, if they were all working for the Chinese why this complicated exchange business? Why bring Winterton into it at all? Once they had sprung Carter all they would need to do would be to dump him on this ship and hand him over in a Chinese port. Then, pathetically, that one crumbled. I, in my innocence, would still have to be supplied with a valid reason for it all. If I had just been told to hand Carter over to the Chinese I might have started to think—and that would be the last thing they'd want. Perhaps there was no question of an exchange. I handed him over—and then, as Carter had suggested, got quietly knocked off—my usefulness, such as it had been, ended.

But would they have gone to all this trouble, the years of training, just for this? Hardly. No—I was just a gullible starry-eye who thought he was working for his own country. Probably there were many others in the same position. Pawns being moved, without any clear ideas of who was doing the moving. Carefully conditioned not to question or reason why. Taught to regard our own real security services as our worst enemies. This job was a natural for me. It just cropped up—and I was in the right place at the right time. And boy—was I expendable!

So, assuming all this to be right, what the hell was I to do now? Was there a choice in the two evils of turning Carter over to the Russians in preference to the Chinese? I just couldn't answer that one.

How about throwing the whole thing when I got to Hong Kong? Going to the police and making a clean breast of it? Telling them I had been acting in good faith—and naming names? Then I started to sweat afresh. Suppose I wasn't right, and that all this was fantastic theorizing, and I blew the whole thing needlessly?

No—anything but that. I shuddered.

I finally fell into a fitful, bedevilled sleep, and woke shivering and damp as day was breaking.

Carter was awake when I went to the cabin. I avoided his eye and swore at him when he said good morning, but knew he could see what a lather I was in and was marking it up as a point to himself.


## Chapter 15

I avoided him all that day. I avoided Sonia too—by the simple expedient of being just plain damned rude to her when she spoke to me, which distressed Kjaer. He saw me and said: 'What the hell goes on? Sonia bloddy mad at you. She asks me to go in a hole by herself when we go through the Canal.'

'Good idea,' I said. 'You do that.'

He shook his head. 'Can't put a lady in the bilges. Bloddy big rats down there, and it stinks like hell.'

'Well, put her somewhere else.'

'Not so. Only two really safe places on this ship, if the Gyps got nosey.'

'All right—I'll go in the bilges.'

'You're nuts,' he said. 'But please yourself.'

That meant the three others would be together, cooking up God knows what, but they could do that anyhow on a long trip. This way it meant I didn't have to talk to anybody.

But Carter still made it. He corralled me in the cabin two hours before we came up to the outer bar in Port Said.

'What about it?' he said without preamble.

'Not a chance,' I answered.

'You're forcing my hand, Wainwright.' He was looking straight at me, unwaveringly.

'And you're breaking my heart—but the answer's still no. And don't try slipping any of the crew a note without the piecee-money. They know they'd never collect it afterwards. I've warned Kjaer.'

'Wainwright, listen to me,' he begged. 'There's one thing I haven't told you——'

'Save it.'

'—one last thing which I hoped I wouldn't have to tell. But the position is desperate now. I'm working for the British. I always have.'

I laughed. 'I'd have said the Krauts on that. It was Hitler who said the bigger the lie the better its chance of being believed, wasn't it?'

'It's true.'

'All right—so it's true. But what difference does that make? I'm working for the people who pay me. In this case it's the Chinese. You told me that yourself. They're paying me to deliver you somewhere on the hoof. Skip it, Carter. That one wasn't up to your usual standard.'

'Wainwright—*it's the truth*,' he repeated—and by God he was almost convincing me. I've never before or since heard a man put so much conviction into three simple words. Once more I was standing on shifting sands, but I fought back.

'Maybe you were—once—but you went over, didn't you— first to the Chinks, then to the Rusks—and the British caught up with you and you were clobbered with thirty years.'

He stepped forward and took my arm. I could feel his fingers digging into the muscle like steel prongs. His voice and his eyes were steady. This was no frightened man begging for his life.

'Just listen to this. It will give you something to think about in the comparatively short time you've got left, if nothing else. I went over to the Chinese. With my back-ground and antecedents that was easy. White Russian—anti-Red. I was a natural—on the surface. But I was already in a Red cell. I doubled for the Russians right from the begin-ning—long before the split came. Then I was uncovered in Amoy and had to skip for Russia. My admittance was

138

already bought, paid for and guaranteed by ten years' solid and valuable work for them—but naturally I was useless in the Far East. But I still had a potential in the West. They did what we were banking on—and sent me to London. I did a good job for them there too—but of course I was leaking it back to our own people——'

' "Our own people" being the British?' I interrupted.

'That's right.'

'Then why the bloody hell did "our own people" give you thirty years?'

'If you'll listen a little longer I'll explain,' he said. 'In terms which even you might understand. I was blown by a China-man in Ipswich. Blown in a manner that our own people couldn't hush up. The police came into it—and it leaked to the newspapers. I was as bare as a badger's arse, shivering in the cold. Our own people had the choice of clearing me, or letting matters take their course. But it really wasn't a choice. Clearing me would automatically have blown a whole string of other people—a chain reaction through at least fifty cells in Russia—with strings leading back to God knows how many more in China. So matters had to take their course. The prosecution was supplied with just enough to make a watertight case against me—and no more. All good straight stuff—nothing faked—but not a hint of who I really worked for. So I went down for thirty years.'

'Without a squawk?'

'Naturally. Even if I'd wanted to squawk, what good would it have done me? Our people would just have denied it.'

'So?'

'So this. One good point about the Russians is that none of their top people are ever caught and imprisoned by the Opposition without their moving heaven and earth to get them out again. Exchange is the usual thing. They offered two commercial travellers and a journalist for me who they'd arrested in Moscow.'

'Why didn't we settle for that?'

'Because none of them was worth a damn. They knew it, and they knew that we knew it too. To the British I was a very big salmon indeed. They wouldn't be likely to exchange me for three tiddlers. They did offer me in return for an American, but the Russians wouldn't wear it. This guy knew too much and could still be very useful to C.I.A. So we just sat on our asses and waited for what we knew would eventually come. A spring.'

Kjaer came along the deck then and put his head into the cabin. 'Time you boys wasn't here,' he said. 'The breakwater's in sight and we'll be having the pilot alongside before long.'

'Just a moment,' begged Carter, and Kjaer grunted and went away. 'The Russians approached the Meisterspringer, and he was ready to do it, but he got a tip from somewhere that it had leaked, so he dropped it like a hot potato. Then they went to a fellow called Wates, who had done three commercial jobs but no politicals. He was cagey at first, but the price went up and up—until he took it on. But now the Meisterspringer had got word of it—and the old bastard sold the tip to the Gaffer, who was already cooking one up for the Chinese. *You* know more about things from then on——'

'Possibly I do,' I said. 'But how the hell do *you* know so much? You were inside—and you've had no contact with anybody other than the girl and myself since you came out.'

He laughed shortly. 'How naïve can you get, Wainwright?' he asked. 'I was kept abreast of every detail, right from the time I arrived in Lanchester. I was a highly-privileged good-conduct prisoner, making myself useful to the screws, working in the ration office and in the school. I was allowed any books I wanted from outside. I was even allowed a radio in my cell—a beautiful transistor job with one of those earplug things—so damned simple that it was laughable. Hold it the right way up and it received. Turn it upside down and it transmitted over a distance of ten miles—twenty if I hung a tiny coil of fuse wire out of the window—on a wavelength tucked away between the BBC and the police and amateur bands. I was briefed right up to the moment I came down that ladder. Wates and another fellow met me and gave me the word I was expecting, and we went off across a field to a waiting car. Then we were jumped—jumped by *one man*— someone was shot—the others hared away like hell into the darkness—and in the confusion I felt a needle jabbed into me and that was it.'

And it fitted. It all fitted together so convincingly. This could so easily be the truth—and yet—and yet——. He pulled a letter from his pocket; the envelope was unsealed. He held it out to me.

'This is our last chance, Wainwright,' he said. 'For either of us. There's a quartermaster—a Swede—Olsen. I've sounded him out. He'll do it—but he's got to have the piecee-money. Give it to him—and I'll take you into Russia with me—or you can shag off on your own—and if you ever want to go back to England I can even fix that too—*working for us*—the British—really this time.'

And then Kjaer was back with us, roaring: 'Mister Jones —for Christ's sake—down that bloddy engine-room and along the shaft tunnel. Mister Smith—find the mate and he'll show you where to go. You think we got all bloddy day?'

Carter gave me one last look. Threatening? Beseeching? Questioning? I don't know. Perhaps a mixture of all three. Kjaer hustled him off. I pushed the letter into my pocket and went forward.

I still had time to do it. Olsen, the sailor who had been on the gangway the first time I came aboard, was along the deck preparing a rope ladder for the pilot to come aboard. My pack of money was tucked inside my shirt. I just had to tear some hundred dollar bills in two and give them to him with the letter. If this was the truth I had been listening to I would be instrumental in getting a top British agent back into Russia—quite apart from probably saving my own neck, and incidentally his. If the Gaffer and the others were what he represented them to be, I'd be blowing them sky-high. If——

But then a whistle sounded from the bridge, and Olsen dropped what he was doing and hurried towards the ladder without a glance at me—and simultaneously the mate descended on me in a crimson burst of profanity and hurried me down into the well deck, and through an iron door, and down into the tween decks, and lower and lower still, until he lifted a trap over a dark and stinking hole and flashed his torch downwards. I dropped through wearily. The decision appeared to have been made for me.

'A jar of water and some grub in a canister. Piss where you like—All yours, mister,' said the mate, and dropped the trap into place. And he didn't even leave me the torch.

I was in complete and absolute darkness, with barely headroom when I stood upright. Oily water slopped round my ankles, and from somewhere the other side of a bulkhead came the hellish din of the engines, but suddenly there was a tinkle of a telegraph and the din dropped to a purr. I

141

pushed upwards on the trap to relieve, if only for a moment, the ghastly claustrophobic panic that I felt welling up, but it was securely clamped down the other side. I groped around with my feet and eventually found the two-gallon jar and a big square canister with a screw top. I turned it on its side and used it as a seat and felt about me for some dry spot above the level of the water to put my feet. I found a stringer at just the right height running between the steel ribs of the ship but then something soft and furry ran over my ankles and squeaked as I yelled and kicked, so I settled for the boot bath again.

I tried to read the letter, but the air was so bad that my matches didn't give sufficient light, then, if that wasn't enough, I dropped the damned thing in the water and in scrabbling for it I dropped the matches also, which put paid to it anyhow.

The engines started up again, ran for half an hour or so, then stopped and stayed still, except for the throbbing of a dynamo, for a long time. I preferred them to run because then one couldn't hear the squeaking of the rats. The place was lousy with them. Eventually we got under way again and I guessed we were now in the Canal, because she was rock steady with the engines throttled down.

But why dwell on it? It went on for thirty-six hours all told, and what with the thought of those rats and the agony of mind I was suffering anyhow, I was as near completely nuts when they let me out as made no difference. I followed the mate up the ladders, howling obscenities at him, but he only grinned. The light on deck nearly blinded me at first. We were well south of Suez now, with the barren shores of the Gulf widening out and receding on either side—and the Red Sea was incredibly blue. I went into the saloon and took three fingers of straight aquavit from Kjaer's private bottle, then staggered off to the bathroom and lay in warm water for nearly an hour.

Carter was lying on his back on his bunk when I came into the cabin, with his hands behind his head. He said, slowly and distinctly, without looking at me: 'You yellow-livered bastard.'

'Why yellow?' I asked him wearily. 'Mine might have been the harder decision.'

'You didn't make a decision, Wainwright,' he said. 'You just let things drift. When they let you have it I hope you'll live long enough to think of what might have been. What *would* have been—if you'd had the guts to hand that letter over.'

'Sure,' I said. 'I might have been handing a golden boy back to the Rusks.'

'And you wouldn't do that because you'd be letting your Chink bosses down, eh? Don't give me that line. Your sort would sell your mothers—if it was safe. You did nothing because you couldn't screw up the resolution.'

'You're wrong,' I told him. 'I didn't do it, because I don't believe you, Carter. You're a liar—a really convincing, bloody clever one—but you've overlooked one thing—and that punctures your whole story.'

He looked up at me quickly. 'What's that?' he asked.

'Find out.'

He swung his legs to the deck and sat up slowly, staring at me.

'I think I *know*,' he said. 'Or rather I think I know what *you* think. And if I'm right then this really is a tragedy—or a comedy—according to what sort of sense of humour you're endowed with.'

'Oh, drop it for Christ's sake,' I said, and prepared to go out on deck. He moved quickly, placing himself between me and the door.

'My story is unpuncturable, Wainwright, for the simple reason that every word I've told you is the truth,' he said very quietly. 'And I haven't overlooked anything. *Not even the possibility that you yourself are a British agent.*'

And he won—hands down. I tried desperately to ride the shock, but it was no good. I felt, and no doubt looked, like a boxer caught by a sucker punch—flat-footed and wide open —and he was reading my face like a book.

'So that's it,' he said, and nodded slowly as if confirming it to him. 'I was pretty certain. You gave yourself away when you blew your top when I mentioned that your father had gone over. A very old interrogator's trick that. Something dropped in quite incidentally—"Your father defected in 'thirty-six"—"Your wife became Robinson's mistress two years ago"—"Your brother had a homosexual relationship with a War Office clerk." It takes a very well trained man indeed to be on his guard against that particular technique —when he's tired, as you were—and when there is a possibility that it could be true. You're *not* very well trained, are

143

you? A crash course at that place up in the Wirral, I should say—and you've been a lone duck ever since.' He grinned suddenly—not sardonically. There was sympathy in it. 'You jumped as if I'd stuck a pin in your arse when I said "Wirral". So that was it, was it? I'm sorry, Wainwright. I'm not riding you for the fun of it. *I had to know*—for the sake of my own neck.'

I had struggled to the surface by this. 'You don't know a bloody thing, you son of a bitch,' I said. 'But if it's going to pass the long hours in front of you by thinking up wild ones, go ahead. Only get off *my* back. You're boring the pants off me.'

'I'm not boring you. Confusing you, maybe—even scaring you a bit—but not boring you. *You've* got some long hours of thinking ahead of you too.'

'Carter, you flatter yourself,' I said. 'I'll be spending my long hours sleeping in the sun.'

'*And* wondering. Wondering how the hell I could possibly know as much about you as I do—if I weren't what I represented myself to be—a British agent.'

'I've told you—and you don't know anything. You've made some pretty shrewd guesses, and some of them have been a bit close to the mark, and maybe my reactions showed that. But you've read those reactions wrongly. Now suppose you let me pass—or do I have to take a swing at you?'

But he didn't let me pass—and I did take a swing at him—a hard one. His head hit the door jamb behind him and he slid down to the floor, a thin trickle of blood appearing at the corner of his mouth.

I felt a swine. He was still a sick man, and he was booked for the slaughterhouse anyhow. I shouldn't have let it come to this. I hauled him to his feet and lowered him on to the settee and got some water and a towel. He opened his eyes and shook his head slowly from side to side as if trying to clear it.

He said thickly: 'What does that settle, Wainwright?'

'Not a thing,' I said miserably. 'I'm sorry—but for God's sake stop it, will you. I've got my orders—and I'm going to carry them out. Nothing can alter that.'

'But you've got your doubts too, haven't you?'

'Not a doubt,' I shook my head firmly.

'Yes you have,' he said. 'But you're clinging to one thing.

One thing that shoots my entire story down in flames. Shall I tell you what it is?'

'What difference could it make?' I asked. I handed him the wet towel. 'Stay there and I'll get you a drink from the saloon.' I moved to the door again.

'One thing,' he repeated softly. 'How, if we're both on the same side, could your orders be to hand me over to the Opposition?'

'That's it,' I acknowledged. 'The clincher. You've said it yourself. Now, shall we let it drop?'

'One minute more,' he begged. 'Then I will let it drop —because there's nothing more I can say.'

'Go head,' I sighed.

'I accused you of working for the Chinese,' he said. 'You didn't deny it.'

'I didn't confirm it either.'

'You didn't need to—then—because I was positive I was right. It suited your book at the moment to let me go on thinking that. There wasn't a reaction from you.'

'I'll get you that drink,' I said, and started to open the door. He wriggled upright and grabbed my sleeve.

'Wait—But when I changed my tack and mentioned the possibility of your working for the British—you *did* react. My God you did. That wasn't faked. It was only a shot in the dark, but it landed right on target.'

'So we're back where we started,' I said. 'Somebody in the higher reaches has made a balls of things and set dog on eating dog. Too bad. But it doesn't alter a thing. I've always been taught to obey the last order.'

'Nobody has made a balls of anything. But *you've* been made the goat. You *are* working for the Chinese, you pitiful bloody fool, *but you don't know it*.' He was gasping and shaking. If he was putting on an act of a man who had been groping in the dark and suddenly found himself in blinding light, he was certainly doing it well. In fact he put it into those exact words: 'Wainwright—I'm beginning to see the whole thing in the light now. Listen to me, for God's sake.' He started to enumerate off his fingers: 'One —those names I've given you—Gaffney, Kempson, Walters, Blackman, and yourself, who I thought right up to this minute was one of them—one of them knowingly, I mean —you'll admit that I've got those right, won't you? You were all blown at the same time. I told you—I had you all on the last list I got before leaving China. But it wasn't positive. You were all working for us—the British—but there was a possibility that one or all of you were leaking stuff to the Chinese. I was told to investigate from the Chinese side. I found out nothing—but Winterton did. It was I who interrogated him in Amoy. The very last job I did before I was blown myself, and had to skip to Russia. He named you all. I told you earlier that I passed the information back to Hong Kong. I did—but I never got an acknowledgment, and I certainly hadn't time to check whether it arrived. The fact that you're all still at large rather makes me doubt it now.'

'Couldn't you check from Russia?' I asked.

'I couldn't risk it. I was too busy establishing myself there. I was under rigorous screening for the first six months, anyhow. And it was the same when they sent me to London. I was under the closest rubber-heeling and I certainly couldn't afford to interest myself in something that was no longer in my parish.' He paused to take a deep breath. 'Right—Two—Winterton did, in fact, mention the possibility of your being a starry-eye doing low-category courier work without knowing the side you were working for—but that's a normal recruiting procedure. Three—and believe me I'm sorry about this, Wainwright, if it really hurts—but you couldn't be on any regular British intelligence roster, because of your father's defection. That, at least, is true.'

That one went home again—right under my ribs, in a cold, sickening stab—and I didn't even try to cover it this time. He didn't miss it.

'All right then, I'm not asking you to give me any answers, but I do want you to ask yourself these four questions: one—have you ever had an M.I.5 Positive Vetting? Two—have you ever met a departmental Head or Deputy Head of any regular intelligence agency whom you knew without any shadow of doubt to be such? Three—have you ever been controlled by anybody but the four men I have mentioned? Four—have you received your pay and expenses into your banking account by cheque—*and paid income tax on it*—or has it just been slipped to you in cash? If the answers to all those are in the negative, and you still think you're working for the British, you're *really* in cloud cuckoo land, and I'm sorry for you.'

He lay back and closed his eyes tiredly.

'I could do with that drink,' he said.

And he wasn't on his own. I went out and along the deck with my knees nearly buckling under me—and I was sorry for myself.


## Chapter 16

My God—and how sorry for myself. The more I went over things during the next few days, the more I realized how far out on the limb I was. His whole story was incontrovertible. I tested it link by link, but couldn't find a single flaw—except, perhaps, that school in the Wirral. Surely a spy ring couldn't run as elaborate a show as that right in the heart of England, and get away with it? The two main regular agencies—M.I.5 and 6—were being pilloried in the Press at the moment as inefficient and complacent—but could they possibly be as dumb as that? And the students themselves? Damn it all, with the best will in the world I had nearly blown the place twice myself. What were the other students, anyhow? All starry-eyes like myself—or was I the only mug who thought he was working for the British?

No—that school was genuine. I remembered once seeing a discreet police guard put on it when some high-up came down from London to lecture. But couldn't that have been rigged for some devious purpose of their own? Phoney uniforms——?

That was the whole pattern of it. Every time I thought I detected some slight inconsistency I found myself putting up counter theories to refute it. But that one persisted—and in the end I took it up with Carter—springing it on him one morning while he was still only half awake.

'The school, Carter——?' I began, but he didn't even let me finish.

'A kindergarten with a failure rate of eighty per cent—of which I should imagine you were one,' he said without hesitation. 'What about it?'

'You're asking me to believe that a set-up that size could be run in England without—er—our people—getting wind of it?'

'I'm not asking you to believe anything. I've shot the lot to you now. How much you accept, or reject, is up to you.'

'I reject that anyhow. M.I.5 would have been bound to uncover it sooner or later.'

'M.I.5 run it, you bloody fool,' he said drily. 'They took it over from SIS after the war.'

'SIS?'

'God—you don't know an awful lot, do you? Secret Intelligence Services—back in the days when Five, Six, Admiralty, Foreign Office, S.O.E., Special Branch—the lot—were centralized. Any one of those agencies can nominate a promising recruit to it for *ab initio* training. I imagine Gaffney would have put you in there as a possible for M.I.6—Far East—then picked you up later after you failed to make the grade.'

'Nobody ever told me I'd failed to make the grade,' I snapped.

He chuckled. 'They never do. Shake hands, pat on the back—"don't call us—we'll call you." Isn't that what happened?'

And it was, I reflected sadly.

'Was Gaffney M.I.6?' I asked.

'Was? Probably still is—and likely to stay that way after the balls-up you've made of things. M.I.6 ultimately control everything outside the British Isles. You know that office of his in Portman Square?'

'Yes——?'

'You're a liar. He never had an office in Portman Square. Where *does* the old bastard work from nowadays?'

'Get stuffed,' I snarled.

He chuckled again. 'That's better. Actually it used to be from a building near Waterloo Station—but I bet he never called *you* there. That's genuine M.I.6 country.' He climbed out of his bunk and started to shave. 'I'm willing to bet that you always saw him in some hole-in-the-corner bang in the middle of town—always at night—and that the one thing that you were really trained well in was the art of throwing a tail—and that you never called him except at prearranged times—on an ex-directory number. Right?'

I caught his eyes on me in the mirror. Of course he was right—and he knew it.

'Poor bloody Wainwright,' he said. 'You don't know whether you're on your head or your arse, do you? And I'm sorry. Believe me, *I'm sorry*. I'm not trying to take the mick out of you. I'm trying to make things easier for both of us, but what more can I do? I've told you everything now. If you don't trust me, I can't make you.'

'You've given me nothing I could check.'

'You could check on every single thing I've told you—by radio. But who would you check it *with*?' He turned and looked at me. 'You might have a telegraphic code address —but I bet it would only be to one of the four men I've named. What good would that be—if what I've told you is the truth? If they are still in circulation and you asked for fresh orders, you'd merely have your old ones confirmed. To hand me over to the Chinese. Where *am* I to be handed over, by the way?'

'Vladivostok,' I said obstinately. 'To the Russians.'

'Screw that. We both know it's not true—or if those really are your orders, you'll have them changed long before we reach there.' Again he was right. He turned back to the mirror and carried on shaving in silence. I sat chewing my nails for a long time, then I said, 'There's one way out of this, Carter.'

'I know,' he answered. 'Let's see if we're thinking along the same lines.'

'Hong Kong's the next stop,' I said. 'I go to the police there and make a clean breast of everything.'

He shrugged. 'Given the choice, I'd prefer that to being handed over to the Chinese—but have you considered all the implications?' He looked at me sharply, and saw that I hadn't.

'I'll give them to you,' he went on. 'All that will concern the Hong Kong police is the fact that I am an escaped convict—a very important one—and I'll be extradited by air to England and shoved straight back into gaol to finish my thirty years—in a *real* top-security nick this time. That puts paid to my usefulness to our people, because I'm pretty certain the Russians would then abandon any idea of an exchange.'

'You'll have to take your chance on that,' I told him. 'Somehow I can't see "our people" leaving you inside indefinitely.'

'I wouldn't bank on it. People in our line of business are pragmatists—on both sides. If you're unlucky enough to be caught you're expected to take what's coming. We know that when we take the job on.'

'Well, anyhow, that way your head stays on your shoulders —and not on top of one of Chairman Mao's flagpoles,' I said.

149

'There's not much in it either way really,' he said quietly as he wiped his razor. 'The thought of thirty years in prison makes my flesh crawl. That's something you'll discover for yourself, although I shouldn't imagine you'd get more than five.'

'Why me?' I said, startled.

'You're not deluding yourself that you'd get away with anything, are you?' he asked. 'You'd be for it either way. If I'm telling lies and Gaffney and Company *are* on the British side they'd disown you, and your story would be put down as fantastic guff. They'd have to.'

'But if, on the other hand, you're telling the truth my information would unmask them,' I said hopefully. ' "Our people" would owe me something for that, at least.'

'Don't count on it. You're dealing with some pretty experienced men. They would probably involve you up to the neck in it, if only to discredit your evidence in the eyes of the jury—and you'd be made to look like a willing cooperator who had got cold feet and spilt the beans at the last minute to save his hide.'

'Queen's evidence——' I began.

'Doesn't apply in two cases—murder and treason.' He turned and grinned at me. 'Didn't you get any civil law at the Wirral? I did.'

'What was the lecturer's name?' I shot at him.

'Aileen Fernberry,' he said without a moment's pause. 'Middle-aged woman with a gorgeous figure—viewed from astern—but with a face like the back of a bus and a pronounced impediment in her speech which ruled her out for court work. And if you're still trying to test whether I was there—law lectures were held in the small lecture-room upstairs in the stable block—north side.'

I gave in. 'And still are,' I sighed.

'Oh, yes, I was there all right,' he said. 'That's where it all started. Only I made the grade and went on.'

'Where?'

'To use your own words—get stuffed. As I said—the Wirral was a kindergarten. There's a Middle School above that—and then a university. I'm not surprised that you've never heard of either.' He grinned again. 'No offence meant—but I'm not giving away anything that I don't have to. What I'd be likely to say if the Chinese ever did get to work on me seriously is another matter. That's mainly why I'd like to avoid being handed to them.'

'You won't be,' I said. 'Even if I have to throw the whole thing into the lap of the police.'

'Well, thank you for that, at least,' he said quietly. 'May I ask you one final question? Don't answer if you've got any lingering doubts left whatsoever. It's just this. They must have given you *some* reason for handing me over. What was it?'

'In exchange for Winterton,' I said.

He stared at me open-mouthed. 'For God's sake!' he exploded. 'Winterton's *dead!*' He died before I left Amoy—and what's more our people know it. I reported it myself —*and got an acknowledgment.*'

'Then why wasn't it announced? That would be news,' I said.

'I know perfectly well why it wasn't announced. The Chinese hushed it up. Since I was one of the very few there at the time who knew Winterton's real identity I'd have been number one suspect if the news had been published, and my position was already pretty rocky. But that doesn't alter the fact that our *Intelligence* knew.'

So this was another clincher. The final one. If this were true then everything else he had told me was stripped of the last vestige of doubt. Even a fool like me would have questioned the reason for a straight handover. There had to be an exchange to make it valid.

He was reading my thoughts. I don't suppose it was a very difficult task. They must have been written plainly in my face.

'So you see,' he said. 'Even if you're still gagging at the thought of Gaffney being a double agent—even if he's as clean as the driven snow—he *knows* Winterton is dead—everybody in M.I.6 Far East knows it—and yet he sends you—does that make sense?'

'It *mightn't* have got back,' I said feebly. 'You said yourself that other reports had missed—the one naming them.'

'This one didn't miss. I told you—I got an acknowledgment. The other was different—I was on the run—and so were my last two couriers. They may have been scuppered before crossing.' He lit a cigarette and gave me one and sat drawing smoke down deep into his lungs, considering.

'Wainwright,' he said at last, 'you're probably still not entirely satisfied that I'm on the level. I don't blame you in the slightest for that. If I could prove to you that Winterton did in fact die on that—wait a minute—yes—the twenty-second of April last year—and that M.I.6 were made aware of it within a matter of days—would that satisfy you?'

'Completely,' I said. 'But how in the hell *can* you prove it?'

'Coded radio to M.I.6.'

'London?'

'Hong Kong. I'd need the books for London. Hong Kong I can do from memory with a sheet of paper, a pencil and an hour's quietness.'

I thought for a moment. 'All right—and if you did that —and the answer came back confirming it? What then?'

'Isn't that rather up to you? I should imagine that you then should let me report my exact whereabouts and ask for orders. But the main thing is to let them know where I am.'

I tried to pick holes in this, mulling over it for a long time and then asking questions. I asked them aloud, but I was really interrogating myself more than him.

'So they know where you are—and you ask for disposal orders for yourself? What would they be likely to do? What *could* they do?'

'I think we could safely leave that to them,' he answered. 'My guess is that we would be intercepted somewhere at sea, and I'd be taken off.'

I thought again. This was a pretty big order. To pick up one ship in the vast expanse of ocean we had ahead of us before Hong Kong. Once again he seemed to guess my thoughts.

'They'd undoubtedly call the Navy in,' he said. 'There's nothing difficult about getting a fix on a ship once we've reported our last noon position, course and speed.'

'Maybe not,' I said. 'But an operation as big as that would be bound to leak.'

'You can leave that to them, too. Clamping a security gag on the Navy at sea is a vastly different thing from trying to muzzle the police and Press in a port like Hong Kong.'

That was valid, of course. I nodded. 'All right. But there's just one thing more. The address? I take it you wouldn't be sending it to "M.I.6, Hong Kong"?'

'Naturally not. The telegraphic address is "Lok Sam, Kowloon".'

And there I put my heels in. 'I'm sorry,' I said firmly. 'But I've got to be absolutely certain. As far as I know "Lok

Sam" could just as easily be "Ivan Ivanovich"—and the warship that intercepts us, a Russian one.'

'In other words you still don't believe me?' he said.

'I want to—but as I said, this has got to be one hundred per cent.'

'So what do you suggest?'

'You'll have to break procedure and address it *enclair*.'

He shook his head. 'Not a hope in hell. The Wireless and Cable Company would bounce it straight back at us— "Addressee Unknown—please clarify"—or at best it would be sent round to the Hong Kong Police Special Branch, and that's something we have to avoid, isn't it?'

'We'll just have to take the chance.'

'But there *isn't* a chance, Wainwright,' he said patiently. 'Even supposing it did reach them, they wouldn't act on it. And could you blame them? Every bona fide agent has his own telegraphic address. It's part of his identification. A signal to "Lok Sam" could only originate from me. If I sent it to M.I.6 they would assume that somebody had got hold of my code and had broken it—or that I was sending it under duress, and was giving them the tip by not using the code address. See what I mean?'

I did, unfortunately. I tried again: 'Then direct to the Governor. Surely to God *he* knows the M.I.6 people.'

'I'm bloody certain he doesn't. He wouldn't *want* to know. It's not a case of trust, or lack of it—it's just that M.I.6 are not answerable to him, and the less he knows about them the less he is likely to be embarrassed if they act outside the strict letter of the law—as they do most of the time. Do they still tell that story at the Wirral about George the Fifth and Pecksniff?'

I nodded. It was a venerable chestnut told during the security lectures—probably apocryphal, although they swore it was true. George the Fifth is alleged to have asked the titular head of his Secret Service during World War One, 'Who is the *real* head of the Secret Service, Pecksniff?'

'Sir, I cannot tell you,' answered Pecksniff.

'What if I said, "off with your head," Pecksniff?'

'Then, Sir,' answered Pecksniff, 'my head would roll, but my lips would still be sealed.'

It illustrated Carter's point perfectly. The Governor was out—and that being so, who the hell else was there to go to? But I still tried desperately.

153

'But surely the Governor would have to be brought into it if the Navy was to participate?' I said.

'Not of necessity,' he answered. 'M.I.6 deals directly with London. The Navy would get their orders from the Admiralty.'

He had stopped every runway. There was no other argument I could put up. I rose from the settee.

'Make out your signal,' I told him.

'Thanks,' he said quietly. 'You've made the right decision —but I know what sort of load you're carrying at this moment—and I can sympathize. May I offer one last word of advice?'

'What's that?'

'For her own sake, don't take Miss Malcolm into your confidence about any of this.'

'So you know who she is?'

'The Mesterspringer's daughter?' he said. 'Oh yes—I know her, or rather of her.'

'Why "her own sake"?'

'For the simple reason that she *is* the Meisterspringer's daughter, and as such, unreliable. He works for whoever pays him. At present he's working for the Chinese. His next job could be for the Russians—or conceivably even for us. When this is over you're going to be debriefed by our people. That means anything up to a couple of months' screening and intensive interrogation. The sort of thing I was put through when I went from China to Russia. They'll have everything out of you—*everything*. At the same time they'll be doing it to her. If I succeed in getting back into Russia, and they had reason to believe that she or her father knew I was a British agent I can see it being a very long time indeed before they were back in circulation.'

'That could go for me as well,' I said, startled again.

'It could indeed—but at least you'll have a lot working for you. I can speak for you—I couldn't for them. I believe in your good faith—I tested it by the offer of a heavy bribe and an easy way out, but you stood firm. You only co-operated when I convinced you of my bona fides. All those are points in your favour. But it still isn't going to be easy for you. At the present moment only you and I on this ship know where I really stand. Don't make it harder for either of us by letting it out to anybody else.'

'I see what you mean,' I said. 'But there's a wild joker
154

aboard. Wetten. Where does he stand—and how much does he know?'

'I wish I could answer that,' he said thoughtfully. 'On the face of it I should say that he was planted by the Russians when they realized I had been hijacked. It would have been a routine measure. There are half a dozen skippers who do this sort of thing. They would probably have whipped a man on to every one of them that happened to be in a European port at the time. Their orders would be to report it by radio or to get word ashore at some port as soon as they were certain I was aboard—but Kjaer, the crafty bastard, has stymied this one with his master-switch.'

'If that were so, wouldn't Wetten have made some approach to you?' I asked.

'He hasn't, although I've given him every opportunity of doing so. That makes me wonder. He may either be put on by the Chinese to keep tabs on you—that's just the sort of thing they might very well do—or even be completely in the clear.'

'You can scrub that one,' I told him. 'That bump on his bean was put there by me. He followed me from this ship the night I first came to see Kjaer. I thought I'd got rid of him, but the police put him back aboard at the last minute.'

'That settles it then. He's not in the clear—but we don't know who he's working for. We'll just have to play it by ear —but I'll want to be standing over him when he's transmitting in case he whips a quick one in to somebody else. Better still, I'd prefer to be on the key myself.'

We went along to breakfast then. We were late and only Sonia was there. She looked altogether lovely—fresh, healthy, tanned—and she was wearing a simple blue cotton frock, one of the half dozen she must have brought aboard rolled under her peajacket. She looked up at us and smiled. She and I had made peace again after our last fight and I would have given a lot to have gone out on the deck with her and along to our place at the stern, and to have talked this over with her. She had always been so sane—and her decisions had all along been right. I think I would have done just that had it not been for Carter's warning—but I saw the force of his reasoning and fought the temptation down, knowing that it was going to place a further strain on me. However much we had quarrelled up to now we had at least trusted each other.

Usually after breakfast we walked a statutory twelve complete circuits of the ship for exercise, but this morning I was glad when she said she had some washing to do, and went off and left us. Carter took a sheaf of stationery from the saloon rack, nodded curtly to me and went back to the cabin. I sat out on deck for the next couple of hours until he came and collected me, and I went back with him. He handed me a sheet of paper.

'Lok Sam, Kowloon, H.K :' I read. 'Following cotton staple quotations received ex Manchester exchange. Advise earliest how compare local prices.' Then followed blocks of letters and figures. It was obviously a code, but just the type of thing that trading companies work out between themselves. I had seen a lot of this work myself at the bank, and I knew that in the ordinary way it would excite no suspicion. I looked at him and nodded. He handed me a second sheet: it was the translation.

'G 327 aboard *Nurma*. Co-operation escort Wainwright secured provident upon answer one question, namely present condition with significant dates Winterton. Further signal upon receipt. Axiom.'

He said, 'I'll take you through it if you wish,' and pointed to a pile of other sheets which had been ruled out into squared grids, with letters along the horizontals and figures down the verticals. 'It's a bit complicated, but try and bear with me. Right—ten sheets, each ruled into four verticals and ten horizontals—forty squares per sheet. Four hundred basic words plus two proper names, yours and the ship's, which have been anagramized—I'll show you that later. Now, if we take the sheet number——'

But what the hell was the use? I tried to follow, and fair play to him he was very patient, but he lost me. It had been the same at the school. I was just no good at ciphers. He realized it and his temper frayed in the end.

'Wainwright, for Christ's sake try and concentrate, will you? It's no good just looking intelligent and nodding. It's only a simple slidex after all,' he said.

'I'll take your word for it,' I mumbled ruefully.

'Up to you,' he shrugged. 'You're not cut out for this work, are you? Are you still wondering why you were dropped at the Wirral?'

'No, and I don't bloody well care either,' I snapped. 'It's not the work that gets me down. It's the bastards one has
156

to mix with. Give me the message. I'll go and fix it with Kjaer.'

'I've got to be there when it goes out,' he insisted.

'You don't need to be,' I told him. 'I'll be standing over Wetten and I'll karate the son of a bitch if he departs from that by one letter. There's nothing wrong with my Morse even if my ciphering is lousy.'

'Well, just remember that it's your neck as well as mine if things go wrong,' he answered, and gave me the coded sheet.

I went up to the bridge. Kjaer was having a pre-lunch nap in a deck-chair. I shook him gently and handed him the sheet. He cocked an irritable eye at it.

'What's this?' he asked.

'A message. I'd like it sent out—just like that,' I said.

'Just like that, eh?' He passed the sheet back to me. 'Fok off, Mr Smith,' he said, and closed his eyes again.

## Chapter 17

I began softly and reasonably, but he wouldn't budge. Then I went over to money—raising my own bids to the limit of what I was carrying and even above that. But he just wasn't having any. Then I started to rave.

'You bloody, stupid, square-headed bastard,' I swore. 'What possible difference could it make to you? It's purely to let our people in Hong Kong know we're aboard—so they can make arrangements to get us off.'

'Arrangements should have been made already, mister,' he said mildly. 'If they haven't been, then I make my own —bloody quick—but I ain't telling anybody beforehand that you're aboard. No goddam fear. No messages, Mr Smith.'

'Look——'

'I looked plenty. I tell you *no*. You think this the first bloody time I run blackbirds?'

I made the mistake then of grabbing a handful of his shirt and hauling him to his feet out of the deck-chair. His belly looked round and flabby but when he butted me with it I thought I'd been hit with a bag of concrete. I skittered backwards across the deck and finished hard up against the rail.

'You do that again, Mr Smith,' he said very quietly, 'and I'll have you in irons and down the bloddy bilges quicker than a Hamburg whore can get her drawers off on payday.'

And I knew he meant exactly that. Sadly I went back to Carter. It was a measure of the man that he neither blew his top nor looked dismayed. He just sat thinking for some minutes, rubbing his chin and gazing into the distance.

'I can't altogether blame him,' he said at last. 'If the news leaked and he were caught running illegal passengers he could be barred the port, have a thumping fine smacked across him and be damned lucky not to have the ship seized into the bargain.'

'How the hell could the news leak, if the signal is to who you say it is?' I demanded.

'It wouldn't leak, but he's not to know that. The bloke's only taking sensible precautions. I wonder what his own arrangements for getting people ashore are—if he doesn't like what's been laid on?'

'Ask the son of a bitch,' I suggested.

'I don't suppose for one moment he'd tell me. Pity. No—we'll have to try it another way. That signal's got to go out.'

'All right—you tell me another way. He's got a master-switch in his cabin.'

'Where?' he asked quickly.

'Forget it. It's in a locker with a heavy steel door—in fact I think it's also the ship's safe—and he carries the key on him.'

'So that rules out an attempt while he's in at dinner or up on the bridge. Oh, well—only one thing for it.'

'What?'

'We'll have to get into his cabin when he's asleep—slug him—engage the switch and go along to the radio shack and send it ourselves.'

I stared at him. 'You must be joking,' I said.

'Can you think of anything better?'

'I can't think of anything at all—but I know that's out. A. His cabin is up on the bridge and there's always an officer on watch and a quartermaster at the wheel. B. The radio shack is just abaft the wheelhouse and they could hear the key going. Damn it all, you can hear it down here when Wetten is sending.'

'Yes, Wetten does send from time to time,' he said thoughtfully.

'You can forget that, too,' I told him. 'The skipper or the third mate is always with him when he does.'

But he still reconnoitred the position—for days—and only gave up when he was convinced of the complete hopelessness of it, by which time we were across the Indian Ocean, through the Malacca Straits and standing up towards the China coast—with only two days to go before reaching Hong Kong. Then he asked me for my gun.

I said, 'Not bloody likely. What do you want it for?'

'When we get in,' he said. 'He's bound to put us down below until after the port police, medical and customs have been aboard and given him clearance. Right?'

'I should imagine so.'

'After that I should think it would be a foregone conclusion that we would be going ashore at night. You agree?'

I nodded.

'All right,' he went on. 'Well, try and picture it. We will either be anchored out in the stream, waiting for a berth—or we'll be alongside. In the first instance whoever is coming for us would be in a launch—two or three men. They wouldn't risk a big party because it would be conspicuous. It would be unnecessary, anyhow, as you're on their side. Agreed?'

'The probable circumstances, yes,' I said. 'But what do you think you could do about it? Start a gun battle in the middle of the harbour?'

'No, but I'd certainly make a run for it when we got near the shore—and a gun would give me a better chance.'

'Nothing doing,' I said flatly. 'I'll keep the gun—*and* the responsibility of using it, or not, as I think.'

He said, 'Sorry, Wainwright—but I don't think you'd have the resolution.'

'Go on being sorry,' I told him. 'That's the way it's going to be.'

'So after all, you really do intend handing me over tamely if all else fails?' He shook his head slowly. 'You're a funny bloke, Wainwright. I once called you yellow. I don't think you are really, but you're incapable of making up your mind—of setting yourself a course and following it. You let circumstances take control and just drift with the stream —hoping to God something will turn up to get you out of the mulligatawny.'

And he wasn't so far wrong at that. But this time I *had* got some sort of idea.

'I don't intend handing you over,' I said. 'I told you that. If the worst comes to the worst, I'll call the police in.'

'You may not have the chance. You'll be in the same boat —literally.'

'Sure—but as you said yourself, unsuspected. Anyhow we may not be in a boat. We may go down the gangway on to the wharf. Whichever way it is there'll be police all over the place—patrol launches on the harbour—armed police on the docks. There always are. They won't be able to get too rough in the early stages. You've been drawing pictures—lots of them. Let me draw just one. Wherever they take us, it has to be by car. Right? Very well—that's the limit. We don't get into any cars. If you haven't had a chance to make a break for it I'll start shooting if necessary. *But that decision has to be mine.* I've got more than your hide to think of.'

'The girl?' he said. 'That's what I'm afraid of.'

'I haven't gone soft on her, if that's what you mean.'

'It wouldn't pay you to. She's tougher than her old man, and he's nobody's tenderhearted chicken, the bastard.' He shook his head. 'No, that wasn't what I was thinking of. The thing that worries me is that you are still instinctively thinking of her as an ally. She's *not*. She's on *that* side.'

'How do you know? She may be a starry-eye, like me.'

'Starry-eye my rump,' he snorted. 'What's *she* got to be starry-eyed about—except the cheque at the end of it? Listen, Wainwright—if she saw that cheque walking away from her she'd pull a gun—*and* use it—on you or anybody else who got in the way. She's got a gun, you know. I saw the shape of it in the hip pocket of her slacks when she was getting her stuff out of here. I wish I'd jumped her for it. It'd be about the only thing I *would* jump her for. I like mine a bit exclusive.'

'Cut that out, you dirty-mouthed bastard,' I said.

'You do give yourself away, don't you?' he said calmly. 'I don't make cracks like that normally. But it proves my point. I'm not accusing you of going soft on her, as you put it, but I *am* afraid that in an emergency you might act the gentleman at the wrong moment and get both our blocks knocked off.'

'You *wouldn't* act the gentleman under any circumstances I take it?'

'Not likely. I was cured of that for all time in 'fifty-five. I went to the assistance of a lovely young White Russian
160

nun on the Bund in Shanghai. She was being roughed up by a bunch of the younger Comrades. She was very grateful —until I got her back to the convent door.'

'What happened then?' I asked, interested in spite of myself.

'She side-swiped me and then nearly debollicked me with a bloody great cleaver she was carrying under her robes—and got away with my despatch case. The bitch had been working for Chiang Kai-shek for years.' He grinned impishly, and for a moment I almost stopped disliking him.

'Don't worry about Sonia,' I assured him. 'Actually she was only sent along because her father thought there was a chance of her being snatched in London.'

'By whom?' he asked.

'The Russians.'

He shook his head over that. 'That's not the impression I had,' he said. 'That girl works for Poppa.'

'Unwillingly. I told you—don't worry. She'll do as I say —so long as she doesn't think her father is being put in any danger.' But I could see that he was more uneasy over the girl than over any other aspect of the business. He kept coming back to it all through that last day. He wanted me to persuade Kjaer to put her down below and take her on to Amoy, but I turned that down flatly.

And then the whole thing was taken out of our hands.

We sat over dinner very late that last night—all of us jumpy, even Kjaer. Carter caught my eye several times and signalled me to come out on deck, but in the saloon I was safe from further argument so I acted dumb and pretended not to understand. But then the mate, whose watch it was, blew down the bridge speaking-tube urgently. Kjaer listened, and I saw dawning panic in his face. He reached the door in two bounds and shot up the bridge ladder. We followed him out.

It was a perfect night. There was no moon, but the stars gave a lot of light and the sea was like a mill pond. We saw the flashing light immediately. It was ahead and slightly to port of us. Carter and I started to read aloud, confusing each other, so I moved to one side out of earshot. They were giving the 'I say again' flash, which meant that they had completed their first transmission and were going to repeat.

'Query name and registration,' I read. Overhead on the wing of the bridge I could hear Kjaer and the mate jabbering excitedly in Finnish. Carter raced past me and yelled up to them, 'Ask who they are. Stall! For Christ's sake, stall!' and Kjaer took time out from arguing to tell him to mind his own goddam business, but told the third mate to do that nevertheless. The bridge Morse lamp flickered the 'Declare identity' signal but before we had finished they were flashing us to heave to. I strained my eyes into the darkness, but it was impossible to make out the other ship. She was just a blacker bulk against the loom of the coast. Carter went up the bridge ladder two at a time, and I followed close behind him.

'Don't heave to,' he shouted, and that seemed to accord with Kjaer's own view, although he told us both profanely to get the hell off his bridge. He blew down the engine-room tube and bellowed in the ship's patois to 'Hurry up like bloddy hell—*Schnell! Schnell! Schnell!*' and I felt the steady throb of the engines increasing. Then the other ship stopped flashing and there was a stab of flame that lit the water between us for a split second. I started to count instinctively, but only got to three before the boom reached us, and there was a hell of a splash dead ahead of us. And that decided Kjaer. I don't suppose one could blame him. After all, he was part owner of his ship. I heard the telegraph sound faintly down below, and the engines ceased abruptly and then went astern in a crash stop that had us all nearly off our feet.

I felt my sleeve being tugged. 'Listen, mister,' he implored tearfully. 'I give you your money back—the lot—only you got to say you're stowaways. You say you sneaked aboard in the Canal, eh?'

'If you'd let me send that signal this mightn't have happened,' I told him with malice aforethought. 'Who do you think these people are?'

'Who the hell could they be, but the Navy or maybe the police?' he asked dolefully. 'What about it, mister? It don't make any difference to you now. You say that—all of you. I'm in plenty of trouble already.'

'Maybe it's only a routine check,' I said hopefully. 'In that case they won't search you. If we're down below——'

But he shook his head. 'No good. They flash our name first and tell us to confirm. They know who we are.'

Carter said, 'How could they know unless you'd reported your position to them first? It's your own fault, Kjaer. Better do as we say. Put us down below and try and bluff it out.'

'I don't report to nobody,' Kjaer raved. 'That's why I don't let you send anything out. I was going to say our radio had packed in because we don't have a proper Sparks aboard. My way *nobody* would have known until we arrived there. I was going to put you ashore nice and quiet at night and there wouldn't have been no trouble. Mister—you've got to help me—you've got to. I played straight with you.'

'Fifty-fifty,' Carter said. 'You put us down below. If it's only a routine check and you don't get searched, fine—nothing's altered. If they do know we're aboard and we get hauled out, we'll say we're stowaways. How's that?'

'Lousy,' Kjaer snapped. 'They'd know bloddy well that four people couldn't stow away from the Canal to Hong Kong without me knowing they're aboard. They'll want to know why I don't report it to the officer as soon as he comes up the bloddy gangway. No—no good—I got to report you as illegal passengers right away—and no hiding.'

'In which case I'll sell you downriver, you bastard,' Carter said, and Kjaer moaned sorrowfully. We could hear the engines of the other ship as they closed the distance between us.

'What about it, Kjaer?' I asked. 'You've got a chance our way—and you get paid—in full.'

I was beginning to feel sorry for him. A fat man in dire trouble is always pitiful. He said, 'God forgive you. If I lose my ship and my ticket, *I* don't. I'll bloddy kill you. The lot.' And he told the third mate to get us below—all four of us, because Wetten was just as slimy a son of a bitch as the rest. I grabbed a few things from the cabin and chucked a few others over the side and ran along to collect Sonia, but there was no need, because she had heard everything and was waiting for us at the bottom of the bridge ladder—once more bulky under her peajacket—and probably the calmest of any of us. The girl was a wonder, and I found myself warming to her afresh.

The three of us scurried down into the engine-room and along the shaft tunnel into the hole, but there was some delay about putting the steel plate back in place because they couldn't find Wetten at first—but eventually the mate brought him down, and his right eye was swelling badly and there was a trickle of blood coming from his nose. The mate said murderously: 'Beat the damn hell out of the bastard. We catch him trying to signal with a torch from the stern.'

They slammed the plate back in position. Carter looked at Wetten. The German, though battered, was not nervous. He didn't need to be. He shrugged and sat down on the deck with his back to the bulkhead. Carter kicked him heavily in the ribs. I saw no use in this and disliked it intensely on Sonia's behalf. I said, 'Cut it out, Carter. What good will that do?' He didn't appear to hear me.

He said to Wetten: 'Do you want to live?'

Wetten was gasping and retching, but he managed to spit in the general direction of Carter. I got in between them, and stopped the second kick with my own leg. It made me angry and I swung at Carter, but he saw it coming and dodged.

Sonia said coolly: 'If you really want to find out anything from this man, I suggest you stop crowding each other. What are you trying to establish, Mr Carter?'

'Just who these people are,' he answered.

'Is that going to make any difference at this moment?' she asked.

'It could—a little,' said Carter. 'Ask sonny-boy here to stop interfering, will you?'

'Sit down, Carter,' I told him. 'We'll know soon enough. If it's just a routine check by the Navy or police, we'll be under way again before long. If it's not, we're going to be hauled out of here. What's the use of kicking the daylights out of this bloody rat in the meantime?'

'Thank you, Mr Smith,' said Wetten. His English was fluent but accented. 'If it makes you happier, Carter, it's a Russian destroyer—down from Vladivostok.'

'You're a liar,' said Carter.

'All right—I'm a liar,' he answered. 'Is kicking my ribs going to make me truthful?'

'How did they know where to pick us up?' Carter asked quickly, and Wetten looked tired.

'Oh, for God's sake, I've been in touch with them for the last three days.'

'How?' I demanded.

'I bypassed that damn switch when I fixed the television aerial,' he said with a certain expert's pride. 'But I had to cut it a bit fine. I couldn't transmit direct to anybody that mattered until we came into range.'

164

'They'd have heard you from the bridge,' I challenged, but he shook his head and smiled.

'Remote key from down astern, Mr Smith,' he said. 'Now suppose we all relax? Mr Carter goes where he wants to go—so do I. Mr Smith and the lady stay on board. What trouble you're in with your own people is your own affair.' He sighed. 'Bloody awful life, isn't it?'

Carter spoke to him in rapid Russian—far too rapid for me. Wetten answered him in the same language. I looked a question at Sonia, but she was too interested in what the others were saying. I felt out in the cold. I butted in with an inconsequential question in English.

'If you were in radio touch with them over the last three days, why were you signalling with a torch just now?'

He smiled at me again. 'Just to save a little time,' he said. 'I told them where we'd be. I could only rig the bypass when the third mate was out of the cabin.'

No joy. I had been vaguely hoping that he was still lying and that the Navy was here, but this fitted. It even seemed to satisfy Carter. He took a deep breath and looked relieved. So now I was back in my old familiar role of Joe Soap. The experts had taken over again. I tried to avoid Sonia's eye, but I needn't have bothered. Once more the three of them were talking in Russian. All Migs together—Old Home Week —working for different bosses maybe, but still brothers and sisters under the skin.

Then we heard the bolts being unscrewed the other side. I tried, pathetically, to make a last gesture. I said, 'Whatever the outcome of this may be, gentlemen, I trust that Miss Malcolm will be kept out of it. She's not here of her own free will.'

The plate was being lowered. Carter and Wetten were standing watching it, their backs to us. Sonia reached out and took my hand and squeezed it. I thought for a moment that it was a friendly little gesture, just a small acknowledgment of the fact that I *had* tried. She leaned towards me and I, like a fool, thought she was going to kiss me, but her lips went to my ear rather than my cheek, and she whispered, 'Watch it. Both these bastards are lying like hell.'

Then the plate came down with a crash, and Carter planted a haymaker under Wetten's jaw that dropped him like a sack of wet sand.

## Chapter 18

Two of them pushed in—short, chunky Cantonese in sloppy olive green uniforms festooned with bandoliers, and carrying burp guns. Outside I could see the shaft tunnel was crowded with others, and all were yelling. Whoever says the Chinese are a silent, inscrutable race has never been further east than Southend Pier. They hauled Carter, then me, through the hole into the shaft. I turned, trying to make way for Sonia so that they would have no reason to start manhandling her, but all I got for my pains was a smack across the back with a gun that knocked the wind out of me. They raced us along the shaft into the engine-room and up the steel ladders to the gratings, then up again and out on to the deck. Alongside I could see a big motor junk, the low waist crowded with more Chinese troops. Kjaer was standing by the rail looking sick and miserable. I thought at first that it was out of sympathy for us, but his first words disabused me of that.

He said: 'I done my part of it, Mr Smith. I suppose you couldn't see your way clear to slip me what you owe me?'

'Ask your pals to loose my arms,' I said unfairly, 'and I might be able to do something about it.'

They swung me over the rail. It was a good twelve-foot drop to her deck and I landed in a heap, with Carter on top of me, then, as we were trying to sort ourselves out, Wetten was added to the pile. At least we made a carpet which broke Sonia's fall. The junk's powerful diesel was chugging in neutral. It roared on a louder note and they cast off, and we headed away into the darkness. I watched the deck lights of the *Nurma* receding, and felt very lonely indeed. Then we were pulled to our feet and hustled along towards the junk's high poop.

There was a large cabin under it, furnished with a table, a chair and an oleograph of Mao Tse Tung, and nothing else. A man sat at the table. He looked up as we were shoved in front of him. They don't wear anything so undemocratic as badges of rank in their army, and he was dressed like the others, even to the burp gun lying on the table in front of him, but he was obviously an officer. He grunted something to our escort and they dived on us each in turn and searched us—first me, then Carter, then Wetten, who had now come round. They got my gun, of course, and the pack of money and my passport. Carter and Wetten didn't yield much except cigarettes and matches. The officer studied the passport intently, but he was bluffing, because he opened it at the back page and solemnly read forward to the beginning, but of course the photograph pinned it on to me. He flicked through the money, but plainly that was beyond him and he told one of the escort, in Cantonese, to fetch Hung Tai, who turned out to be an unpleasant youth with Red Guard patches on the sleeves of his tunic and a lot of food stains down the front of it. He counted the money by the numerals but clearly had no idea of the actual value of it, because he told the officer that it amounted to over a million Hong Kong dollars. Then he grinned and spat right in my face and called me a capitalist-imperialist something in excellent Hong Kong pidgin. The officer looked at us each in turn and said inquiringly, 'Kahtah?' The youth identified me from the passport as 'Win-li', which shifted things to the other two. He kicked first Carter and then Wetten hard and repeated, 'Kahtah? Which piecee-one Kahtah? Hully—chop-chop—dirty bastahd.'

Wetten pointed to himself and said: 'Ganz,' and mimed tapping a morse key. 'Buzz—buzz-buzz—buzz-buzz-buzz.' That made him buddies with the youth immediately, because he pointed to himself and went into the buzzing routine and then shook hands with him. Wetten pointed to Carter and identified him and then shook hands with the officer, and everybody seemed delighted—except Carter and myself who promptly got another salivation from the youth. I was relieved though, because in the general exchange of pleasantries they forgot to frisk Sonia who, as a mere woman, was standing well to the rear of us. The officer then told the escort to put us down below—Carter, myself and the one he named as the shameless-concubine-who-battened-upon-the-blood-of-the-people. It's all one word in Cantonese. They rushed us out and along the cluttered deck and down into a hold which smelt even worse than the bilges of the *Nurma*, and slid the hatch over us.

We sat in silent misery for quite a long time, then Carter said bitterly, 'If you two hadn't butted in I'd have kicked the truth out of Mister Bloody Wetten before they boarded us.'

'Satisfying, no doubt,' Sonia said icily. 'But what would it have achieved? They'd have got us out in the end.'

'Sir Bloody Lancelot here had a gun and a packet of spare rounds. They could only come in one at a time, and they couldn't fire round corners. We could have held out for quite a while. If it comes to that, you have a gun yourself, Miss Malcolm.'

'And I intend keeping it,' Sonia said.

'To save yourself from a fate worse than death?' sneered Carter. 'Don't flatter yourself. Sex is bourgeois decadence to these types. Give it to me and I can at least put it to some use.'

'Such as?' I asked, just for something to say.

'Drop a couple when they come for us,' he said. 'With luck we might get their sub-machine-guns. Better than just waiting for it without doing anything. Or do you feel more comfortable letting things drift?'

And the best I could put up against that was swearing—and even that wasn't as fluent as it might have been, because Sonia's presence cramped my style.

We each drew into ourselves after that. I tried desperately to sleep, but it was no use. This was the worst yet. Almost there, and shot down by that lousy little East German rat. Why the hell hadn't I thought of that possibility? Why hadn't Carter, for that matter? He'd been shooting his superior mouth off about his two-way radio in prison, hadn't he? I saved this one in case he started on me again.

The diesel chugged on interminably. I tried to speculate on the course we were taking. As far as I knew we had been about seventy or eighty miles to the south-west of Hong Kong when we were intercepted. The China coast would have been roughly twenty miles on our port beam in that case. This thing probably made about ten knots so, if we had been heading for the nearest point on the coast we should have been close inshore long ago. Then the edges of the hatch started to lighten with the dawn—much stronger on the starboard side and to the front of it than the others. That would appear to indicate that we were heading north and east still—on much the same course as the *Nurma* had been on already. I tried to recall the maps of this part of the coast. There was little of importance along here—just an occasional fishing village as far as I could remember. Canton was the nearest port of any size. Yes—quite obviously that was where we were making for. Canton, ninety miles up the Pearl River. It didn't cheer me in the slightest to think that to make the mouth of it we would, if they were disposed to take any short cuts, be in British territorial waters for a short period between Macao and Hong Kong. We never interfered with Chinese shipping unless it was behaving suspiciously.

More light came down into the hold as the day wore on. I was tortured with thirst and guessed that the others must be also. They say that misery loves company, but it didn't seem to apply in our case. We each sat as withdrawn from the others as the confines of the hold would allow. I stood up to ease my cramped limbs. The deckhead was quite low—in fact even on the keel itself I couldn't stand completely upright. To let a little more air into the place I risked lifting the hatch an inch or so. I looked out on to the deck. As so often happens after a very clear night in these latitudes, a heavy sea mist had clamped down and I could barely see the length of the junk. I could see, however, a twenty-millimetre Czech Oerlikon gun under a tarpaulin. That was evidently what they had fired the warning shot from. Christ—it wouldn't have made a dent on the plates of the *Nurma*. If only the windy old devil had clapped on speed earlier and made a run for it.

I looked aft towards the poop. A group of them were clustered round the helm. I could see the officer arguing with the youth Hung Tai. They seemed jittery and nervous. Looking forward I could see why. The fog was a solid wall in front of us and we were belting straight into it at speed. The youth, in the manner of his kind, East or West, seemed to know it all. The others, including the officer, obviously wanted to throttle down a bit. I couldn't hear exactly what they were saying for the simple reason that they were saying it all at once, but then the youth's voice rose above the others. 'Leave it to me. I know, you windy lot of bastards,' would be a reasonable paraphrase. Then he went on to say that he was guided by the sayings of Chairman Mao, and produced a little red book to prove it. That held the officer and most of the others for a time, but not the old boy at the helm. He looked like a Hakka to me. They are fishermen, and nobody's fools.

He said: 'My arse to Chairman Mao, and you, you snotty-nosed little Wanchai brothel bastard,' or words to that effect, and put the helm over and tugged at a rusty lever protruding from the deck. The throb of the diesel dropped, and her bows

169

paid off to port. There was a hell of a row then. The youth hauled a pistol out and shoved it in the old man's ribs. The old man clipped him hard, skittering him into the scuppers. I thought I detected veiled approval among the others. It certainly cheered me quite considerably. Then, as in the manner of those bewildering fogs, it lifted suddenly and dead ahead of us I saw the long, lean grey shape of a frigate. I even saw the white ensign fluttering in the stern. She was about a quarter of a mile off and moving very slowly at a tangent to us. Her signalling searchlight started to blink immediately. I made out dot-dot-dot-dot—dot—dot-dash —H-E-A- before the blasted fog clamped down again, blotting her out. Clearly it was the beginning of an order to heave-to.

The officer leapt for the lever and shoved it forward, and the beat of the diesel rose. My affection for the helmsman dimmed a little. If we'd kept on the original course at that speed we'd almost have collided with her.

But as I have said, the Hakka fishermen are no fools. When they are not fishing they are smuggling, pirating, and running prohibited immigrants from the mainland to Hong Kong, and they are quick thinkers. He knew that the frigate had seen us swing to the west so he held the helm over until he had completed the full turn and were running due east. Unless the Navy realized what we were doing, we would now be heading away from each other.

I felt movement beside me. Carter had come up and was looking towards the stern. He said: 'If only I had had the gun I might have been able to do something when they were all preoccupied then. Speak to this bloody woman, will you?'

'Why you?' I asked sourly. 'You haven't shown up so brilliantly so far.'

Behind us through the fog we heard the dull boom of a gun. There was no following whine so I guessed it was a blank. The helmsman looked astern and made a rude gesture with two fingers, which means the same in China as in Chelsea. The old rip seemed to be enjoying it—but he was a little too previous, because we hit something at that moment—and damned hard. It pulled us up dead and threw Carter and me into a heap at the bottom of the hold. The gang on the poop were raising merry hell, each trying to out-shriek the others. We pulled ourselves up to the look-out again. The helmsman had shoved the lever into reverse and the screw was churning like mad but we seemed to be held fast—then, looking ahead, I saw why. We had run hard aground and right in front of us was a sheer cliff—so close that I could see outcrops of scrub on its rocky face. Between us and it there didn't seem to be any water at all—just hard white sand. The gang on the poop were lookng at each other in comical dismay. From behind us came another boom.

The officer was the first to regain his wits. He yelled to the others and leapt the poop rail, running towards us. We dropped down into the bottom of the hold quickly. They threw the hatch back and half a dozen flat yellow faces were looking down at us. One of them dropped a bamboo ladder down. I looked at Carter. Was this a chance? But it wasn't. The officer fired a burst. It splintered the keel right alongside my feet. I stepped aside and gallantly indicated the ladder to Sonia. She went up, looking very angry indeed. I followed her—then came Carter. The officer stuck the gun in my belly and harangued me urgently. The youth translated into pidgin. He didn't need to. I understood perfectly. We were going over the side chop-chop and we were going to run like bloody hell with guns at our arses—and if we stopped running before we were told, the guns would go off.

We dropped on to the sand. Half the junk was out of the water but she didn't seem to have sustained much damage, and the bar was obviously tidal, and eventually they might be able to float her off without difficulty, but they were taking no chances with us in the meantime—and looking at it strictly from their point of view one could hardly blame them, because the fog was lifting rapidly now—not just clearing in patches—really lifting.

They hustled us across the sand—six of them and, to my sorrow, the youth was one of them—until we came right to the foot of the cliff. Close up it wasn't as sheer as it had appeared from further out, but sloped at a steep angle. They prodded and shoved at us until we had climbed about a hundred feet and the fog was a flat-topped blanket below us. We could see the frigate clearly. She was about half a mile offshore and halted, and they were swinging a boat out. Immediately below us the junk seemed almost afloat again as the tide was rising rapidly. I heard the officer grunting and gasping that if only that stupid old bastard would get her off and make his way up-coast he would lead the chase away

171

—and come back for us when the thrice-accursed capitalist-imperialist running-dogs had departed. I wondered what he was worrying about, because our people would never dream of making a landing on Chinese territory. Orders are rigid on the subject. This certainly wasn't Hong Kong island, nor any part of the British leased mainland that I recognized—and I knew most of it by sight.

They halted us in a clump of she-oak, and the officer unslung his binoculars and studied the frigate for some minutes. The boat they had put out was still hidden by the dispersing fog, but I caught a brief glimpse of it in a rift. It was proceeding cautiously towards the beach and the junk. The latter was now partially afloat again, its propeller churning sand and water into a porridge, and as we watched it slid a few feet seaward and backed off—but it was too late. The frigate's boat loomed up behind it and I saw a white-clad officer and half a dozen armed ratings swarm aboard. I was sweating and praying inwardly that they would guess someone had landed and would venture ashore after us, but it was a forlorn hope. The swiftly rising tide would have obliterated our footprints. I was on the point of risking everything and yelling, but that bloody Oriental Flower Child was watching me, and hoping, I think, that I would do just that, because he was toying lovingly with the pistol he had frisked from me.

The officer lowered his binoculars and grunted again and they prodded us onward up the hill to the flat ground at the top. Above us, a few hundred yards away, another line of hills rose, covered with scrubby pines. We crossed the flat ground and started to climb again, and then suddenly, without warning found ourselves in cultivated land. It was just a knife-slash running round the contour of the hill which had been terraced by rough stone walls into rice paddies, and across the other side there was a huddle of thatched mud huts. A man was ploughing through the knee-deep mud with a wood and bamboo contraption pulled by a pair of water buffaloes, and a line of women straggled behind him planting rice shoots in the sloughy trench it made. They wore, both sexes, muddy black tussah trousers and smocks, topped with cartwheel straw hats, which told me exactly nothing because that is the coastwise peasant dress from one end of China to the other. They stopped work and watched us dumbly as we came out of the trees and walked along the top of a bund between the paddies towards them. The officer started to jabber rapidly, in a language I didn't know but which had the odd Hakka word in it. The man with the plough called to an old woman. She climbed out of the mud and beckoned to us and led us through the tiny village and further up the hill until we came to a goat track which crossed our line of march at right angles. We turned on to this and kept going until we came to another huddle of huts in a valley which cut back into the range. I looked over my shoulder towards the sea, but only for a moment. I would have liked to have looked longer because the view was breath-taking, but the youth clobbered me hard with the butt of the pistol, then screwed the muzzle of it into the back of my neck. I had noticed earlier that the safety catch was off and the damned thing was cocked, so I took the hint without arguing and kept my eyes to the front thereafter. But I had seen in that short time that the frigate was still in sight, steaming very slowly close inshore parallel with the coast.

They separated us here, shoving me into the first hut and taking the others on further. My hut was a granary, half-filled with rice in matting sacks, and the last thing I saw before they slammed the heavy wooden door was a huge snake coiled up just inside, and the hair on the nape of my neck stood upright. The youth giggled and hissed realistically. I remembered then that this was common practice with the rice farmers and fish-driers of the coast. The snakes they use are a variety of rock python, non-venomous and even friendly in that they are said to curl up beside sleeping people for warmth—that is sleeping people less jumpy than I. They keep down granary rats far more efficiently than cats, and don't pee on the rice or eat fish.

There were no windows in this place, but the door was made of rough planks which had warped into inch wide cracks. I spent the first hour with on eye glued to a crack and the other swivelling round behind me in the general direction of the snake. Unfortunately I couldn't see seawards here, so I had no idea of whether the frigate was still beating up and down or had made off. I could see the officer and the youth though, and occasionally one or other of the soldiers as they patrolled along the edge of the clearing. They were all certainly on their toes, and the watch they kept was alert and thorough—even nervous.

The day dragged on. In the evening a couple of women

came up from the other village with food. The off-watch troops sat in a circle and produced chow-bowls and chopsticks and fed in full view of me. I wished they wouldn't. I wasn't conscious of hunger, but thirst was by now just about driving me mad. But finally they brought me some rice and dried fish and a big bowl of the Chinese peasant's staple drink—hot water—and dumped it down inside the door. I cheered up considerably, because I had heard somewhere that the Chinese, to whom food is sacred, would never dream of feeding anybody they intended to bump off within the next twenty-four hours.

The food was a twofold blessing, because it loosened the tongues of the others, and soon the officer and the youth were arguing like hell. The youth, I gathered, was all for going down to the shore as soon as it was dark, grabbing a boat and pressing on. The officer, on the other hand, wanted to wait for the junk to return. The youth asked what the hell was the good of that? The old bastard wouldn't come back while the frigate was hanging around, and although it was out of sight now, how did they know that it wasn't tucked away round a corner in some bay or other? The officer said they didn't know—but they'd still wait. The youth asked why, since they were inspired and upheld by the Thoughts of Mao, couldn't they spread out and walk round the island until they either saw the frigate's lights or were certain that she had gone? One of the soldiers asked wearily why he didn't do something anatomically uncomfortable with the Thoughts of Mao and then belt up? That enraged the youth, who pulled his gun and threatened the soldier. The soldier knocked him arse over head and took the gun from him, thereby endearing himself to me, and the officer told them *all* to belt up and set a sentry on each of the three huts, with one at the end of the valley to watch seaward. The youth was on the first watch, outside my hut. He sulkily asked for his gun back and the officer gave it to him, first, I was delighted to see, unloading it and keeping the rounds.

Then Wetten came up. I'd been wondering about him. If the Navy had got him I hoped they might have made him talk. But those hopes were quickly dashed. The officer brought him across while the youth translated from pidgin English to Cantonese.

No, the Navy hadn't got him. He'd reached the shore before

174

the boat came up to the junk and had hidden in the scrub. What were his orders now? The officer asked him if he could get through by radio to Canton to report the position. Wetten said sourly that he couldn't. The youth, apparently, hadn't kept his batteries topped up, and the charging motor was kaput. The youth didn't translate this bit truthfully. The officer then said that they would wait here until the frigate had definitely departed. The junk could anchor offshore. Wetten said he was going to sleep on board in that case because the junk stank less than the village. Then he went off.

I sat on a sack of rice and considered. So we were on an island, and, since the frigate was here, that island was inside British Territorial waters.

You'll have to bear with me a little here, while I give you a brief rundown on the Territory. Hong Kong is itself an island —nine miles by six—lying a mile off the mainland. The city, properly called Victoria, is on the north side of the island. The nearest part of the mainland is the site of another city—Kowloon—bigger in area but not as impressive as Victoria. The main docks are on the Kowloon side and the stretch of water in between is perhaps the finest deep water harbour in the world. If you put the point of a compass on Victoria and extended the other arm twenty miles and drew a circle, you would roughly enclose British Territory—half of it land, half sea. The land, except for the city of Kowloon itself, which was permanently ceded to Britain with the island, is known as the New Territories and we hold it on lease from the Chinese. The lease is up in 1977. In the seaward half are a number of islands, nearly a hundred, ranging in size from one, Lan Tao, bigger in area than Hong Kong itself but only sparsely populated by peasants, to tiny uninhabited bits of rock. Where the devil the seaward line runs exactly, nobody, not even the Navy, knows, and consequently we and whatever government happens to be in power in Peking are always arguing about the ownership of some of the smaller islands on the outer fringe. In the days of gunboat diplomacy it didn't matter a damn, but nowadays things are different, and we don't push our claims too hard, but the Chinese *do* push theirs.

So we were on an island. The question was, which? At the present moment I could have been sitting on my rump anywhere from two to twenty miles from that holy of holies, the

Hong Kong Club. The thing was to find out. And to find out I had to get out.

By the time I had reached this momentous conclusion darkness had fallen and I could hear some full-bodied snoring coming from somewhere—and that bloody youth was sitting on his backside leaning against the door. But I knew that his fangs had been drawn, and that his gun was like those of the Guards outside Buckingham Palace—for moral effect only. But he could still yell.

Skirting the last known position of the snake, I climbed up on top of the rice sacks and explored the possibilities of the thatched roof. It wasn't a formidable obstacle in itself, but the rushes were dry and they crackled loudly as I started to make a hole by the eaves on the side furthest away from the door. But I persevered and eased handfuls out as gently as a beautician working on a wealthy client's eyebrows until I had a space I thought wide enough to wriggle through. It sounded to me that I made a noise like a steeplechaser crashing through a brush jump, but it didn't reach the snorers who kept on with a steady *basso-profondo* throughout.

But junior was more on the job than I gave him credit for. I was just picking myself up from the drop when he came gum-shoeing round the corner on tiptoes, the gun at the ready. I reached him before he had time to cut loose with the yell that must have been forming in his throat. I didn't like doing it—not to a kid—even a horror like this—but one can't judge the weight of a palm-edge chop across the Adam's apple—not to a nicety, and certainly not when time is of the essence. I don't suppose the poor little sod ever knew what hit him. His gun rattled on the stones at my feet. I grabbed it, useless as it was, and started in towards the other huts—but then I saw movement by the nearest of them, so I had to nip round the other side smartly.

My first thought had been to loose the others, but I let that go quickly. I hadn't a hope. The sensible thing would be to get help—any sort of help—so I settled for that. I made for the path towards the first village, but then I saw the pinpoint of a cigarette and heard a cough. That way was out. And then the snoring stopped and I realized that the second watch was being called. If they went round to relieve sentries now I'd had it. I took about three seconds to worry things out. They would, I hoped, assume that I'd made for the seashore, and that's the way they would start the chase. I therefore did the opposite and went up the valley, fast.

And for once I wasn't wrong. I hadn't gone a hundred yards before I heard all hell break out behind me. They'd obviously found junior.

## Chapter 19

I let caution go to the winds and really pelted up the slope until I thought my lungs would burst, but for once it seemed that I was getting a break and nobody was on my heels, although I could hear excited voices and see torches flashing far below me. I reached the top of the hill and stopped dead.

They say it's the most beautiful night sight in the world. Try and picture it.

Broadway, Piccadilly and Coney Island rolled into one huge neon cluster and planted in the black velvet of the China Sea and sky—riven through the centre by the darkness of the harbour and repeated on the other shore—Hong Kong to the south and Kowloon to the north—with a jewelled necklace of arc lights surmounting the former, outlining the road up the Peak, and the grim hills of China itself surrounding the latter.

I saw immediately where I was—on Lan Tao, seven miles across the Lamma Channel from the Colony itself. I could place myself by an isolated patch of lights in the shape of a dumb-bell which I knew to be Cheung Chau right in the centre of the channel. Yes, I was on British territory all right —but that didn't help much at the moment. There was a police post here, I knew—but where exactly in its ten miles by ten miles area I hadn't a clue, because this was one of the few bigger islands I had not visited. There was also one on Cheung Chau, but that didn't help either, because I *had* been there and I knew that the post was manned by a Chinese sergeant and a handful of constables—splendid blokes no doubt, but not, I should say, strong on imagination. I'd probably find myself shoved inside until morning if I applied there. No—it was Hong Kong, and the fountainhead that I wanted now, because I knew for the first time what I was going to do.

Far below me I could see a cluster of dim lights on the

shore, with brighter ones moving out to sea. It was, I guessed, a fishing village, with boats lit by acetylene flares operating from it. I plunged downhill, falling into gulleys and ravines and getting snarled up in the scrub, but making the village more or less in one piece in about half an hour.

It was just a tiny place—half a dozen huts and a rickety pier jutting out from the beach and, except for a few dim lamps in the windows, it seemed deserted. But as I stood looking round trying to take stock, a harsh glaring light sputtered into being at the end of the pier as somebody lighted an acetylene lamp in a boat. I raced along towards it.

There were two Hakkas aboard coaxing a balky petrol engine into life. I jumped into the boat and gabbled that I wanted to get across to Hong Kong chop-chop, but they just stared at me blankly—even when I promised them more than they'd make in half a year fishing—so in the end there was nothing for it but to pull the gun on them. They understood that all right, poor devils, and shrugged resignedly, and after a few abortive coughs the engine started wheezily and we got under way. I made them dowse the lamp and I sat right up in the nose where I could watch them both.

It took us an hour and a bit to make it, with me prickling with frustration the whole time, but eventually they landed me by the Sulphur Channel, under the shadow of Mount Davis. I told them I'd keep my word and the dough would be sent across to them at their village—then I hopped out and made my way up to the motor road that circles the whole island a few feet above the sea. I was about four miles due west from the centre of Victoria here, so I started to pad east as fast as my leaden limbs would carry me, but then I managed to flag a prowling taxi. The driver looked at me dubiously and didn't want to take me at first and I had to wave that wretched gun again. I could hardly blame him either, because I must have been looking a hell of a sight —three days' growth of beard—a filthy shirt and jeans and bloody scratches all over my dirty face and arms. But, like the fishermen, he was Chinese and philosophical, and took me along the Praya, round the Cricket Ground and up past Murray Barracks towards Magazine Gap.

We stopped where I told him—three-quarters of the way up the Peak. I got out and looked down. The view of the city from here is, if anything, more bewilderingly beautiful than from across the water. But I had no time to admire it now. I told the driver to wait if he wanted his money and walked up a path which led to a large white villa set on a shelf in the hillside in an ordered riot of huge azaleas. Far below I heard three o'clock strike on the cathedral chimes, and somewhere a dog was barking.

I knew his room. It was the one over the porticoed front door. For a moment I thought of climbing the porch and really surprising him, but I discarded the idea. This place was wired. So I rang the front door bell prosaically, and got no joy for a long time until a light appeared in a downstairs room, and then the door was opened cautiously on its chain. It was old Fut Su, his number one boy, and for a time he blinked at me muzzily and didn't know me, but when he did he flew into a flutter and opened up. He said he'd go and call Mastah, but I told him not to bother and took the stairs three at a time.

But 'Mastah' had heard the noise and was already waiting for me at the top, in pyjamas and dressing-gown—and he wasn't even surprised. He just said: 'Where the hell have you been?' and led me to his study without waiting for an answer. He locked the door and went straight to the drinks cabinet and poured me a stiff one, then turned. And now he did look surprised, although not unduly so, because I had the gun on him.

He said: 'A little melodramatic, Wainwright, isn't it? What about this drink? Do you want it?'

'I could do with it,' I told him, 'but it had better wait, Mr Walters. Right now I'd like you to take me to the Colonial Secretary.'

'Might I ask why?' He moved to his chair by the desk but I motioned him away with the gun and then did what I should have done in the first place and went round behind him and frisked him. He wasn't carrying a gun, but I kept him in the middle of the floor just in case he had one stashed away in a drawer. The moral effect of this one was working perfectly, but I still felt horribly vulnerable.

'Because I knew very well that I'd never get in to see him looking as I do now,' I said, taking up his question. 'You're by way of being my passport, Mr Walters. My guarantee in other words.'

'And what do I guarantee, Wainwright?'

'Just my name and identity,' I told him. 'I'll do the talking after that.'

179

'And what are you going to talk about?'

'You're asking too many questions,' I said. 'Get moving.'

'May I put my trousers on?' he asked plaintively.

'You can do that,' I agreed. 'Walk ahead of me, and be sensible or I'll blow your head off.'

We went along to his room. I took a pair of slacks and a jacket from a dumb-valet, I looked through the pockets and threw them on the bed. He said severely: 'You're going to allow me a little privacy to change, surely, aren't you?'

'Not bloody likely,' I said. 'Get bouncing—we're both big boys.'

He stripped off his pyjama pants, looking as outraged as a spinster, and pulled on the others, then put the jacket on. I had a brainwave and moved to his bedside cabinet—and it paid off. There was a Browning .38 there. I took it and left the empty one without his noticing. I motioned him to the door. He gestured towards the telephone.

'I'd better ring him first,' he said. 'I don't think he'd see even me at three in the morning without some sort of explanation.'

'No telephones,' I said. 'We'll risk it. I'd be obliged if you'd bring a little money. There's a taxi to pay.'

'Why not my own car?' he asked.

'Just do as I say,' I said sharply. 'Time's getting short.'

He sighed. 'I hope you know what you're doing, Wainwright,' he said. 'Or that you can persuade an understanding doctor to certify you, if you don't. I'm afraid it will go hard with you otherwise. Very hard.'

'I'll have to risk that too,' I said. 'Get moving, Mr Walters.'

We went down the stairs and out into the darkness.

The taxi was still waiting, the driver curled up asleep in his seat. The Colonial Secretary's house is only a short drive up the Peak Road. There was a police guard at the gate, and there we struck trouble. The Chinese sergeant flatly refused to ring the house until he had first called the European sub-inspector from the Magazine Gap station. So there was another wait, and another argument—but eventually we got in.

The C.S. received us, frostily, in his drawing-room. He looked inquiringly at Walters and distastefully at me. Walters didn't help. He just gestured towards me and said: 'I'm sorry I can't enlighten you, John. This young man brought me here at gunpoint.' The C.S. pressed a bell hastily.

And then I felt a complete and utter bloody fool. The whole thing seemed so absurd in this last citadel of British colonialism, with two elderly gentlemen looking at me disapprovingly and curiously.

So I plunged. I said: 'I have been doing certain highly confidential government work, sir—both here and in England. Here I have received my orders from Mr Walters—but I have recently had reason to believe that he is not what he represents himself to be—and that I have unknowingly been working for—well, the other side.'

There was a knock at the door and the European police officer looked in. The C.S. told him to wait outside and then said to me: 'What you're saying is that Mr Walters is your Controller but you think he is doubling—and you've been furbled in reverse, is that it?'

It took me a good half minute to find words—because here was this completely unquestionable senior official using the common jargon of the trade. Actually I *didn't* find words. I just gulped and nodded. The C.S. went on: 'All right—spit it out, boy. What are your reasons for doubting him?'

'I'll have to ask you a question first, sir,' I said, and my voice sounded squeaky—like that of a schoolboy accusing his house-master of something nasty to the Head.

'What?'

'Where is Winterton?'

The C.S. looked at Walters. Walters said promptly: 'He was in Canton Central Gaol on Monday, but we think they moved him downriver on a junk that evening—to await our half of the bargain.'

'I was told that he died in Amoy some months ago,' I said, 'and that the fact was reported back here.'

'It was,' Walters said. 'By Carter. We didn't acknowledge it because lines were cut and Carter was already on the run. It was fortunate we didn't—because we found later that *Carter* was being furbled. They let him think that Winterton was dead as a test to see whether their suspicions were correct and he was leaking back to us. Where did you hear all this?'

'From Carter himself,' I said miserably. 'During the voyage.'

'And you accepted it without corroboration and came in here waving a gun like the sheriff of Deadman's Gulch?' Walters said mildly. 'Amazing. What else did he tell you?'

'Everything—or at least I think everything.'

'Including his doubling for us with the Russians?'

Again I nodded.

'In which case he's told you the truth—although I can't think why,' the C.S. said. 'What was it? Moonlight on the boatdeck or something? Girlish confidences?'

'Carter isn't like that,' said Walters primly. 'And neither is Wainwright. They've both been screened and cleared.'

Well, that at least was something, I thought wryly.

'Aren't we all rather wasting time?' the C.S. said. 'Unless, of course, this young man would like the bloody Governor to vouch for *me*. Incidentally, why did you ask for me, specifically, to vouch or otherwise for Walters?'

'You were the most senior official I knew personally, sir,' I said.

'*Do* you know me?' he asked, raising his eyebrows.

'I was introduced to you when you presented the rugby cup last year at Happy Valley,' I said and felt like a charwoman claiming the acquaintance of a duchess on the strength of a prizegiving at the Women's Institute.

'Ah—you play rugby,' he said, as if that explained a lot. 'I thought some fool had blown me. Four people in this damned Cheltenham-with-chop-suey can do that now. You're the fourth. Watch it, young man—unless you want your next posting to be on Immigrant Control in Wolverhampton. Still—that's not the point. Where the hell is Carter?'

'On Lan Tao,' I said.

'What did you leave him there for?' he asked. 'Malcolm wanted him taken off the ship in the Lamma Channel.'

'There's been a slight box-up,' Walters said nervously. 'He wasn't on board the *Nurma* when Wilson got out to her in the launch—and the captain denied all knowledge of the party, naturally. I had hoped that Wainwright would have explained by now—but things have been rather confused, as I think you'll agree.'

'Actually we were taken off by a party of Chinese,' I said helpfully. 'I managed to escape and get across here——'

I rather admired the C.S.'s self-control. He merely belched as if he had been punched in the belly. Walters I thought was rather unfair.

'You goddam bloody idiot!' he screamed. 'You've wasted half an hour before telling us *that*? I thought you had him holed up in a place of your own contriving—just to show how clever you were! When did you leave him? Who's actually holding him?'

'About five hours ago—a party of six—no five,' I stammered. 'The junk was chased by a frigate and ran ashore——'

'Probably to hell and gone now,' the C.S. said sadly. 'So they've got them both. Lucky Chinese. When are you due for retirement, Walters?'

'Be funny later, John, will you?' snapped Walters. 'At the moment I need help if there's the remotest chance of snatching even half a chestnut——'

'Navy?' asked the C.S.

'Take too long scratching their arses and asking for Admiralty sanction,' said Walters. 'No—I'll need your weight to deal with Malcolm. He's in the Hilton now, refusing to do anything more until he knows where his daughter is. Where is she, anyhow?' he demanded of me.

'On Lan Tao with Carter,' I said.

'Well, that's something,' he said and made for the door. 'Come on, Wainwright. John—call him before we get there and tell him we want full co-operation and no bargaining —or else.'

'Will do,' said the C.S. 'Wainwright, you've earned yourself a commendation: "Tries hard—means well".'

We jumped into the taxi and hared off down the Peak to the Hilton. I wondered vaguely what sort of impression a furious old gentleman in a scratch collection of garments and a battered sailor would make on the night reception clerk, but Malcolm was waiting for us on the kerb outside. He got in and said tersely: 'All right—John's told me. We want a fast launch. We're probably too late to do anything—but Wainwright—if anything has happened to that girl of mine, I'll cut your bloody throat with my own hands.'

It just wasn't my night.


## Chapter 20

It *was* a fast launch, and we made the crossing back in something over a quarter of an hour from Murray Steps —the three of us with a party of ten Chinese plainclothes men under a Yorkshire detective-superintendent. I thought at first that security had now gone by the board, but I realized after a time from the directions Walters was giving them that these were no ordinary police. We landed at the fishing village and I led the way up the slope, hoping to God, but by no means certain, that it was the way I had come down. Fortunately it was, more or less. I offered to do a recce at the top, but Malcolm said not bloody likely, I'd ballsed things up enough already. He just wanted me to show him.

I led them down into the valley. It was now getting light and I could see the huts plainly long before we crept up on them. I knew, of course, that the birds had flown even before we saw the doors standing open and the stamped-out fire they'd had going in the shelter of the rocks.

I looked miserably at Malcolm. His rage seemed to have left him. He was just blankly white-faced and expressionless. I felt the ashes of the fire, feeling silly and boy-scoutish. They were quite cold. Then the superintendent, who had been looking down towards the sea, pointed. A motor junk was standing inshore to the beach. The frigate was nowhere in sight.

The superintendent said: 'That anything like the hooker you arrive in, sir?'

'It might well be it,' I answered. 'The bloody things all look alike to me.'

'Don't take any chances,' said Walters. 'Let's get back to the launch and move round this side—fast. We can cut her off before she gets outside territorial waters. Come on—*move.*'

Malcolm said, 'I'm going down this way on foot. You can pick me up on the beach when you arrive.'

'Do you think that's wise?' Walters asked a little nervously.

'Just leave me alone, Walters,' Malcolm answered flatly.

'I'll leave a few men with you, sir,' the superintendent said.

'I don't want anybody with me,' Malcolm answered—then added. 'Yes, you, Wainwright. You told us you came through another village. You can show me the way there.'

Walters gave in and led off back up the hill. I went along the path ahead of Malcolm, feeling prickly at the back of the neck. Was this just to get me on my own, I wondered?

But I was still on my feet when we reached the edge of the paddy, which was perhaps fortunate for all of us, because the old boy was a bit myopic, and I saw them before he did. I signalled behind me for him to drop and flung myself flat behind a bund.

They were just coming out of the village—the officer and one of the troops—then Sonia and Carter walking in single file—then two more troops bringing up the rear. At the far side of the paddy the remaining soldier was waving a white cloth down to the junk.

We lay there until they had disappeared down the slope into the scrub, then rose and followed. An old man came out of the nearest hut and stared at us. Malcolm addressed him as Honoured Grandfather and told him we were following the *maskee daimen* who had just left, and hoped that none of the villagers would be unkind enough to shout a warning down to them, as there were other soldiers coming shortly and he would prefer not to be put to the necessity of having the whole village decapitated. The old man kowtowed politely and said he hoped so too, but not to worry—this was where the three monkeys originally came from, or words to that effect—in beautifully articulated Cantonese.

We went off after them, sweating now, because the junk had hove to a few yards out and the party in front only had a couple of hundred yards to go, and there was no sign of the launch. I could hear Malcolm alternately swearing and praying in Russian in a strangled undertone.

He said: 'If the worst comes to the worst we'll have to start shooting before they get on board—but intelligently. Drop the officer first. The others won't know quite what to do without orders.'

I thought what a hell of a hope. Two pistols against five burp guns, but I didn't argue.

He went on: 'There's always the chance that they'll shoot the prisoners if they're cornered—in which case I'm afraid I will still have to hold you responsible, Wainwright.' And again I didn't argue.

We were close up behind them now, but still with plenty of cover. They dropped down on to the sands and started to cross to the water's edge. Malcolm doubled forward like a stag and gained the brink of the last drop—and then, thank God, the launch came roaring round the next headland, half her length out of water and a bloody great bow wave creaming up each side of her. The troops stopped and gawped at it, but the officer turned and came running back, roaring at them to hurry. Sonia, the quickest-witted of them all, promptly sat down and refused to move. The officer levelled his gun at her. It was the last thing he ever did, because Malcolm shot him straight through the head. At thirty paces! I'd never have believed it if I hadn't seen it. One is taught to aim for the thickest part of the body, and even then one is lucky if one raises the dust within five yards of the target's feet. Ten paces, yes—but not *thirty*, and while running.

The remaining four reacted more or less to expected form. Two of them started to spray the air in our general direction with their burp guns. The inevitable weak sister one gets in cases like this, broke and ran towards the junk—but the remaining one, sustained no doubt by the Thoughts of the Chairman, remained steadfast to his duty. He came back to the prisoners with his gun cocked—and Malcolm missed this time—and so did I. But fortunately Sonia didn't. She got him in the guts with her chromium toy before he could squeeze the trigger—and twice again before he hit the ground. The weak sister was easy meat. His own outraged comrades got him from the junk, and he finished as a messy splurge in a foot of water.

But then they were pretty well preoccupied with the launch, which had closed right in and was brewing them up with a spigot-mounted Bren. The two sprayers had to stop eventually to change magazines—and even I couldn't miss then.

Carter said: 'If you expect me to say "bloody good show" you can forget it. None of this would have happened if you'd done the proper thing in the first place.'

I said something filthy and turned and looked at Malcolm and Sonia. He had her in his arms and was crying. Sonia was looking rather bored.

The men on the launch had secured the junk by her cable and had boarded her. Some diehard started shooting again. There was a final blast from the Bren, and then everything was quiet. I felt sorry for the old helmsman—and maybe even for Wetten.

Walters came up and said: 'We'll have to get attention for Malcolm. He's bleeding like a pig,' and only then did I realize the true cause of his emotion. It was rage. He'd been hit in the arse again—by an absolute wild one. A soldier's disgrace —twice in a lifetime. I sat on the sand and laughed until I was sick.

But Walters was a hogger for business. He drew Carter and myself to one side and said, 'We haven't got much time left. As far as I know the exchange is still on and it's arranged or two o'clock this afternoon—at Bias Bay—and that's the other side of the wretched Colony.'

'What exchange?' asked Carter.

'You for Winterton,' Walters told him. 'What else?'

'Winterton's dead,' Carter said flatly, and it was nice to hear Walters telling him he was talking cock, and giving him the real facts.

Carter's jaw dropped. 'I'm not doing it,' he said. 'Damn it all—it's asking too much. Russia's one thing—these bastards are a different proposition altogether. They'll have my hide on the barn door—and you know it.'

'With safeguards, naturally,' Walters wheedled.

'What safeguards?'

'It's all laid on. You know the Tai Tun sandbank, a couple of miles off the Bias shoreline? They will put Winterton there, just before high tide. One boat—three men only. We're allowed the same. You pass half-way—you to their boat —Winterton to ours. If there's anything else in sight, the deal's off.'

'It's off already,' Carter said. 'What the hell are you thinking of, Walters? Anyhow, why wasn't I told all this beforehand? Why did you allow a nit like this to break it to me? Why, if it comes to that, wasn't I told the truth about Winterton at the time? Why——?'

'Carter, will you let me finish?' Walters begged. And it was also nice to hear *him* taking it instead of dishing it out.

'Nothing doing,' said Carter. 'I undertook to go back to Russia—and that's a big enough risk to take, God knows —but not this. You're mad even to think of it. If you can't play straight with your own people——'

'Play straight?' Walters's voice was trembling with indignation. 'What about all these absurd stories you told this wretched fellow about us, eh? Bloody unethical—and it came perilously near to wrecking everything.'

'Necessary at the time,' Carter said. 'The clot is allergic to the simple truth, so I had to improvise like mad.'

I said: 'That bit about my father defecting? Was that improvisation too?' And I had difficulty in keeping my voice steady.

'I wish to God it had been,' he said nastily. 'We wouldn't have been stuck with *you* then.'

I swung a round-armed haymaker at him that would have had his block off if it had connected, but the Superintendent

187

pinioned me from behind and clucked reprovingly. Carter turned his back on us and continued as if I wasn't there.

'But that's beside the point, Walters. I'm not playing—so what are you going to do about it? Send me back to finish my time?'

'Until we can infiltrate you back to Russia,' Walters sighed. 'You're making it very difficult for us.'

'Difficult for *you*?' exploded Carter. 'Have you ever seen one of these public trials in Peking? Have you ever seen what a man looks like when he's really been under intensive interrogation—the Chinese way? Have you ever seen——?'

'Damn it, Carter,' Walters interrupted. 'You won't *be* on trial. You won't ever be in their hands——'

'What do you mean by that?'

'I'm trying to tell you. We've got the place plastered——'

'With what?' Carter demanded. 'More M.I.6 bullshit?'

'With naval frogmen. Twenty of them, working in relays from a submarine resting on the bottom a couple of miles offshore. They've been there for three days.'

I saw the change come over Carter's face, and I shuddered inwardly. He was hooked. What is it that motivates these people? I'm damned certain it's not bravery. Not bravery as I understand it, anyway. Just the terrible fascination of thin ice, maybe. 'Go on,' he said.

'The bank is about eight hundred yards long at half-tide,' Walters explained. 'The two boats meet half-way out to it—for mutual recognition purposes. We'll be even-stevens as I said—three men in each—that is, two besides the principals. When both are satisfied, the boats proceed to opposite ends of the bank. The principals get out and start walking towards each other—you with a certain reluctance until you're threatened with a gun. You'll pass half way—and then you'll yell to Winterton to drop flat—and you'll do the same—because at the first sign of treachery they'll undoubtedly open up with rifle fire. They'll try to shoot both of you.'

'What's to prevent them doing that anyhow?' Carter asked. 'As soon as they've got us both in their sights.'

'They'll only do that as a last resort. They want you alive if possible,' Walters said.

'You can say that again,' Carter said with feeling. 'Go on.'

'As you both drop—the frogmen come up behind their boat. Need I say more?'

'*Bloody* good!' Carter said with even deeper feeling.

And that is what happened—almost. Malcolm and I were supposed to be the ones in the boat—but Malcolm was now out of it, although fair play to him he did volunteer, provided we could find him an air-ring to sit on, but Walters was adamant—and came himself. Carter voiced certain objections to my coming—and I had reservations about Walters—he was pretty doddery—but I *didn't* voice them.

The launch took us round to Bias Bay, picking up a sampan with an outboard motor at Aberdeen, and then casting us loose a couple of miles short of the bank and making off.

We saw the other sampan coming out from the shore. Bias Bay, incidentally, is Tom Tiddler's ground. We have a loose suzerainty up to high-water mark, and they're supposed to own the foreshore—but it's a barren place, and nobody lives there.

We closed up to within about twenty yards. There was a soldier and a man in black peasant clothes in the other boat—both patently Chinese—and we began to think we were being short changed, but then a scarecrow looked over the gunwale and waved feebly—and I heard Carter catch his breath.

'Holy Christ!' he said. 'Yes—that's Winterton. You see what I mean, Walters?'

Carter stood up, wobbling with the motion of the boat. The man in black clothes studied him keenly, then nodded, and without a word we put our helms over and headed for the opposite ends of the long whaleback bank.

Carter did it very well, arguing and pleading realistically, and we were conscious of two pairs of binoculars on us from the other boat, but they wouldn't let Winterton move a step until our man was on his way. I climbed out and stuck a gun in Carter's back, and he started to move then, slowly, with his shoulders slouched—a picture of a man who has come up to the brink of hopelessness, and then gone over. And I still say the bastard was enjoying it—like a fellow I knew in the Parachute Regiment who used to crawl and gibber before a drop, but who tried to cut his throat when he was transferred to a line battalion.

They got to the crossing point and we heard Carter yell and saw him drop, but Winterton's reactions were blurred and he hesitated a fraction of a second, and when he did drop it was

189

with a bullet in his back. We could see their shots kicking the sand up all round them, but the hump of the bank gave them just that tiny bit of dead ground that hid most of their shapes from the other boat.

Walters had the outboard going by this time. I thought he was leaving them to it, and I got my gun out, but he swung the sampan into the smooth water on the shoreward side of the bank and roared towards the other boat. He was mouthing something I couldn't hear over the noise of the engine, and pointing with his foot to a khaki haversack on the floorboards. I opened it. There were six Mills bombs in it. I saw what he meant then.

The Chinese had stopped firing at the others and were now concentrating on us, but Walters was jinking the sampan violently from side to side, and as we came round the end of the bank I managed to get the pin out and lob the first bomb. It missed badly, but put them off their firing for a moment. The second one did all right. It landed smack between them.

It was a pity that I had drawn the pin from the third one because it wasn't necessary, and the blast from the second made me lose my footing on the slippery bottom boards of the sampan, and I dropped it. They say you've got three and a half seconds with this type. I scrabbled frantically for the damned thing, but lost my footing a second time. I probably got it and threw it clear in three seconds, but it wasn't enough and I've got half an ear and a silver plate in the side of my head to prove it. Walters was never able to prove anything again. He had no head at all.

Yes, that's how it happened. Just as the old gentleman had said. Except that there were no frogmen.

In spite of the chunk out of my dome I wasn't out to it —not then. That came later. I managed to turn the sampan and get back alongside the bank. Carter came down a little way to meet me—and then fell flat and stayed there. I crawled out and up towards him. He'd been hit twice—in the leg and the shoulder—but was quite conscious. I went on to Winterton. He'd got his smack between the shoulder-blades —but wasn't quite dead as far as I could make out. I dragged them both down to the sampan, and somehow managed to get them into it, with Carter bitching at me the whole time. Then I started for home, but we didn't get far before I passed out, and Carter had to take over with his sound arm. I came to after a time and managed to bandage both him and myself roughly with our combined shirts. Winterton didn't need bandaging, because he wasn't bleeding out of either of the two neat holes in his back or his chest and I thought he had handed in his chips, but he was still breathing when a naval launch picked us up outside the harbour boom. I remember a young sailor being sick as they lifted what was left of Walters out of the sampan.

Unfortunately they shoved us all into the police hospital and somebody recognized Carter before it could be hushed up, but the C.S. had Winterton and myself spirited out of it the same night and I was flown back to London in an R.A.F. plane.

They took me by ambulance to a small and very discreet nursing home in the country, and the Gaffer came down the following day. He stood at the foot of the bed and sucked his horrible teeth, grinning nastily.

'True to form to the very end,' he said. 'One gigantic balls-up.'

'I got them both out,' I said with dignity. 'And if we're on the subject of balls-ups, what about the bloody frogmen we were promised?'

'Frogmen my arse,' he said. 'That was just to put Carter's mind at rest. He was supposed to go over—and you brought him back, you goddamned idiot.'

I nearly vomited. 'You filthy lot of bastards,' I spat at him, but it didn't wipe the grin from his face.

'A bit devious at times,' he admitted. 'But the Chinks wouldn't have knocked him off. They wanted to swap him for one of their own that the Russians are holding. Another Mig—fellow by the name of Kowalski. It would have suited us lovely if it had come off. Winterton out of hock—Carter into Russia—and Kowalski back in circulation. He's been doubling for us for years.'

It was too much for me. I just stared at him, my mouth opening and shutting, but nothing come out of it. But he still didn't spare me.

'Can't even lob a bomb decent,' he went on accusingly. 'Carter says you let that one off right alongside poor old Walters's ear'ole—and then bloody well brought *him* back as well. Why the hell didn't you put him over the side? Caused us more trouble than anything, that did.'

'How did you explain it?' I asked hollowly.

'They put out a yarn that he'd met with an accident

dynamiting fish—but it didn't go down well at the Hong Kong Club, I can tell you. He'd got the Deepsea Sportsman's Cup last year, or something.'

'Gaffney,' I begged. 'Do me a favour. Go away. *Please go away*. I'm tired.'

'Is that all the thanks I get for coming down to cheer you up?' he asked, injured. 'All right—I'll be back tomorrow to debrief you. But you're not to see that girl of yours in the meantime. Understand?'

I sat upright. 'I take it you mean Miss Malcolm,' I said. 'Where is she?'

'In town, screaming her head off to know where you are.' He winked lasciviously. 'Carter reckons you were laying her on the ship. She must like it.'

'I'll get into Lanchester and kill the lying bastard when they send him back!' I screamed.

'You won't you know,' the Gaffer said calmly. 'They're not sending him back. The Meisterspringer is getting him over the wall of Hong Kong Gaol as soon as his leg's out of plaster —and shipping him on to Vladivostok. Must be costing the Rusks a bloody fortune.'